# TWISTED TALES OF HALLOWEEN HORROR: CARNIVAL OF CARNAGE

THE SISTERHOOD OF THE BLACK PEN

Before you read…

We all want to escape into a world of fiction, but the ones filling these pages may never let you go. They will haunt you long after you've closed the book. Readers, beware.

This anthology contains a collection of truly horrific short stories featuring blood, gore, and explicit content. It is absolutely not intended for those under 18. Readers, please review the following triggers and put this book down or shut off your ereader if it's going to upset you. We're not out to traumatize anyone, just to scare the shit out of them We're twisted, not terrible

Trigger List:
Amnesia
Suicide
Self Harm
Domestic Violence
Blood-Gore
Death
Dub con
Non con
Cheating

*Dedicated to those of you who take their horror with a heavy hand of spice.*

*We've got your ticket right here...*

# contents

# PUMPKIN SEEDS

A.C. Salazar

*2002*
*Talon, New York*
*Halloween night*


*The little house had been condemned for longer than any of them had been alive. Peeling paint on the door and seething masses of weeds did nothing to ward off the giggling band of teenagers hiding poorly in the bushes outside. One of the older boys, the would-be leader who had so daringly raided his parents liquor cabinet already, had gone ahead to look for a way in. Of all those who waited for their intrepid hero, only three of them didn't know the house's bloody history. The rest had grown up hearing the story from their parents and grandparents, some of whom had been there when the news of what had happened first broke all those years ago.*


*When at last they spotted the signal to join their intrepid hero they crawled into a dank and rotted place. The air was heavy with the smell of earth, retro decor eroded down so much it was nearly unrecognizable. There were hushed murmurs of delight by all those assembled. It would be the perfect haunt for the scariest night of the year. So they made their way carefully up the creaking steps, into the room where it happened.*

*They pulled clinking bottles out from under their costumes, gathered round a single flickering flashlight, and just as they were ready to regale the newest of their members a rather unexpected discovery was made.*

*A pumpkin.*

*It looked for all the world to be a perfectly normal pumpkin, save for the curious location it was growing. Undeterred, delighted even. It was cut from its thick stem and brought to the center of their little circle. A dog howled somewhere in the distance, the house groaned on its foundations. The story about to begin.*

A chill had crept into the air, welcome relief after the swelter of summer. For Irene there were few things that she enjoyed more than fall. She luxuriated in dancing gold and ruby leaves, cozy shawls, and the breeze running through the park reminding her to take a deep breath. In and out. Slowly. It's all she could do to bear the burden of her husband's company.

Roland Keller was the worst mistake Irene ever made. Like most of his poor customers, she had given him the benefit of the doubt. He was a good-looking fast talker who made pretty promises, after all. It wasn't until the contract had been signed that her raw deal came to light. It has been seven of the worst years of her already difficult life. She just wants a moment without his voice interrupting the sound of the crows. Sharp pain sears in her shoulder as the arm she had looped through his is yanked abruptly.

"What does a man have to do to get a bit of sympathy, huh?" he says with enough vitriol that Irene feels spittle land on her cheek. "I spend all damn day working myself to the bone to keep us afloat and you can't even fake being grateful?"

"Dear, I wasn't trying to make you feel that way. It's just so lovely out here. Why not try putting your job out of mind for tonight and come back to it fresh tomorrow?" She tries. Mentioning the pulsating ache suddenly taking up residence in her shoulder is pointless, she knows. He never cared before; it seems unlikely for him to start now.

"You would think something like that wouldn't you, lazin' around all day, not a care in the fuckin' world? Some of us don't get to put it outta our heads. Some of us have to pay the God damned bills."

She fights to keep her eyes down. If he sees the flash of indignation behind her hazel gaze it won't end well for her. Irene works more than he does, she knows. Keeping the house spotless, watching her neighbor's children to bring in some extra income, all of it on top of the late-night hours spent mending clothes until her fingers are bruised and raw for those extra few cents that sometimes are the only reason she can feed herself after he's drunk everything else away for the month. He spends his days in a plush office occasionally making dirty sales, and his nights fondling anything in a skirt down at the bar. She bites all of it down, trying to think of a way to soothe his temper when something bright flutters on the wind to land atop her boot.

A red flier. Now where had that come from? Pulled out of her miserable thoughts, she bends down and grabs it without hesitation. *One week only! Come join the carnies at Lady Rosavier's Carnival of Frights! Halloween delights that are not meant for the faint of heart! Freaks and fabled feats guaranteed. Games and prizes around every corner! Alcohol free with admission!* Irene barely has time to skim over the printed words before Roland snatches it from her fingers.

"What the hell is this? You pick up garbage in the park but can't manage it at home?" Yet he reads it too; she can tell because he has to squint. Irene used to find it endearing. Now she just wonders why they bothered buying him glasses when he refuses to wear them. She looks around while he's distracted. Some ways up ahead is an odd figure. It must have been them who had dropped the paper. A satchel with red peeking out of its half-secured pouch is slung over their shoulder. The outline seems to be a man, though it's hard to tell from this distance. They look strangely proportioned—lumpy, if one were forced to say. They trudge their own path with a broken gait that feels painful just to look at. As though every movement were a great strain. Something about it seems so intensely wrong, even if she can't think why. A limp is not such a frightening thing. Though she realizes the more it moves away that she is holding her breath.

"A carnival? Look here, they'll tell you the booze comes with admission, but they ain't gonna say how much the admission is, now are they? Ya can't fool a salesman with a trick that simple. No how." Roland sneers.

"Can't get one over on you, darling." She agrees in an absent sort of way. The response is automatic on her part. She's long since learned that listening to his self-aggrandizing is better than having to submit to his never-ending list of grievances. If it puts him in a good enough mood, he might even go to the bar tonight and leave her well enough alone. It gets them moving again at least. Down a different walkway than the one that odd man had taken.

He manages to take up the rest of the walk, as well as the journey home, regaling her with stories about all his most recent cons. Sales, in his mind, but she knows better than that now. Irene takes pains to make sure she flatters in all the right spots. It manages what the stunning colors of fall cannot. He's in the best mood she can remember since his last major scam was dismissed in court. She's surprised however, when just as they arrive at the house, he seems to come to some epiphany.

"Yeah, a guy like me knows what's what. More than some penny pinching transient ever would. A guy like me knows the real value of things, knows how to haggle, how to persuade." He grins, lets go of her to hold the peeling blue door open. Irene blinks, too surprised to remember she's supposed to play along. He hasn't held the door for her since their honeymoon.

"Go on and get dressed, gorgeous. I'll show these rubes who's the king of the sale. Go on, get dressed, nothin' too fancy now. That brown rag yer ma left you, that's the one! Yeah, and the shoes with the shoddy heel. What you slackjawin' me for? I told ya to get dressed."

"Roland, why on earth do I need to put on different clothes to make dinner?" She asks despite herself.

"We're going out tonight, ain't that a treat? Now hurry it up, and don't you make me ask ya again." He grits out from clenched teeth.

Irene, still baffled by the wild swings of his mood, goes upstairs and does as she's told. She's further concerned when she comes back down to see he's left the good coat he'd worn that evening for his oldest, thinnest jacket. Somehow there's smudges of dirt on his person that weren't there when she'd gone to change. The crumpled bright red paper sticks out of his now somehow dusty trousers.

She can't parse it out. Roland's pride could very well rival Lucifer himself. There was no way he'd want either of them seen in public like this. Even if he really did want to go to the carnival—she assumed that must be it if he hadn't yet thrown away the flier—he had no reason to make them look even worse off than they already were.

"Roland?" She hedges, unsure if she should risk asking directly for a second time. He looks her over and nods in approval at her threadbare wardrobe.

"That's the ticket, or it's gonna be anyhow. Never mind the details, hon, just follow my lead."

He grabs her by her still-tender arm and marches her out again without so much as a coat or gloves. October is far less pleasant without them. A setting sun plunges the crisp temperature down to a bitter cold. Yet the pair walk on. They don't take the trolly, though she wishes they would. Not until she's nearly numb from the cold, far into the industrial district, do they at last find what Roland is looking for. Irene hears it before they round the buildings. What sounds like a wheezy accordion playing its tipsy tune on a loop. Blinking lights can be seen reflecting in what few windows remain unboarded.

Set up in a large stockyard between closed factories is indeed a carnival. There are caravans parked along the perimeter, brightly colored tapestries and banners drawn between them to stop unpaying visitors from seeing much of what lies beyond. Yet peeking up from the farthest point back Irene can make out the sight of a big top tent. Like the kind she had seen at the circus as a girl.

Only one vehicle is faced out to the street, its wooden exterior ornately decorated and painted in fantastical colors. There's a large open window with drawn curtains along the length of it, the sill set with a service bell and a sign she can read even from a distance. *Lady Rosavier's Carnival. Thirty cents a ticket. Drinks unlimited.*

"Thirty cents! Oh, they really think they can pull a fast one on me, aye? Well we'll see 'bout that. Remember, just go with what I say, and don't say nothin' unless I'm askin', got it?"

"I— yes. Yes, dear, of course."

"That's what I like to hear." He keeps her close, strolling up to the bell and ringing it without hesitation.

Bells, Irene reflects, were not something she associated with good things. The bells of the school yard had been a constant invitation for either teachers or classmates to torment her. The church bells rang goodbye to her loved ones with the same finality as they did the day she became a bride. Wind chimes never seemed to sing until they caught the first warning of storms. Every morning that Irene awoke and saw Roland still in bed beside her, it was the shrill cacophony of the alarm bell that forced her away from the blissful escape of sleep.

This bell echoed with a force its small size wouldn't suggest. Irene could hardly shiver more than she already was, yet something in her gut warned that they had just caught the attention of a beast much larger than themselves. Before she could pluck up the courage to ask her husband to take her back home, the thick curtains parted with a flourish. A woman, skin like cinnamon bark and eyes the color of fresh-poured whiskey, stood framed before them dressed in fashion Irene finds glamorous, if foreign. Metal rings have been woven into her hair to secure thick braids. Robes arranged in layers both protective and provocative alternate between opaque silk and sheer chiffon and make her seem almost bare. Jewelry gathers on her fingers, climbs up her arms, kisses her neck, and whispers with fine gems into her ears. The effect is dazzling.

"Welcome, dear travelers. You arrive on a most beautiful night. The cost for two tickets is sixty cents, but in return I promise my carnival will change your life forever. The heavens have deemed it so. If you would like to come inside and see for yourself?" Even her voice feels luxurious. Like velvet slowly slipping into Irene's mind. She can't recall a time she has ever felt so deeply taken by another woman's charms. What she wouldn't give to have such a voice saying her name. It clearly rattles Roland as well. It's a full five seconds before he finds the ability to talk again. A record, no doubt.

"Oh, well, you see ma'am, I hadn't realized— To tell you the truth, I'm awful embarrassed." He rubs the back of his neck, looking apologetic as he produces the red paper from his pocket. "The thing is, my wife and I saw your flier here, and she just wanted nothin' more than to come here and forget our grief for a while. See, it's been hard for us since we lost our baby. Been nothin' but misery to tell ya straight. Well, I just hadn't seen her light up like that since I got her back from the doctors. I went and promised her I'd scrape up enough for us to come tonight. 'Cept this ad don't have the prices on it, see? I didn't think it would quite be this much. Don't ya think it might be in yer heart to maybe cut us a deal? I would never ask ordinarily, but I don't think I could bear to disappoint her again."

She very probably should have seen this coming, but if Irene said she had it would've been just as much an outright lie as his story was. In fact, the only reason she isn't staring incredulously at him is because she still hasn't been able to tear her eyes away from Rosavier. The Lady's stunning features have not changed expression whatsoever. Calm, steady, with no sign that this improvised tale has made any impression on her at all. An eternity goes on before those lustrous orbs slide away from Roland and land upon Irene.

"You poor creature. There has been much suffering in your life, yes? Come, show me your palm. I will see what cannot be seen. The Sisters of Destiny will tell me then what to do with you."

Somehow, she had the feeling that Lady Rosavier wasn't talking about Roland's conjured story. Finally looking at him, Irene thinks he must still like his chances with this particular farce. He has an unnatural look of forced tenderness to him and nods slowly for her to do as the soothsayer asks. Fine then, she thinks, if they end up denied he can hardly blame her for not having the right palm. Her fingers are stiff from the chill as she reaches up and presents herself to be examined.

Lady Rosavier leans forward, taking Irene's hand in her much warmer ones. Everything else fades to the background. It feels so wonderful it's almost shocking. More than just temperature, those hands are soft and gentle as she traces patterns into Irene's skin with such practiced ease it's a wonder she's able to stop herself from whimpering. Like a street weary mutt must feel when meeting a kinder, more loving new master. Those mesmerizing eyes concern themselves only with their mysterious diagnosis for a minute or two before they find what it is they are looking for. The artful stroking slows to almost nothing, but the Lady doesn't release her as she finishes the reading.

"You have a gentle nature you learned from your mother, a trusting heart you inherited from your father. Both were separated from you too soon. In their absence, these quiet strengths have been taken advantage of by others. Like a garden, you have much to give, for you find joy in giving, but there is an infestation in your midst. Those who take more than what is offered. They destroy and rot what you seek to nurture. This will not do. Luckily, there is time yet to change your fate. A decision is coming, sooner than you might be prepared for. When that time comes, you may feel the need to stay with the company of the parasites, for they are a familiar companion to you, but do not let the unknown stop you from reclaiming what should rightfully be yours."

Irene is left mouth agape at the enchantress. How on earth had she known about her parents? The Lady spoke with such certainty. She'd never been given to think much of fortune telling up till now, yet it is as if Irene had told her deepest woes to this woman. How strange.

"In light of this I can think of only one way to set you on the path that will bring you back to happiness. Both of you may enter tonight. Free of charge."

"What a woman! I can't tell ya how grateful we both are!" Roland exclaims, giving Irene yet another start. Somehow, she had forgotten he was there.

Roland puts both hands on her shoulders and starts steering her away from the window to the entrance, forcing Irene to let go of Rosavier's lovely caress.

"Ah, thank you, my Lady." She manages, then feels foolish at once. It had to just be a part of her stage name. There was hardly any reason to actually use a grandeur title like that to address her. Still, as she and her husband round the corner Irene can swear she sees a small smile curving up the corner of her painted lips.

"What did I tell ya, doll? Does your man know how to deliver, or what? Now let's see what we're working with here."

Past an archway made from strings of glass beads, they at last see the grounds. Irene's first impression of the place is a strong reminder of how uncomfortable she'd been before meeting its proprietor. A thin fog swirls around their feet as they enter. Enormous pumpkins and dark barren trees break through cracked pavement at random. The large space is completely encircled by a fence made from game booths and tents. At the center of the patch stands an impressive, if filthy, fountain. The waters look a brownish yellow, with the acrid stink of beer coming from it, and Irene can make out mugs in every shape and size set out on its ledge. A rather literal way of having your drink "flow free," she thinks. Roland only has one thought, and it doesn't surprise his wife in the least.

"My good God. I'll be damned! Would you look at that? Ha! This is the best idea I've ever had! Free, unlimited drinks? Let's see how it tastes!" He races for the rather questionable waters like a desert wanderer coming upon oasis.

Irene is slower to approach. No amount of pointing out how unclean this must be will stop him from trying it. If it suits his fancy, he won't be dissuaded from having his fill. If it's not satisfactory, he's just as likely to be furious with her as anyone else. Considering there doesn't seem to be anyone else around, she'd like to wait for his verdict from a distance. There comes another shout of delight from him though. Safe, it would seem. At least from her spouse—is it her imagination or is someone watching them? She tries to shake it off, there doesn't seem to be anyone here yet. With some trepidation, she walks farther into the gloom to find Roland has already claimed a large glass, filled it, and is drinking deeply.

"Darling, shouldn't you pace yourself a bit? We've only just gotten here. Maybe we might play a few games and have a look at the show? I'm sure there will be peanuts or something you could eat. We skipped dinner, remember? Aren't you hungry?" she wheedles. If he blacks out, she doesn't know how she's going to get them home.

Roland lowers his mug with a loathing glare at her. "You're really going to nag me when I'm trying to enjoy a hard-earned drink? You keep your trap shut, woman, and leave me alone. Here!" He pulls something from his pocket and throws it at her feet. A small handful of coins scatter around, and Irene is left to scramble after them. If she loses any, he'll be screaming about it all week. He'd blackened her eye once for dropping a few nickels into a storm drain by accident.

"That's all you're getting outta me, got it? Now go find something to entertain yourself with. I don't wanna see your mopey mug till I call for ya, understand?"

"Yes, dear, thank you." Well that sorts it then—she'll call for a cab if need be. Until then it's a waiting game to see how long it will take him to pass out. All she needs to do is stay off his radar till then. Without a backwards glance, she walks through the thickened air to the nearest booth. The mist makes all the surrounding lights seem hazy around the edges, but it's more than visible enough to make out the sight of what looks to be a shooting gallery. As she approaches, there seems to be no attendant, but there are stools. The only thing she'd be more grateful for would be a warm change of clothes. Except, no, there is someone. Someone holding a rifle.

Her step falters for a moment, ice locking in her gut. That outline. Almost like a person, but not quite. It's without a doubt the person from the park, and they seem to be wearing a costume for the occasion. If they were to hold perfectly still, she might have even mistaken them for a decoration. A ghastly jack-o'-lantern mask covers their entire head. It almost seems like vines extend from under it and disappear beneath a tattered shirt and overalls. A scarecrow. Appropriate choice though it was, it would seem more effective on her than any bird.

She forces herself to breathe. It's only natural that someone who works here would have been out earlier that day to hang fliers up around town. The gun in their hand is a toy to play in the gallery with. It's all completely understandable. There's nothing for her to be frightened of. Nothing logical in any case.

"Um, excuse me? Would it be alright if I sat here? I've been on my feet all day you see, and I promise to move once you get customers," she squeaks out, recovering from her surprise.

The figure doesn't respond. In fact, they don't bother to look at her. She might have thought they hadn't heard her timid voice if not for the way they came to a halt in their cleaning. Only the strangled sound of the accordion music floating ominously on the air fills the silence. It's unnerving, how utterly still they've gone.

"Ah…hello? Are you well?" Irene asks.

No reply. Her stomach starts to fill with heavy dread as long seconds go by. She wonders how they can see from inside there, and she's sure that they can. Despite herself, she takes a tentative step closer. It must be a mask, but why does it look so real? Like it's just beginning to rot. There's a droopy, fleshy quality to it. The face carved into it might once have been laughing. Now it's difficult to tell from how concave it's becoming. She reaches out carefully, curiosity and fear competing within her.

The pumpkin-headed person senses her approach. Slowly, it begins to lift its head to look at her. What *is* that? Something is wrong with the eye holes. If she didn't know better, she'd swear that a worm is wriggling around in there. It has to be a trick of the light. She's nearly leaning on the counter now. It's rude, no doubt, but what if they're ill? This close she can make out a rattling breath coming from inside, and a twitching muscle in their hands.

"Don't mind the handyman, he's the simple sort," says a deep voice just beside her.

Irene lets out an unflattering yelp. She spins on the spot to see there are not one but two new faces looking at her with interest. A cowboy and a knight.

The cowboy is the one she assumes had spoken. He's rugged, with dark features that are tempered by a remarkably kind smile. The other man studying her meanwhile has the elegant appearance of a fairytale prince. Aristocratic, fair in color, and perfect posture. The chainmail and sword of his ensemble are impressively authentic looking.

"Sorry to give you a turn, ma'am. Meant no offense." Says the cowboy, reaching up to tip his hat to her.

"Oh, no, no offense taken! I was just wondering if it might be alright if I sat here while I waited? If this is your stall, sir?" Irene sputtered.

"Well of course it is, and by all means you may. I'll be mighty glad for the company. This dusty old Brit is getting on my last nerve." He throws out the last part with a lighthearted nudge to his companion as she sits.

"Dusty? So says the ungrateful yank in dirty boots," the other replies with a playful smirk. "I know manners are hardly your forte, but perhaps we had better introduce ourselves to the young lady?"

The first man snaps his fingers. "See, now I knew I was forgetting something. Name's Amos Wicksloe, miss. It's a pleasure to be making your acquaintance. This here's Bastion Finchley."

"Charmed to meet you. Though I do apologize for our colleague. You'll find a great many of the workers here a bit empty headed, but so long as they work hard, Lady Rosavier keeps them around," the knight says with a dismissive wave to the gourd-wearing mute.

"I see, well, that's very kind of her. It's hard for anyone to find work nowadays. Oh, but now I'm the one forgetting manners. I'm Irene Keller." *I'm here with my husband*, she was going to say next, but then she thinks better of it. There's every possibility they passed by Roland on the way here and saw his rather shameless indulgence. It's mortifying to think of admitting he's her spouse when he might very well be splashing around in a public fountain in the next hour or two.

"Irene, huh? Beautiful name for a beautiful lady. It suits you," Amos says with a warm gleam in his eyes.

She feels herself go pink at his words. Behind him Bastion raises an amused eyebrow at the exchange. "Well now, my dear fellow, I believe I had best get prepared for the first show of the night. Speaking of which, I do hope to see you in the crowd tonight, Ms. Keller."

"Show?" she asks.

"Oh yes. I perform with the freaks, you see. Have some rather unusual talents, if I do say so myself," he preens. "Though, of course, there are plenty of other acts you'll want to see. For instance, we have the strongest woman in the world."

"The eastern fire breather. The Boneless Brothers. Madame Mirror, the Boogeyman, the Harpies." The cowboy counts them off on his fingers as he goes.

"My word, that certainly does sound exciting. I hope I get to see it later," she hedges, knowing full well she won't be able to afford it with what's in her pocket.

"Until then, Ms. Keller." Here Bastion bows deeply. Not just to her, but also to his leather-clad companion.

"Happy sword swallowing, Finchley. We'll be there, front and center, don't you worry about it."

Irene smiles weakly as the knight walks away into the fog, before turning back to Amos. "Forgive me, but I don't think I'll be able to attend. I hate to disappoint, but I really can't afford it at the moment."

"Well then, I guess you're just gonna have to win it," he replies easily.

She blinks. "Win it? You can't possibly mean here? I've never held a gun in my life."

"Seems a good night to try though, doesn't it? I'll show you how to get started. Vince, give that here. " Irene turns back to the jack-o'-lantern. They give the rifle over without hesitation, twitching on occasion. Looking at them makes her skin crawl in a way she still can't explain. So she turns back to Amos, far more pleasant by comparison.

"You tuck it into your shoulder, see? Like this. Left hand on the stock, and you're gonna pull on it to pump in the air to fire with. Your right hand will be down here. Keep your finger off the trigger till you're all lined up. The sights will help you aim. Take a nice deep breath and then you can fire. Ain't much to it." He has green eyes, she realizes, an earthy green that reminds her of the pine tree forests she'd grown up near.

"Well, if you insist." Irene says, doubtful.

He hands it to her. It's surprisingly heavy. Doing her best to copy what he demonstrated, she looks at her targets. The range is made from lots of small moving paper figures, and it seems to be telling a story. A late-night saloon on an open dusty street is painted on the back panel; scantily dressed cartoon ladies in distress are being chased by both men and demons. All the people have points on them. For the damsels, she can be expected to lose a point if she clips them, for the others it could be anything from one to five points depending, it seemed, on how difficult the shot would be. Eventually Irene lines up the sights on the cut-out of a devil scampering back and forth at regular intervals with a little "+3" on his back. She takes a deep breath, counting in her head every four seconds, when the rascal will pivot on his track and double back the way he came. He walks right into her sights.

*Pching!*

The metal bb tears through the center of the paper doll with ease. A perfect shot. Despite herself, Irene grins. She only wished it were that simple in real life.

"We've got ourselves a natural! Why not try helping out the little lady there with the nice man offering her a back rub?" He crows delightedly.

There's a bearded man grabbing a red-haired girl from behind, his +5 only an inch or two from his victim's -1 as the pair twirl on the spot in their struggle. Every other second, he and she swap places. So Irene aims, and counts, and after a beat, shoots.

*Pching!*

The villain continues to dance back and forth, now missing his face. Irene revels in the way Amos claps for her, the way he praises her as she takes out target after target. Not a single shot misses. By the time she runs out of evil-doers, there is a growing crowd of delinquents in the square. It would seem that most of them are like Roland, only concerned with the fountain, stumbling around with mugs in hand. Rowdy chatter is now the easiest thing to hear, and the fog has thickened, swirling faster than ever because of all the foot traffic. Irene hardly notices any of it. She feels as though transported into a dream. Especially with the way her cowboy is looking at her.

"Now I know you have to be trying to pull one over on me. I think you might be a better shot than I am, and I grew up with a barrel in one hand and a cattle whip in the other."

"I swear on my life I've never done this before. In any case, I should hardly think this is comparable with true marksmanship." She giggles, flattered anyway. "Now then, I have some fifty-two points. Is that enough to earn me a ticket?"

"Funny thing about that," he leans in on one elbow, close enough that she now knows he smells just as good as he looks. "You have enough for two. I'd be more than happy to take you myself while Vince here resets the range. What do you say?"

She should say no. She knows she should say no. Even if Roland treats her like an unwanted pest, she made a vow. There's a voice deep down, however, that points out that while she had kept those vows every day, her husband hadn't kept them for longer than a month. Was it possible to still betray someone after they had betrayed you for years? Even if it was, should she care?

Does she?

"I think that would be lovely," Irene answers.

The rest of the night is a brilliantly bizarre blur. They walk to the show leisurely, talking about anything that comes to mind in a comfortable back and forth that charms her so thoroughly she doesn't notice the many carnies in jack-o'-lantern masks, all watching her from the shadows as she passes with her new beau. Once inside the dark embrace of the big tent, the freaks perform stunts that have her hiding behind her hands one moment, then clapping the next. Bastion starts the exhibition. At first swallowing small daggers whole, and by the end has his own broadsword down to the hilt in his gullet before a chain is lashed to it lifting him up into the air. Irene thinks it will slice him in two leaving nothing but the gore of her brief friend behind on the straw-strewn floor. He touches back down without so much as a scratch.

Rhona the strong-woman lifts the bleachers with the audience still seated on them. Without warning. All of the patrons scream, whether with delight or terror, the proud smile on Rhona's face suggests she's pleased either way. When the dragon man follows, he breathes fire that wraps around him in shades of emerald green. He doesn't burn, though Irene thinks it must be because of the scales upon his body. They had seemed tattooed, yet the fire brightens them to a gleam as his eyes become reptilian.

Yet it's the Boneless Brothers who are the first to make Irene look away completely, the incredible flexibility so unnatural it looks as though they are breaking one another down into bundles of twisted limbs. She feels queasy by the time they bow out. A few of the freaks are unavailable for the night, so the Harpies, a troupe of women with deformed arms just like wings, end the night for them. They fly overhead, throwing their voices to create a haunting concert punctuated by occasionally swooping down and screeching at an unsuspecting audience member.

If Irene thinks she will trickle out with the rest of the attendees she's mistaken. Both Amos and Bastion insist on introducing her to the others. All of them greet her with an interest and kindness she can't recall ever having experienced before in her life. They laugh and tease and swap outrageous tales for what must be hours. Eventually there is no denying that it is time to press on. It must be dreadfully late, and she can only hope Roland will be too drunk to fight her about going home. The thought douses her good mood at once, and her cowboy is quick to notice as they exit the tent.

"Hey now, that beautiful smile looks like it's wandered off. What's wrong?" He asks softly.

Just the way he says it, no harsh impatience painting his tone, no grabbing her by the arms like an old toy that's lost its novelty, makes an ache build up in her throat. It's not fair to have someone so wonderful for only a fraction of time. She wants to keep him so much longer than a night. If not him, than someone, anyone, who would treat her like this. Unbidden, Lady Rosavier appears in her mind's eye. The freaks, all smiling and waving and making room for her in their lives is weaving itself into her fantasies with every step she takes away from the real thing. Irene can feel the all too familiar sting of tears beginning to well up.

"It's nothing to do with you, Amos, I promise. Only I can't recall the last time I had so much fun. I'm sure I must have, a long time ago, but the memories seem to have gone fuzzy on me." She hopes he can't hear the way her voice wobbles as she confesses. Saying it outright makes it harder to keep her face straight.

"Then we'll just have to make this a regular thing then, won't we?"

"I would dearly love to know how."

"So would I, and were I a betting man, my money would be on Rosavier. Never steered me wrong, that woman. She's never left a wrong un-righted either, so far as I've ever heard." He takes her left hand, examining the wedding band on her finger with a pinch of distaste in his eyes. "I can't picture anything more wrong than leaving you with this chain around your neck."

Irene colors with distress. "You— you knew about my husband?"

"Everyone does. The way he was talking to you, we could all hear it. There wasn't anyone else here yet. How could we not?"

"You still asked me to the show." She points out.

"Yes, and I'd do it again."

"You would?"

"Yes."

Irene likes to think she isn't the kind of woman that would be doing something like this. Maybe because, once upon a time, she hadn't been. The years have made her bitter, she realizes at that moment. Now she thinks that maybe being that kind of woman wouldn't be so bad. Between staying miserable and alone, with nothing to show for it but a failed marriage, or being a happy and free woman again with a broken promise, she sees only one person worth being.

"Do you really think she can help me?"

"I know she can. She's done the same for me, for all the folks who call this carnival home. If you want to have a place here, then all you have to do is ask."

A few minutes later they stand at the back of Lady Rosavier's caravan. With an encouraging nod from Amos, Irene lifts her hand to the door and knocks. It really is like rattling the cage of a tiger, she thinks. Gaining the attention of a magnificent beast and hoping it will find you too lowly a prize to bother hunting, yet desperate to see just a little more of the creature within. They wait for only a moment before the door glides open smoothly. No one stands ready to greet them. Irene can make out walls covered in unusual trinkets and the warm light of fire from inside.

"Enter, Mrs. Keller. Amos, you are to wait there unless called for," calls out a velvet voice.

Irene starts at this, looking to him for his reaction, but the cowboy looks as relaxed as ever. This must be fairly normal then. With a deep breath, she steps up into the small space. At least, she had thought it would be a small space. The interior is no house, but it is far more comfortable than the outside would suggest. Rather like stepping into a little cottage. There's a nook at the back that looks to be for sleeping. The vaulted ceiling is hung with drying herbs and flowers. A rustic looking table set with a tea kettle and two mugs is pushed against the opposite wall from the little wood burning stove. A long window runs along one side, but it is covered with thick curtains at the moment. The door closes gently, and Irene spins round to find Lady Rosavier standing behind her.

"Welcome back," she greets with a small smile. "I take it the gunslinger has convinced you to seek control of your fate. This is pleasant news. I will be honest, I wasn't sure you'd have enough fight left for it. Come sit at my table, I've prepared a warm drink for you."

"You did? How did you know I would be here?" She didn't even know she would be here.

"I have my ways. Come. Sit." The Lady beckons, taking her own seat while Irene does as she's told. "Now then, I am going to ask you some questions. You may ask your own, but not until I've finished mine. Do you understand?"

"Y-yes, ma'am," she stutters.

"Good. Drink your tea, dear. It will help with your nerves."

Irene looks at her mug. The liquid inside is a warm amber color, just like Lady Rosavier's eyes. When she lifts it to her lips the first taste floods her with a wave of nostalgia so palpable she nearly stops breathing.

"My first question: What do you taste in that blend?"

She very nearly asks what the Lady means by that. Except she had just very explicitly been told not to ask anything until it was her turn. Very well then. If this is some kind of test then she is determined to get it right, and if it's not then there's no harm either way.

"I taste vanilla, cinnamon, and molasses. Like the little cakes my mother would make when we had some money left after expenses. I taste..." She has another sip, to see if it helps her describe the sensation any better. "I taste the fall, all the harvest has given, the calling of winter telling me to rest."

Irene blinks, startled by her sudden bout of poetry. What is she saying? She hadn't meant to say it quite like that. Then, without any intention, she continues.

"I taste all the dead things that are gone, the beauty of decay. I taste the end of the cycle as it comes back to its own beginning. The endless wheel that dooms us and gives us hope. The death of my past self and others that will give birth to new life."

Irene claps a hand over her own mouth. She feels as though something has possessed her. Where did all of that come from?

"Perfect. I thank you for your honesty. Now tell me, what is it you would seek from me?"

"Freedom from my chains, refuge from the mundane, pleasures I have never known," she admits at once. Mortification fills her, yet she can't look away. This is some kind of spell. It has to be. Irene has never said something so bold in all her days.

Lady Rosavier's smile changes then, causing a low simmer to start taking hold in Irene's center, seeing the look on the other woman's face.

"Now tell me, what will you give me to receive what you ask for?"

She fights not to answer. It's debased. The truth of what she's willing to give. Just as before, the words come anyway.

"My loyalty. My love. My body."

"Deal." She raises back to her feet, coming around the table to stand before Irene. With one hand she takes Irene's chin and tips her face up. "There is no need for shame now. From this day forth you are one of us. You will have all you need and more. I am your mistress, and you are my beloved servant."

"Yes, my Lady," she breathes.

Her obedience is rewarded. Rosavier leans down, and for the first time in her life Irene tastes another woman's kiss. It's an intoxicating thing. So soft, so inviting. Irene might very well have felt her legs give out on her were she not already seated. She lets slip a small, desperate noise as they part.

"Have patience, my pet. I have sworn to give you pleasures you have never known. I will not let you leave this place unsatisfied." With a wave of her hand, the door swings open once more. "Amos, come. Our newest addition is famished. I believe you are more than capable of giving her what she needs."

Irene feels her heart slam against her ribs. Lady Rosavier couldn't possibly mean what she thinks she means. The simmering heat is quickly coming to a boil, taking over her body. What remains of her logic shies away from the implications, yet the rest of her shudders with excitement. Hands comb soothingly through her hair as the man reappears. He doesn't look upset in the slightest to see her already touch-drunk with someone else. If anything, he looks bemused.

"I'm glad to hear it's all worked out then. So tell me, how may I be of assistance?"

"Take her to my bed. The poor girl is feeling a bit weak."

He comes to her at once. His broad figure looming over her doesn't feel threatening like it does on the rare occasion Roland seeks her out. Irene indeed finds it comforting, how carefully he lifts her into his arms. She can't keep down her deepest urges. That smile, like he's been waiting for her his whole life. She kisses him with abandon.

He returns her affections without hesitation. The roughness of his stubble, the hunger of his tongue tasting hers is so different from Lady Rosavier. She finds she can't pick a favorite. By the time he sets her on the bed he has her gasping. It's a wonder that there's room for all three of them to fit. Yet they do. Slowly her new lovers strip away her clothing. Their touch is practiced and unhurried. Each brush of skin leaves her begging. Rosavier steals Irene's breath with a wicked tongue. Amos savors the symphony of noises he pulls from her as his hands map out the planes of her body. His fingers stroke her perfectly. Every sensitive spot ruthlessly searched for and found. Irene cries out. It's so good, but not what she yearns for most. Finally, when none of them can hold back any longer, he settles himself between her legs.

Where one begins and ends is a mystery over the next few hours. The delicious friction of Amos filling her over and over again is more than she has ever dreamed. Filthy praises being sung in her ear by Rosavier's otherworldly voice has her on her knees. She is left sobbing as she finds countless releases in their hands. Yet she begs for them to continue, until her mouth is too busy to form words. It's only when the sun begins to crawl back up that they are too exhausted to go on. She rests in the afterglow while her mistress explains everything and answers every question. Irene lets herself drift off. She knows now what she needs to do.

Roland Keller wakes up in his bed with the mother of all hangovers. It hooks at the back of his throat before he even opens his eyes. His attempt to roll out of bed and stumble to the bathroom is more of a half-hearted lurch that stops at the nightstand. He retches a thick, repulsive pool of stagnant beer and bile onto the floor. Only the luck of losing his balance backwards stops him from landing in his own sick.

"Roland?" A feminine voice asks. Alice? No, he hadn't seen her since last week. Harriet, maybe? No, that was stupid. He hadn't bothered with her since she'd started putting on weight. Fuck, it's his damn wife. He cracks open his eyes barely enough to take in a blob that looks enough like her for his arm to swing out at before slamming his eyes shut against the stinging daylight, missing her by a mile. Still he swings again, and misses again just as well, completely blind.

"Ya wanna keep your fucking voice down, you inconsiderate bitch?" He growls at her.

"I'm so sorry, darling. I just thought you might want these. Pumpkin seeds from the carnival last night. They were giving them out to everyone who had drinks. It's supposed to be very good for clearing up after-sickness."

"Do I look like I want some cheap street food? Those bozos probably dug it outta the garbage. Go make me a real fucking breakfast and get this mess cleaned up. It smells to hell and back."

"Yes, dear. It's going to be ready in just a few minutes. I'll just leave these here for you and some water. Please give them a try. They've done wonders for the others."

He can hear her heels clicking on the hardwood as she leaves again. The sound irritates him. Of course she'd be wearing the loudest possible footwear while he's hung over. It's the little stuff like that he can't stand. When he does peek open his eyes for a bare second, he notes that despite saying she wants him to take the little remedy, she left it on her side of the bed. Does she really think he doesn't notice stuff like that? The way she constantly makes things as difficult as possible even after he's told her exactly what he expects. It's her own fault really—a man can only have so much patience.

Swearing to himself he's not gonna hold back this time, not until she learns her lesson, he reaches with a pained groan to the cup of water and downs it. The cold helps a bit, but overall it just makes him feel like he has more to puke up. He looks again. A little plate is set out with roasted pumpkin seeds on it. It tickles something in his mind about last night. Something about pumpkins. No, jack-o'-lanterns. There had been a whole lot of both as Roland partied with the other fountain drinkers. They had smashed them, he thinks. Then the carnies had come around, probably to tell them all to calm down, though he can't remember any of them actually talking. Those creeps had gathered up some of the mess but left most of it for he and the others to throw at each other in their drunken revelry.

So they had been collecting the seeds, it would seem. If it was a cure-all for drinking, he supposed that would make some kind of sense. He had to admit, giving stuff out for free might be a losing strategy for making money, but it probably would get folks to come back twice. That bleeding heart of a dame might be pretty to look at, but she was a lousy businesswoman. He bet he could get back in a second night for free, and if he played his cards right maybe even see what was under that funny-looking dress. Yeah, that was an idea. He grabs some of the seeds off the table and eats them quickly. They taste like…

They taste like a backwards deal, like a pretty face that's never been lied to before, or maybe like standing head and shoulders above the rest. They taste like the best kind of feelings, all of Roland's proudest moments, rolled into one.

Damn it was good. He eats the rest for good measure. By the time he's done savoring the nostalgia he finds he can open his eyes just fine. His ears don't seem so sensitive either. In wonder, he pops up to his feet like a dandelion through the sidewalk. Good as new, who would have guessed? Suddenly feeling much more forgiving, he makes it downstairs, away from the nasty mess he'd made in the room. She'll still need to clean it, but to his surprise he comes downstairs to something half decent.

Irene is dressed properly, in one of her last remaining tailored dresses, hair pinned up and makeup done. The table she put together has toast, bacon, hash, eggs over easy, and fried tomatoes set out.

"So the seeds worked. That's wonderful. Absolutely wonderful." There's something about the way she says that. It gives him a pause. A light is twinkling in her eyes he hasn't seen in years. It shouldn't worry him, but for some reason it does. He frowns at her but takes his seat anyway. It's stupid to be scared of a little thing like her, so he decides he isn't.

"Looks like you're not tryin' to starve me for once. Have that mess taken care of by the time I get home though, ya got it?" He takes a bite of his food. It's good. One of the only reasons he hasn't kicked her out yet is her cooking. It doesn't scratch the same itch those little pumpkin roasters did, but it will at least fill his stomach.

"Of course, Roland, I'll go clean it now. When do you think you'll be back?" she asks lightly, leaving her much smaller plate untouched to go grab a bucket from under the sink.

"When I get back," he seethes. Fuck, he hates it when she tries to keep tabs on him. If he wanted to marry his mom he'd dig her up first. She just nods and goes upstairs, but not before he notices a little smile pulling at her face. He looks down at his food with suspicion. No, she wouldn't have the brains, let alone the guts to do something like poison him. Would she?

He'll get something at the coffee shop. Yeah, the coffee shop, then work, make a few sales till sundown, and then head straight to the yards in time for the carnival to open. That's a plan, he thinks to himself. He doesn't bother saying goodbye or putting anything away, just gets his jacket out of the closet and heads out while absently picking at his face.

He's far away by the time Irene is done with her unpleasant task. She puts away the cleaning supplies, careful to leave them somewhere handy, then washes her hands twice before taking her husband's seat at the head of the table. Though it's long gone cold, she eats her fill of his barely touched food with satisfaction. All she has to do now is wait.

For Roland, the week leading up to Halloween flies by. He goes to work, goes to the carnival and charms his way in, drinks his weight in booze, then wakes up at home with some pumpkin seeds ready and waiting to cure him. It's damn near a perfect dream. Only there are some things that are niggling in his mind.

For one thing, he never can remember how he gets home every night. He goes to the carnival on foot, so it's not impossible that he's walking back and forgetting about it. It just bothers him that it's the one thing he can't remember. Yet he always wakes up tucked into bed.

More pressing is Irene's unusual behavior. It is great, for the most part. She makes herself either useful or scarce, just how he likes it. It's more the way she's going about it that gets to him. He catches her grinning to herself, at random times, like there's some inside joke she's keeping. Other times she just stares at him, an intense kind of expectation on her face like she is waiting for something to happen. If she wants him to compliment her for doing her job as his wife, she can damn well start doing better, he tells her one day. She says nothing in return, just nods and walks away humming a tune he can't pin down.

Lastly, and most recently, is the rash. Roland isn't quite sure where it came from, but in just a few days it becomes more that he can stand. From his first return to the carnival he's been itching and picking at random patches of his skin. Normally he's able to ignore it after the first few mugs, but soon his arms, legs, chest, back, neck, and face all get clawed so raw that it becomes a constant agony. His whole body feels like a scab, and all the little nooks and crannies he can't get to are like hot barbed wires rubbing against him. From the back of his eyelids to the spaces between his toes. Sometimes he almost thinks he can feel something, under the surface, something moving around in the spaces between his muscles and skin. If he had another drink it would make it go away, but he knows full well he won't be able to get his hands on one in this condition.

Come Halloween morning, he wakes to find Irene sitting at his side, once again the picture of expectation. He wants to slap that look off her face. But he can't move so much as his fingers without tearing the thin layer of protection his dried blood has formed, without searing waves of pain racking him. He wants to scream and curse at her, but then he'll rip all the delicate flesh of his face open. So all he can do is glare at her. She must know it too, because she smiles down at him in return.

"Darling, I can't tell you how happy I am. Tonight is going to be the beginning of a new life for us. One where I get to be happy, and you do all the work quietly, while I have fun and take lovers whenever I want."

There are no words for the rage that fills him. He splits his lips immediately when he hisses, "What did you just say to me, you worthless little whore?"

"You heard me the first time, Roland. Don't make me repeat myself," she says, a level of command in her tone he's never heard before.

To hell with everything else. His pride is willing to pay the price of pain. He launches himself from the bed and grabs her by the throat, sending a wall of fire up his body as they fall to the ground together. He delights in her desperate gasps, covets the sound of pain as her head hits the floor.

The only thing missing is the look of fear she used to have. He tries to force it from her, tightening his grip so she knows her place before he beats her unconscious. Instead, as her face goes red so do her eyes. Not bloodshot but enraged. In a motion swift as a cat she scratches at his face. It might not be enough normally, but he shrieks in pain as the skin there comes cleanly away.

Instinctively, he lets go of her in some desperate need to try and put the hanging flap of skin back. Then he feels her nails at his chest. His body feels like it's falling apart with all the integrity of wet paper. He recoils at once, trying to get away from the agony. Somehow, she is still attacking him, pulling away at his insides mercilessly. At least he thinks she is.

Until he feels the vines under his skin.

Blinking thick blood out of his eyes, he falls back and looks down at his own chest. It's open, the skin gone, and dark vines have woven themselves into everything he can see. He holds out shaking arms to examine them. From what remains of his flesh, roots are sprouting out at random. His muscles contract on their own as the tendrils move freely throughout his body. Shock steals away his screams; he can only twitch and whimper as his wife gets back to her feet. She stands over him with pure loathing.

"You're probably wondering what's happening to you. Don't worry. I would love nothing more than to tell you," she croaks, rubbing at her already bruising neck. "Ever since you dragged me to Lady Rosavier's Carnival I have been planning this. Finally some revenge for all the hell you put me through. Finally freedom from this miserable life!"

She kicks him as hard as she can, heedless of the gore that splashes up her leg as a result. "My Lady has taken me under her wing. It was always her plan to have you rooted, but she let me in on how to perform the ritual myself. It's only right, she said, that I was the one to curse you."

She kicks again, this time squarely between his legs. His manhood rips apart like an old apple being thrown at a brick wall. A guttural howl of pain forces its way past the wall of protection his shock has given him so far. "All of the jack-o'-lantern carnies are cursed, you see. All of them are bound to obey Lady Rosavier and any who have received the mark of her blessing. You did most of it yourself honestly, I just sowed the seeds. You even took care of watering yourself. Returning over and over again to the fountain without any encouragement."

She takes a breath, smoothing out her ruined hairstyle and tugging her rumpled clothes back down. "It all starts with the fountain, you know. It's like fertilizer for the plants. The pumpkins actually. You see the ones that are growing in the earth produce a type of seed that has exceptionally powerful magic. While abundant, it can't be replanted directly. It needs to be planted into living human flesh to fruit. Those seeds are the ones that can then be planted back into the earth to start the cycle again. All the while the incubator must remain hydrated with the fertilizer for an entire week. The time to harvest falls on Halloween every year."

She goes to her dresser. He can hear over his own shaking gasps of air that she's looking for something. He tries to get his limbs to move. Tries to crawl away while her back is turned, but the roots fight him. They contract at random, slithering around inside him. Desperation manages to flip him onto his belly and he reaches out for the foot of the bed to pull himself along. Her heel comes down on his back, spearing into him and stopping the pathetic amount of distance he'd gained.

"You know, when carving a proper jack-o'-lantern the first step is to hollow it out and collect the seeds." He feels something heavy press against the back of his head. "There's probably a cleaner way of doing this, but I think it gets points for style. I'm told I'm a good shot. Don't worry, you're going to feel everything."

He does feel everything.

He feels the top of his head explode. Watches his own mind as it sprays everywhere, the tentacles that escape from his cranium in the aftermath. He expects any moment for the pain to fade away as the world goes blank, except it never does. He can still see, he can't move, or talk, but he can think, and look and feel. Trapped in his own body as his treacherous wife begins to hum her odd little song. It occurs to him only now that it is the very same melody that plays at the carnival, normally being wheezed out by some unseen accordionist. Irene doesn't stop at shooting him though. She pulls out all kinds of strange little tools. She hollows out what remains in his head, putting it into a bucket and making sure to scrape every last little spot clean.

Then she looks around until she finds any last chunks of his brain. She knows he's still there too. She gives him a little wave and sits in his field of sight while she roots around for her prize. One by one she finds large yellow pods in the bucket of red. She counts them out as the plants continue their work, the ones from his head reach down encircling his ruined face, forming a structure very much like.

As the sun goes down, Irene regards her new jack-o'-lantern with pride. His face is carved to remind her of why she was willing to fall so very far. A crying pumpkin face looks back at her in absolute silence. A perfectly obedient husk she'd paid for with seven years of misery. She takes him for one last stroll through the park, then they make their way back home. Not to that awful house but to a carnival at the edge of town. The caravans are loading up with a fresh harvest. The freaks greet her with all the joy she had envisioned. Though their own hands had carved far more jack-o'-lanterns than she had, they all praised her first piece. She'll work faster with experience. It's only her first, after all. They dispose of the mess better than she had too, but there would be years and years to learn the trade. Decades. Centuries, even. She had more than enough time.

She watches the city disappear from view for the last time and wonders idly how long it will take for the neighbors to report them missing. Will the cops knock down that old blue door with the peeling paint? What will they do when they find a bucket of brain and skull fragments in the same sink she had slaved over for years? Will anyone try to pick up the piles of discarded skin on the bedroom floor or wash the blood splatter off the ceiling? She doesn't intend to stay and find out. Irene has a new life to live and a new family to spend her favorite season with.

As it turns out, it takes four days for the cops to come by for a wellness check, three weeks to document the entire crime scene, and only one year for a forgotten seed to produce a very unusual pumpkin in the condemned shell of the Keller home. Sheltered by the fear generated by what had taken place, it sits for longer than it should have. Someone with knowledge of its dark origin, not unlike Lady Rosavier, would have it burned, priceless seeds and all. Yet the Lady knew nothing of it. So it sat. It waited.

Years later, Irene's story would begin to fade from headline to urban legend. Another Halloween night beckons a pack of rather drunk teenagers to do what nearly all teenagers do. When rotten plywood over the windows doesn't stop them for longer than a minute, they crawl in to continue their festivities. Hidden by derelict walls they discover the forgotten gourd. A dare is set forth. A new batch of seeds is sown.

# ABOUT THe AUTHOr

A.C Salazar is an asexual, bi-romantic, latina author with a crippling repulsion for social media. Fresh from her debut short story Hungry she hopes that Pumpkin Seeds will show prospective readers a marked improvement in storytelling. With a love for horror, adventure, fantasy, sci-fi, and many more she hopes that future works will be as varied and unique as her audience. Ms. Salazar is a proud auntie, adopted Oregonian, and a part time potato.

# masked plans

R.C. Lehan

*Man is least himself when he talks in his own person. Give him a mask, and he will tell you the truth.*
*-Oscar Wilde*

# CHAPTER 1

The malevolent glow beckoned Daphne. A mixture of orange and black light dancing in the darkness, it called to her, making her heart race. It was a familiar sensation. One she'd known for years, but it thrilled her every time. With ginger steps, she crossed the threshold.

Inside the carnival, her senses filled to the brim. Bright lights of every color were strewn through the air, dangling off midway games and illuminating rides towering fifty feet high. The aroma of corn dogs, funnel cakes, and popcorn mingled in her nostrils, while a cacophony of sounds flooded her ears. Bells and whistles going off as people shouted after winning a coveted prize muddled the screams echoing from the ride patrons.

Yes, the annual Halloween carnival was in full effect. Everything was as it had been every year prior. Even the chilly breeze was familiar, if not a bit uncomfortable.

"Ugh, next year I'm wearing fuzzy pajamas as my costume," Lynnette complained, pulling her thin cardigan tighter across her corset top.

Daphne laughed. "Yeah, right. You really think Janna will let you?" She nudged Janna's side.

Janna rolled her dark eyes behind even darker eye makeup. "Of course not. We have a group dynamic. We're not changing that."

"Pffft," Lynnette spouted. "What's our 'group dynamic'? Sluts in black?"

Daphne couldn't help bursting into laughter, her sides splitting. Lynnette and Janna were two of her closest friends, along with Emily. The four of them had been close since high school, but even now, in their mid-twenties, Lynnette and Janna still butted heads.

Especially when it came to fashion.

Low-cut tops and short skirts paired with clunky knee-high boots or hooker heels was not Lynnette's preferred style. But for Halloween, Janna *always* chose their costumes.

Janna scoffed, popping her gum. "Then don't complain to me next year when your fuzzy pjs don't get you laid."

"Whatever." Lynnette waved Janna off. "Let's get this night started."

The Halloween carnival was tradition as was the way they always kicked it off–the Ferris wheel. No matter how long the line was, or how hungry they were, it was their first stop of the night.

After they all filed into the bright pink, round car, the ride operator made sure the door was latched. His eyes flicked to the women individually, a sleazy grin sliding over his face as he eyed their costumes. "Don't you ladies worry. I'll take good care of you." With a wink, he stepped away.

Janna fluffed her hair. "See? The costumes work."

"Yeah, as long as you're trying to attract carnies," Emily said, feigning a gag.

"Hey, don't knock them 'til you've tried one."

Their eruption of giggles turned into shrill yelps when the car jerked into motion. Daphne leaned against the seat, staring through the Plexiglas barrier to watch the ground shrink away. Heights were no problem. In fact, the feeling of soaring through the air freed her.

As the car rose, Daphne glimpsed a figure, clad in all black, lurking in the shadows behind the Ferris wheel. He might as well have been a phantom had it not been for the ornate sugar skull mask covering his face. She canted her head, her gaze lingering on him as the car rose higher.

He seemed to be watching the wheel, and even though there was no way to prove it, Daphne could've sworn he was watching their car specifically. The ominous tension in her muscles was almost enough to convince her.

To ease herself, she toyed with the idea of him being an employee simply taking a break. That thought worked for all of five seconds. The carnival workers wore orange shirts, and definitely didn't wear costumes, so who was this weirdo?

A shiver ran down her spine, but not from the cool night air.

"Daph," Janna's voice called. "What do you want to do after this?"

Daphne turned to find her friends all watching her intently. Crinkling her brow, she asked, "Why? What are you all staring at me for?"

"You're the tie-breaker," Emily said. "Lynnette wants to do the midway, Janna wants to go inside to the dance, but *I* want to do more rides. What do you say?"

Daphne smirked. "Rides."

Lynette and Janna groaned as Emily reached across the car for a high-five.

Daphne checked her phone. "It's eight o'clock, the perfect time for rides. Most of the families are leaving, and the adult crowd won't be in full swing until close to ten."

"Fine," Lynnette and Janna said in frustrated unison.

With a satisfied grin, Daphne turned her attention back over the edge of the car. They were on their downward path now. The people below grew in size until they were normally proportioned again, but as the car started back up, Daphne took note of one person missing.

The masked man.

Her gaze flicked back and forth, darting between tents and through the crowds, but he had vanished. Frowning, Daphne rubbed the back of her neck where her hairs stood on end.

"What'cha thinking about?" Janna asked with a pop of her gum.

Not wanting to sound paranoid, Daphne turned to her friends with a smile. "Admiring the view."

"See anything you like?" Janna bobbed her eyebrows.

"No, not like that," Daphne said, flatly. "I like watching the scenery go by. It's cool looking."

"Leave it to you to watch the scenery," Lynette said.

"It's better than looking at you bitches," Daphne said, a teasing tone to her words.

The other three girls gasped, their mouths dropping open as they each took mock swings at Daphne.

"I guess I can agree." Emily settled back in her seat. "But screw the scenery, I'd rather be looking at a hot guy. No offense, ladies."

Daphne joined in on her friends' giggles, but inside she was anything but jovial. Only a year ago, she had done exactly what Emily suggested. Wrapped in her boyfriend's strong arms, Daphne had stared into his deep blue eyes, ignoring every bit of moving landscape as she devoured Thoren's kiss.

His cinnamon-flavored kiss thanks to the gum he always chewed.

Their budding relationship was the best love Daphne had ever known. Thoren was attentive, always listening and never denying her a moment. He had been caring, protective, and never made her feel like a burden. Not to mention he was the best sex of her life.

Between the sheets, Thoren was an animal. He took what he wanted, when he wanted it, but he never frightened Daphne. He wouldn't hurt her. In fact, he tended to her needs before satiating his own desires, but did it with such passion, she swooned every time.

Her heart sank as she clenched her thighs.

"You're not thinking about *him* are you?" Janna asked, judgment in her tone.

Daphne shook her head to clear it of his image. "No," she lied.

Janna arched a skeptical eyebrow.

Daphne sighed. "Okay, fine. Yes, I was thinking about Thoren."

The other three girls groaned. They'd hated Thoren from the start. The tattoos painting his arms made him "bad," and the dark hair that hung in his face made him "grungy." They'd called him clingy and obsessive when he'd checked on Daphne during a late girls' night. She considered it sweet that he'd worried. Her friends thought it was "creepy."

"That loser wasn't worthy of you," Emily chided.

Daphne winced. In her mind, he was every bit worthy of her, and then some.

"Besides, didn't he up and disappear on you?" Lynnette asked.

Daphne's shoulders felt as if two elephants sat upon them. After months of listening to her friends complain about Thoren, Daphne caved. Their concerns took root in her mind, and she questioned whether she was too infatuated to see the red flags they kept harping about.

So, in the late spring, she broke things off.

He was devastated. He begged her to take him back, said he'd change however she wanted him to change. Weeks went by with emails, calls, and texts, until suddenly, they all stopped. The very last thing he wrote her was *One day, we won't have any obstacles, and you'll be mine again.* Then, she never heard another word. It was as if he'd never existed.

"Talk about a *Thoren* in your side," Janna said with a laugh as the Ferris wheel came to a stop. "You can do *so* much better,"

*I don't know how,* Daphne thought sadly as she exited the ride and followed her friends down the ramp.

# CHAPTER 2

After indulging in more rides, including a double round of the pirate ship, the four women opted for a snack. It had been an hour since the Ferris wheel, and though Daphne's stomach rumbled, the sting of Thoren's absence hurt worse.

Janna threw her arm over her friend's shoulder. "Why the long face?"

"You know."

"Eh, nothing a funnel cake won't fix."

Daphne giggled at Janna's joke, though she knew it was partly true. Funnel cakes were Daphne's favorite carnival food, and she'd been craving one ever since they walked through the entrance. It might not ease the pain of Thoren, but it would ease her empty stomach.

When Janna stepped up to order, Daphne stood aside while Lynnette and Emily chatted away. Their conversation about the latest pop singer's number one hit bored her. Daphne much preferred music with an edge to it. Heavy guitar riffs, muddy bass lines, and drums that wouldn't quit.

It was something she and Thoren had in common.

The self-pity sinking in her chest was quickly chased away when someone bumped her elbow. She flinched, tucking her arm to her side, but when she glanced around to find the culprit, she gasped.

The man in the sugar skull mask turned to peer over his leather jacket-clad shoulder as he walked away.

Daphne stared wide-eyed after him, her heart thumping against her ribs. Was that the same guy? She convinced herself it was a coincidence. The carnival wasn't huge, just a small county fair, so it was fathomable she would see the same people multiple times. No reason to get worked up.

"Hey, Daph. What's wrong?" Emily asked, breaking Daphne's trance. "You look like you've seen a ghost."

She blinked rapidly. "Just hungry. Let's eat."

They claimed a small picnic table around the corner and feasted on the heavenly fried pastry covered in powdered sugar. Halfway through their meal, Lynnette asked, "What's next on the list?"

"Ooh, the swings," Daphne said.

Lynnette shook her head. "No way. I'm not getting on those things in this short skirt." She ran her hands down her thighs, stopping on the hem of her skirt that barely covered her ass.

"It's a solid seat, Lynn." Janna rolled her eyes. "No one's going to see your goods."

"You still have that chain that goes right between your legs. It's an STD waiting to happen."

"Well, you're not supposed to hump it!" Janna practically shouted, and they all burst into laughter.

Emily caught her breath first. "How about you come with me, then? Janna and Daphne can ride the swings while you and I do the Tilt-a-Whirl."

All nodding in agreement, the four women finished their treat before splitting up. The swings were another of Daphne's favorites. Though not quite as high as the Ferris wheel, they still provided the excitement of soaring through the air.

After securing the metal latch on her seat, Daphne glanced behind her at Janna, and they shared a grin. Then, the machine's engine roared to life, and the entire mechanism jolted. With a flutter in her chest, Daphne faced forward, eager to embrace the wind whipping through her long, dark hair.

But as the ride took off, Daphne's gaze went the opposite direction. It tracked the masked man standing in the shadows until her spine threatened to snap. When she came back around, he was still there. This time, as her head turned, so did his.

He *was* watching her.

The ride picked up speed, and so did Daphne's heart rate. When she rounded the third time, she almost didn't want to look, but she did.

And he was gone.

Goosebumps ravaged her skin. She slouched in her swing as she released all the air from her lungs. When she inhaled, the cool air refreshed her. It blew across her cheeks and through her hair, reminding her where she was. This was a happy place for her, the swings. She was in the air, able to view the landscape in all directions while the stars twinkled high above her. With a deep exhale, she closed her eyes.

They popped back open immediately. The image of the sugar skull mask had burned itself into her memory, and it haunted her with every blink.

Who was he? What did he want? Was it all coincidence, or was he following her intentionally?

Daphne knew curiosity killed the cat, but she couldn't help herself. All those years of watching horror movies had taught her to fear men in masks who stalked young women. But this wasn't a movie.

When the ride ended, Daphne hesitated to leave the safety of the corral. She searched the crowd surrounding the enclosure, but none donned the brightly-colored Dia de los Muertos mask. Chewing on her lip, Daphne stood frozen in place.

Until someone grabbed her arm.

She yelped, ripping herself away from her attacker's grip.

"Whoa, whoa," Janna cried. "Dude, what's wrong with you?"

Daphne's hand flew to her chest, pressing against her breastbone to keep her heart from bursting free. She swallowed it down as she stared at the concern lacing her friend's face. "Nothing. Except for you sneaking up on me."

Janna arched an eyebrow. "Are you sure? You looked kind of manic during the ride."

As her heart rate slowed, Daphne's rationality took over again. *I'm probably overreacting. No need to worry Janna.* "I was…taking in the scenery."

"Uh huh," Janna said, skepticism dripping from her words. "Come on, let's go find the girls." She linked her arm with Daphne's and tugged her along.

The walk across the fair grounds to the Tilt-a-Whirl had Daphne on edge. Would she glimpse the masked man again? If she did, would she tell Janna?

Daphne decided against worrying her friend until she had better evidence to go on. Besides, the sensation of her best friend's arm against her own ebbed

Daphne's tension with each step. It helped that the sugar skull mask didn't make another appearance. The farther they walked, the less tense Daphne became.

At the Tilt-a-Whirl, Daphne and Janna waited by the exit as the ride began to slow.

"I saw Emily on there, but I didn't see Lynn. Did you?" Janna asked.

Daphne shook her head, a strange sinking feeling gnawing at her gut. The ride stopped and the squeal of unloved metal lap bars rising filled the air. Emily trotted out of her car with a childlike grin on her face, practically skipping down the exit ramp.

When she joined Daphne and Janna, she glanced around. "Where's Lynn?"

"We were about to ask you the same question," Janna said. "Didn't she ride with you?"

"She did once, but I wanted to do it again, and she didn't." Emily pointed behind Daphne. "She said she'd wait over there."

Daphne and Janna turned to find a bench almost completely shrouded in shadows sitting across the dirt path from the Tilt-a-Whirl between two tents. The darkness behind it seemed to stretch forever.

Daphne shivered. "Where would she have gone?"

"Well, the line was pretty long, so maybe she got tired of waiting?" Emily shrugged.

"She probably got bored and went to the midway." Janna pulled out her phone and tapped the screen. "I'm texting her now."

A thickness hung in the air as the three friends anxiously awaited Lynnette's response.

It never came.

"Ugh, fine. I'll call her." Janna raised her phone to her ear, but soon began pacing. When she pulled the phone away, she crinkled her brow. "She didn't answer."

They exchanged worried looks. While it wasn't unusual for them to get separated, especially if a new male friend had come along, it was strange that Lynnette didn't text any of them her whereabouts.

With an exasperated sigh, Janna threw her hands in the air. "Oh, for fuck's sake. Let's go to the midway. She's probably over there."

In silence, they made their way back across the fairgrounds, but a pit sat in Daphne's stomach like a ball of lead the entire time.

# CHAPTER 3

S tanding in front of the midway, Daphne, Janna, and Emily stared at the aisles of games. Three in total, they held all the squirt guns, ping-pong balls, and poorly sewn teddy bears one could ever want. The din of bells and whistles mingled in the air with the game leaders spouting their attraction speeches. For every, "Come one, come all," there were a dozen buzzers sounding off.

"Okay," Janna said. "Let's split up. Emily, you go left, I'll go right, and Daph, you take the middle. We'll meet on the other side. One of us is bound to see Lynn."

Daphne didn't like the idea of splitting up. After all, that's what got Lynnette lost in the first place. And what if she ran into the masked man? If this were a horror movie, she'd be an easy target.

With a deep swallow of her fear, Daphne started down the midway aisle. The crowd had grown from only a couple of hours ago; a peril of Saturday night at the carnival. At ten o'clock, the carnival went into "adult only" mode, where only people twenty-one and older could enter. Not having to listen to the frantic cries and screams of children made the experience more pleasant, but it also meant more adults to wade through.

Daphne slid between bodies, turning her head back and forth as she passed each game. The costumes began to run together. Pink blurs of tulle bejeweled with glittering stones for every princess or ballerina. Fluffy feathers sticking out of pirate hats while long leather dusters hung off dozens of cowboys. They all collided, becoming one big blob of fake personas.

But not one of them was Lynnette.

Daphne tried her best to convince herself that maybe Janna or Emily had found her. Maybe they were already waiting at the end of the midway. Oh, how the relief would flood her upon seeing all her friends together again. The panic and the worry would be all for naught, but she'd welcome the sensation.

A sharp, joyful shriek tore Daphne's attention to the side where a woman bounced up and down as the game leader handed her a gigantic stuffed giraffe.

*Not Lynn.*

The despair within her deepened, gripping her nerves tight. Where the hell was Lynnette? Was she in trouble, or simply playing games? Maybe she'd met a guy and was off in a dark corner somewhere sucking face. It wouldn't be the first time one of the girls had chosen a guy over the group.

Daphne frowned as she thought about the myriad of instances when her friends had accused her of choosing Thoren over them. She had never seen it that way. She had tried to split her time as evenly as possible, but when Thoren would pin her against the wall and kiss every inch of her, it wasn't easy to choose girls' night.

A deep longing thrummed through Daphne. Thoren's touch was seared into her memory, setting her on fire whenever she thought about him. His full lips claiming hers, his hot breath cascading down her throat, his fingers digging into her as if he would never let her go. It was enough to make desire pulse within her.

A desire that could only be satiated by Thoren's—

"Oof!" Daphne crashed into something.

Something hard.

Shaking her head to right her senses, Daphne realized she'd run into someone. "Oh, sorry," she said, but the syllables died on her lips.

The man in the sugar skull mask stood before her, mere inches away. He was so tall, Daphne had to tilt her head back to look at him. Between his height and his broad shoulders, she felt as if he were caging her in as he loomed.

Her entire body seized, her muscles tensing to the brink of snapping. She couldn't move except for the shaking breaths bleeding through her parted lips. Even her heart felt like it had stopped.

As everything around her slowed, Daphne's vision tunneled on the mask. Its cheery design and brightly painted flowers offered little comfort. In fact, they terrified her even more. Would this be the last thing she ever saw?

Daphne's throat closed up. She couldn't breathe. She couldn't swallow.

*He's strangling me!*

Instinctively, her hands flew to her neck to pry his fingers from her throat, but they weren't there. He hadn't moved at all. He stood directly in front of her, staring down ominously.

Still, the vision of the sugar skull fading to black as she lost consciousness played in her mind.

She wanted to scream. Wanted to plead for someone to help her, but she couldn't. All she could do was stare into the fabric covered eyes of the mask and wait for her fate to befall her.

When his arm moved, Daphne shut her eyes, a fearful tear streaking down her cheek.

He brushed it away.

His large, warm palm gently cupped her face, his thumb wiping the tear from her skin. He drug his fingers down her jaw to caress her lower lip before dropping his hand and stepping past her.

With his absence, Daphne's knees gave out. She stumbled to the closest game and plopped down on the stool as she regained her composure. Pressing her hand to her forehead, she studied the ground.

*What in the flying fuck just happened?*

Her breath steadied and her limbs stopped tingling, but her chest still felt tight. That wasn't the encounter she had expected. She had been sure he was going to strangle or stab her, or at the very least, kidnap her.

Now, she was just confused.

"Hey, sweetcheeks. You gonna play?"

Daphne whipped her head up to see the Balloon Pop game worker staring down at her with arched eyebrows. She shook her head.

He frowned, jutting his chin behind her. "Well, then get your cute little ass outta here so a *paying* customer can play."

"Sorry," she whispered, because she had yet to recoup her voice, and left her seat. Daphne trudged down the rest of the aisle, keeping one eye out for Lynette and the other for the masked man.

She came up empty on both accounts.

At the end of the midway, she found Janna waiting with folded arms and her foot furiously tapping the ground.

When she saw Daphne, she threw her arms in the air. "Finally! I thought I'd lost more friends. Did you see Lynn?"

Daphne shook her head.

"Shit. I didn't either." Janna glanced around. "And where the fuck is Emily?"

Daphne still didn't answer. She simply shrugged.

Janna groaned. "What's wrong with you now?"

"I think…" Daphne chewed on the inside of her cheek. "Janna, I think I have a problem."

"No shit, Sherlock. We have two problems." Janna held up a pair of fingers. "No Lynn, and now no Emily."

Daphne shook her head harder, crinkling her brow. "No, Janna. Aside from them."

"What, then?"

"I think someone's stalking me." The words shook from her mouth.

"What!?"

"Mhm. There's a guy in a mask who's been following me around."

Janna's features fell apathetic. "Daph, we're at a *carnival* on *Halloween*. There are lots of guys in masks."

"I know, but I keep seeing the same one. I saw him watching us on the Ferris wheel and the swings. He bumped into me at the food stand, and I just ran into him down there." Daphne motioned toward the midway. "It's got to be more than coincidence."

"Okay, so some guy thinks you're hot. He's probably trying to work up the courage to ask for your number."

"He didn't ask for it just now."

"What do you mean 'just now'?"

Daphne sighed. "When I said I ran into him, I mean literally ran into him. I was busy looking for Lynn, wasn't watching where I was going, and he was *right* there."

Janna's eyes widened. "Did he say anything? Threaten you or something?"

"No, nothing like that." Daphne shuddered, recalling the fear she felt upon facing him up close and personal, but the tension melted away as she remembered his gentle touch. She put her hand to her cheek. "All he did was brush his fingers down my cheek."

"Ew. Creepy."

It wasn't, though. Every rational part of Daphne knew she should agree with Janna, but something about his touch comforted her. It was tender, affectionate. A sensation she'd been missing for a very long time.

But she couldn't tell Janna that. "It was strange."

"Strange, nothing. That's downright bizarre." Janna's gaze flicked around. "Okay, let's wander down the other side of the midway and look for Emily. For all we know she found Lynn and they're still over there." She locked eyes on Daphne's. "Once we find them, we'll go find security. If they can't do anything about the weirdo in the mask, then they can escort us to the parking lot. Okay?"

Daphne nodded, linked her arm with Janna's, and the two of them trotted to the other side of the midway.

# CHAPTER 4

"F uck!" Janna exclaimed as she and Daphne exited the opposite end of the midway. "They're not here." Huffing, she folded her arms. "What do we do?"

Daphne shrugged. "Go to security? We can tell them about Emily and Lynn *and* my stalker."

"Yeah, I guess." Janna scrunched her forehead, but her face relaxed as a heavy bass line thumped in the background. She threw her head back. "Ugh, of course!"

"What?"

"I know where they are."

"You do?"

"Yeah, they're inside the dance hall."

Daphne arched an eyebrow. "How do you know that?"

"Think about it, genius." Janna rolled her eyes. "It's Halloween, and what do you do on Halloween?"

Understanding dawned on Daphne. "Scare your friends."

"Bingo," Janna said, tapping her nose. "Those little conspirator bitches planned this whole thing. And I wouldn't be surprised if they hired some guy to stalk you."

"Seriously? You think they'd go that far?"

Janna hiked a shoulder to her ear. "You're into clingy weirdos. They probably thought you'd eat it up."

Even with Janna's jab, Daphne wanted to smile at the notion her friends were simply pulling a prank, but the idea of the guy in the sugar skull mask being nothing more than a hired goon made her heart sink. After the tender way he touched her, Daphne's fear was extinguished. Her curiosity though, was piqued. "What if the stalker wasn't their idea?"

"Then we go to security." Janna tugged on Daphne's hand. "Come on. I need a drink after all this stress."

With each step they took, the music grew louder, the bass thumped harder against the soles of their feet, and the second they opened the event center door, their ears were assaulted. The music was not only loud, but the acoustics were terrible. Dance beats echoed off the walls, crashing down in jumbled waves.

Daphne's eyes struggled to focus in the ambient lighting. The soft glow of blacklights muted everyone's edges, unless those edges were white. Anything white or neon took on an entirely different look. Daphne felt like she was in the middle of some bizarre post-apocalyptic celebration.

Janna nudged her, pulling Daphne out of her trance. Janna poked her finger into her own chest before pointing to the right, then she poked Daphne and jutted her chin left. The last thing Janna did was make a circular motion and point to the stage. The two women nodded in agreement and set forth on their searches.

As Daphne edged her way along the wall, a sense of hopelessness rose in her. How on Earth was she supposed to find Lynnette or Emily in this crowd? The vast sea of moving bodies on the dance floor looked like one big blob of arms and legs, all swaying with the music. It was impossible.

The only way, it seemed to Daphne, would be to cut through the masses of dancing drunks, but that was the last thing she wanted to do. Fighting through a bunch of sweaty bodies grinding one another sounded like a fate worse than death.

She stared at the crowd with furrowed brows. Should she at least try? Maybe she should head to the stage first. If Janna had found Lynnette and Emily, there was no reason to dive into the throng.

Daphne pulled out her phone. No messages. Barely even a signal.

She sighed heavily, resigning herself to pass through the sweaty dancers, when she glimpsed the sign for the bathrooms.

Of course. That was an extremely probable place for the other girls to be.

Daphne pushed open the door, immediately squinting in the fluorescent lighting. As her eyes adjusted, she found herself in a mess of interconnected hallways. The building was used for all sorts of events; 4-H club, farmer's markets, rodeos, and anything else that could be held at the fairgrounds. So, it made sense that the building would have several different sized rooms. Why each room had to have its own extended hallway was beyond her, though.

At the end of the main hall, Daphne saw the bathrooms. As she strode toward them, the now muffled music softened even more, no longer the brash pounding against her eardrums. She welcomed the quieter setting, relished being away from the immense crowd.

Daphne pressed her palm to the bathroom door and exhaled as she opened it. "Lynn? Emily? Are you guys in here?"

She was met with silence.

With a heavy sigh that puffed out her cheeks, she stepped back and let the door swing shut. She spun around to slump against the wall. Her head fell back, and she closed her eyes.

*What do I do now?*

Clearly, there was only one choice, and that was to find Janna and go to security. Although, she didn't know exactly what security was going to do. If she and Janna couldn't get ahold of Lynnette or Emily, how would security find them in all this mess?

A cynical giggle escaped Daphne as she thought about how to explain to the security officers about her missing friends. *We're looking for a blonde and a brunette dressed like emo goth sluts.*

The giggle faded as the despondency of the situation took root in her chest. This was no time for laughter. Her friends were missing, and no amount of cynicism or wallowing in self-pity would find them.

Daphne gave herself an assertive nod and pushed off the wall. She took two steps in the direction of the dance, but halted immediately. There, only fifty feet from her, stood the masked man. With bated breath, Daphne stared, and the ornate sugar skull stared back, the man unmoving in his stance.

She licked her lips, about to speak, but before she could, the man dipped his chin and side-stepped into a nearby hallway. As soon as he was gone from sight, Daphne panicked. She couldn't let him get away. She had to know who he was, or at the very least, what he wanted from her.

She took off down the hall with her heels clacking against the linoleum, determined to get to the bottom of the mystery. Daphne nearly lost her balance as she rounded the corner, glimpsing him slip through a doorway.

"Hey," she called out, but he didn't pause.

She took off once again, but immediately slowed her pace. This had to be the craziest thing she'd ever done. With leaden footsteps, she crept to the door and gripped the handle. Her heart beat a mile a minute against her ribs, but she opened the latch and stepped across the threshold.

# CHAPTER 5

The door clicking into place echoed in Daphne's consciousness like a clap of thunder. It rolled through her ears, but it was overshadowed by one thing–the masked man.

In the middle of the room, he stood facing her, and she finally got a good look at him. The leather jacket she had noticed earlier, but now she could see everything. He wore black military-type boots and dark cargo pants. His black shirt was pulled tight across his chest, the muscles defined beneath the sleek fabric.

His image screamed dangerous. Even his stance was confident–feet spread apart, arms at his sides, shoulders pulled back. He looked like he was ready for a fight, but Daphne wasn't scared.

Why wasn't she scared?

This man had been following her, staring at her, all night. She should be frightened. At the very least, on alert, but she felt strangely calm.

Not calm enough to approach him, though. "Who are you?" she asked.

The sugar skull said nothing. Did nothing.

She swallowed and tried again. "Have you been watching me?"

Slowly, his chin dipped.

"So, you *have* been following me?"

Again, a slight chin dip, but nothing else.

"You're not going to hurt me." It should have been a question, but the words left Daphne's mouth as a fearless statement.

The masked man shook his head.

"Don't you speak?"

He hiked a shoulder to his ear.

"So, you've been following me all night, watching what I'm doing, but don't want to hurt me?" Daphne licked her lips, her next question trembling on the tip of her tongue. "What do you want, then?"

His shoulders rose and fell with one breath before he took steps toward her. Daphne stiffened momentarily, but refused to let any sort of fear in. She would be strong. She would be ready, just in case he had lied.

When he was within inches of her, he raised his hand to gently trail his fingers down her cheek to her mouth where he caressed her bottom lip. Though it was the same motion from earlier at the midway, the touch was still exhilarating.

Only this time, he tugged on her lower lip as he drug his finger down her chin. He trailed the length of her throat to her chest. Daphne stood frozen in place, taken aback by his brazen touch, even with the familiar tingle zipping between her legs. He buried his finger in her cleavage before snapping the neckline of her low-cut top.

"Oh." She lifted her chin confidently. "What if I say no?"

The masked man tilted his head to one side and backed away. Daphne instantly missed his nearness. The idea of being excited by this stranger was absurd. She couldn't actually humor this behavior. Could she?

Daphne looked up at him through her lashes. "And what if I say yes?" she whispered.

The masked man took tentative steps toward her until there were only millimeters between them. One of his hands cupped the back of her head while the other snaked around to firmly grip her ass. He yanked her body against his, pressing the bulge in his pants to her hip.

Daphne closed her eyes and inhaled deeply. The scent of his leather jacket flooded her nostrils. The heady aroma sent her mind reeling with ideas of what was coming as anticipation coiled low within her. She felt the mask slide down her cheek to nuzzle into her shoulder.

"Do I get to see your face?" she asked.

The masked man lifted his hand from her backside and pulled away from her. Daphne wanted him close, so she clutched the lapel of his jacket, holding him in place. He looked at her hand before turning the dark gaze of the mask to meet hers. She swallowed deeply, unsure of what he would do.

He simply pointed to the mask and shook his head.

A breath bled from Daphne's lips. "Okay, fine. But I at least need something to call you." She pressed her lips together in a flat line before they curled into a mischievous smirk. "How about I call you Sugar?"

The masked man tilted his head, and Daphne giggled.

"Sugar it is, then." She tugged on his jacket, and he gave in. Throwing her arms around his neck, she pulled him to her.

His strong arms wrapped around her and squeezed her tight. He gripped her ass again, but his other hand began roaming her body. The brush of his fingertips left a path of fire on her skin. They swooped from her hips to her waist to her breasts and back. He didn't spend much time in any one spot, but touched as much of her as he could.

Daphne reveled in the passion of it all. Even without being able to kiss him, she felt as if every movement was catered just to her, like this masked stranger knew exactly where and how to touch her. Each squeeze, each caress, was done with care. He wasn't rushing anything. He almost seemed to be savoring the moment.

Sugar pressed his hips and very obvious erection against her, and Daphne moaned. She felt him shudder. It was subtle and brief, but she felt it all the same. It put a smile on her lips. This man was very clearly in control of the situation, but she still affected him. She wondered how far she could take it.

She tilted her head and pressed her lips to his neck, gently kissing the skin above his jacket collar. He immediately pushed her away and held her against the wall by her throat. Waggling his finger in her face, he glanced toward the door as if to say he'd leave as a consequence.

She playfully smacked his chest to challenge his threat.

He caught her wrist as the black eyes of the mask stared at her. Heated intensity radiated from him.

Daphne should have been scared. This masked man could easily strangle her and no one would know, but she wasn't afraid of him at all. Quite the opposite, in fact. Aside from being wildly turned on, she felt completely comfortable in his presence. Even pressed against the wall with his hand around her throat, there was no doubt in her mind she was safe.

Her mind replayed the moment at the midway, the way her fear had melted with his gentle touch. He may be able to harm her, but she knew he wouldn't.

Slowly, she reached up to pull his hand from her throat. He didn't fight. She took his hand in hers, lifting it to kiss his knuckles. With her other hand, she brushed her fingers down the mask as if it were his jaw.

He didn't move. He just stared at her, and she stared back.

As she looked into the emptiness of the mask's fabric eyes, memories of Thoren flashed through her mind. The last time she felt this sort of passion was with him. The last time she felt safe with someone was with him. The last time she wanted anything like this was with *him*.

The image of his tears when she broke things off punched Daphne right in the gut. What a fool she'd been to let her friends sway her judgment. She saw all the good in him. She accepted his flaws, as he did hers, and they were perfect together. So what if he was a little clingy? It showed his commitment, and that was hard to find in a man.

Her own tears stung her eyes, so she closed them.

The masked man gently wiped a stray tear from her cheek.

Daphne's mouth ticked up into an appreciative smile, and she opened her eyes. She may never see the face behind the mask, but it didn't matter. What mattered was how she felt in this moment. Sugar was giving her something she'd been missing, and she'd be a fool to dismiss it. He may not be Thoren, but he'd be an acceptable, albeit temporary, replacement.

The thought of fucking a complete stranger sent a jolt of excitement straight through Daphne, and she clenched her thighs. Plastering on her most sultry expression, she licked her lips and whispered, "Do your worst, Sugar."

# CHAPTER 6

With a deep growl, the masked man yanked her to him. He nuzzled the mask into her neck, so she closed her eyes and imagined he was Thoren. She pictured his handsome yet rugged face. His deep blue eyes pierced hers. She was even able to conjure his cinnamon taste.

Parting her lips, Daphne moaned in delight as she twisted a hand into Sugar's hair.

The hungry prowl of his hands left no inch of her body uncovered. He slid the strap of her tank top down and ran the mouth of the mask to her shoulder, where he pulled the strap more, exposing her breast. He groaned as his palm ran over her hardened nipple.

"I'm guessing there aren't any complaints?"

He shook his head, continuing to play with her nipple.

Daphne panted as his fingers worked their magic at her breast. He dragged the mask up and down her neck while his other hand pulled her top down completely, pinning her upper arms with her shirt straps. She didn't mind. In fact, being restrained was something she'd always enjoyed with Thoren. She knew she was safe with him, and his dominance had excited her.

Tonight, even with this stranger, was no exception.

Sugar slid his other hand under her thigh, pulling her leg up to hook around his waist, and ran his fingers along her damp panties. She bucked her hips. He hummed in approval near her ear. He continued to tweak her nipple before slipping his fingers into her panties and up her wet seam.

Daphne gasped, but melted into his touch.

He groaned as he pushed his fingers inside her. He pulsed them, slipping them in and out at a steady rhythm while his other hand toyed with her breast. Then, he pressed his thumb against her swollen clit and rubbed.

Daphne's head lolled back to rest against the wall.

The masked man pinched her nipple, twisting it between his fingers as he sped up the tempo between her thighs.

Daphne bit her lower lip to keep from screaming in ecstasy as her body shook with release. He held her against the wall, bracing her while she rode out the waves of her orgasm. When she finished, he pulled his hand from between her legs.

Eye to eye with her, he slid his fingers beneath the mask. Daphne heard a distinct sucking sound and knew he had put his fingers in his mouth. With a deep hum, he pulled his fingers out from the mask and dragged them up her inner thigh.

The idea of his face between her legs made desire pool within her again, but she needed something bigger and harder than his tongue to combat the ache. "Can't lick me with that mask on." She arched an eyebrow in challenge.

The masked man just tilted his head.

"So right now," Daphne said, trailing her fingertips along the waistband of his pants. "I think it would be best if you just fucked me."

In a flash, his hands flew to his fly, but Daphne grabbed his wrist, stopping him. His head lifted, and she imagined confusion on his face.

"Don't rush it," she said with authority.

Sugar nodded slowly as if he understood. He grabbed Daphne under her thighs, picked her up, and carried her across the room to a large desk. Setting her down on her feet, he took her chin between his thumb and index finger and drug his thumb over her lower lip.

His hands gripped her shoulders and turned her around, nudging her over to lay her chest onto the desk top. She shivered as the cool surface met her naked torso, but the anticipation of feeling this mysteriously sexy man inside her warmed her quickly.

He slid his palms up the backs of her thighs, pushing her skirt up over her ass as his thumbs grazed the edges of her panties. Snapping the elastic, he tucked his fingers into the waistband and yanked them down.

Daphne tensed to keep from shuddering as she listened to the jingle of his belt buckle and the sound of his pants zipper. She fought the urge to writhe.

The immense desire that had settled between her legs begged for release, but she knew good things came to those who waited.

Placing his hands between her legs, he pushed her thighs apart. He slid two fingers inside her, pumping them in and out.

Daphne tilted her hips, trying to increase the friction. She heard the masked man chuckle as he placed his palm between her shoulder blades and pressed down, his fingertips digging into her spine.

She let out a breathy moan, struggling to move her hips against his hand. "Please…"

He hummed in delight as he pumped his fingers faster.

Daphne wanted to show him exactly how much she wanted him, but being pinned down made it exceedingly difficult. She wouldn't complain, though. This man was the only one who'd touched her the right way since Thoren, and even though Sugar wasn't fucking her at the moment, it still felt pretty damn good.

The crest of an orgasm teased her. It was so close, she thought she might explode. The pressure in her belly rose, deliciously building as she fought the urge to call out Thoren's name. Right on the edge of her release, he removed his hand and plunged his cock deep inside her.

Daphne stifled a passionate scream as she tightened around his hard length, but he didn't stop. He gripped her hips with both hands. Steadily increasing the speed of his thrusts, he pushed harder and deeper with each one. With the pressure of his cock bringing wave after wave of pleasure upon Daphne, her orgasm seemed never-ending.

Then, he flipped her to her back.

Still inside her, he stared at her bare torso as he dragged his hand between her breasts.

"Do it again," Daphne whispered.

He leaned down so the mask hovered mere centimeters from her face. With him so close, she shut her eyes and imagined his kiss, his tongue delving between her lips and dancing in her mouth. He began thrusting again, but this time, he took it slow. The movements were methodical, deliberate.

Daphne's body quaked, but she opened her eyes when she felt him stand upright. She eyed him suspiciously. He had stopped fucking her, but hadn't pulled out. With chin dipped to his chest, his shoulders rose and fell, like he was restraining himself.

*What the hell is he waiting for?*

Then it hit her. "I'm on the pill, Sugar."

With a deep growl and a sharp nod, he resumed thrusting. He ran his palms up Daphne's thighs, around her hips to her ribs to cup her breasts, tweaking her nipples gently.

Daphne closed her eyes, her head lolling back and forth as her moans filled the room. Lost in a sea of bliss, she absorbed every single second.

Until he switched things up.

He adjusted his stance, giving himself a better angle to go deeper. Then, he revved his speed. He pounded into Daphne without mercy, each movement making her moan louder. His hands gripped her breasts so her nipples peeked between his fingers.

This was the best sex Daphne had had in a long time. The masked stranger was giving Thoren a run for his money, but he'd never be able to do better. Daphne opened her eyes, latched her gaze onto the mask, and wished beyond wishes that Sugar could be Thoren.

# CHAPTER 7

The imagined intensity in Sugar's gaze was enough to push Daphne over the edge. She tightened around his hard length, screaming as she tumbled into an ocean of orgasmic waves.

He let out a strained grunt, and after a few quick, hard thrusts, his cock pulsed inside of her. He spilled himself and collapsed on top of her, the mask resting between her breasts.

Daphne welcomed his weight. For months, she'd longed to be crushed by a man's weight, and now, she never wanted the pressure to ease. If only he were Thoren, then everything would be better.

She ran a hand through his hair. "Sugar," she said breathlessly.

He lifted his head, tilting his chin as if to look at her.

Then, the air changed. It grew warm and thick. No words were exchanged, but Daphne felt as if a connection had just been made. Like this masked man had poured his heart out to her without saying a single word.

Daphne's body melted, even though her heart skipped a beat. She imagined Thoren laying atop her chest, staring at her with adoration in his eyes. His lips moved and spoke those three little words she longed to hear again. Words filled with so much truth, it hurt to try and forget them.

Tears formed in her eyes. She'd been alone and in love for such a long time.

Sugar lifted his body, removing himself from her. Without his body heat, the cool air on her sweaty skin gave her goosebumps. When he pulled her up to sit, he slid the straps of her tank top back onto her shoulders before rubbing her arms with his palms. Without a word, he wiped the spilled tears from her face and gathered her to his chest.

Daphne tensed when her phone dinged, but she ignored the chime, instead relaxing into Sugar. He was so warm, felt so safe. Daphne thought she'd bury herself into him and stay there forever.

But he pushed her back and locked the blank eyes of the mask with hers.

The depths of the darkness dragged Daphne inside, threatening to never let her go. "Don't leave me," she pleaded.

His shoulders rose and fell with one huge breath, and Daphne knew their time was over. She hung her head, but he tucked his knuckle under her chin and tugged up. Her gaze met the mask's. Instead of warm, loving irises, she was met with blackness. Daphne pulled his hand to her cheek, nuzzling into his warm palm. She wanted so badly for him to stay. She wanted to see his face, to know him, but he simply took a step away.

She clenched her fingers around his hand, holding him tight against her cheek, but groaned when her phone dinged again.

Sugar brushed his knuckles down her face, again dragging his thumb over her lip before his fingers slipped away and he walked out the door.

When the latch clicked, Daphne's entire body slumped like it had been crushed under a ton of bricks. Her heart turned to lead, sinking in her chest. But she refused to cry. She'd spent too many nights shedding tears over Thoren; she didn't need to spill any over some stranger.

Though, he didn't feel so strange anymore.

Taking a deep, bolstering breath, Daphne took out her phone. She slouched again after reading the messages.

> **JANNA:** *Where the fuck are you? I can't find these bitches any-where, and now you're gone too!*

> **JANNA:** *Seriously! WTF? Helloooooooooo!*

Daphne dropped her face into her palm, sighing. Still no sign of Lynnette or Emily. She sent a text back to Janna, letting her know she'd meet her at the stage, then quickly threw herself back together. Using selfie mode on her phone, she checked her makeup.

Her eyeliner was a bit smudged, so she licked her finger and smudged it more. What did it matter anyway? It was Halloween—everyone looked weird.

She finger-combed her hair, doubled-checked her clothes were covering the right parts again, and strode to the door. With one last longing glance at the desk, Daphne bit her quivering lip and left the room.

Back in the dance hall, she took a moment to allow her eyes to adjust to the black lights. The throng still swayed to the music, though it seemed to have grown in size. She edged her way toward the stage, taking a quick glance at her phone, but saw no more messages.

Hopefully, that was a good thing.

Daphne found no Janna at the stage. No Emily. No Lynnette. Just drunk people dancing. She checked her phone again. The messages all showed delivered, but not one had been read.

*Strange.* The crinkle in her brow moved to her forehead as an idea popped into her mind. *Janna wanted a beer. Maybe she's at the bar.*

Daphne hurried around the dance floor toward the concession stand. The line looked to be a mile long, and every high-top table had someone standing at it, but none of them were Janna. None of them were Lynnette or Emily, either.

Determined not to give up hope, Daphne made a lap around the floor. When she got back to the stage, she checked her phone one last time.

Still no responses.

"Fuck this," she said, and sent four separate messages. One group text to all three women, and one to each individual. Then, she waited.

This wasn't exactly the best follow-up to her strange hook-up. She should still be riding the high from the intense fucking she had just received, not wallowing in worry over her missing friends.

She tapped her toes against the floor.

What would her friends say when she revealed that she'd fucked some guy in a mask? Would they judge her? Call her a slut? Probably, but she had to find them first.

When she saw her messages were yet again delivered but unread, Daphne huffed. She decided to try calling them before heading to security. Glancing around, she found an exit near the back of the stage. As she pushed open the door, she met the cold, Halloween night air head-on.

She shivered, letting it pass quickly. She was on a mission.

Since Janna was the last to contact her, Daphne started there. Pressing "call" on the contact, she pulled her sweater tighter around her. She bounced up and down on her toes. "Come on, come on, connect."

When the monotone ring came through the speaker, Daphne blew out a frustrated exhale. "Fuck, finally."

But her relief was cut short when she heard the distinct melody of Janna's ringtone.

Daphne's eyes darted across the ground as she listened. She pulled her phone away from her ear, the monotone ringing fading into the background. The peppy, electronic jingle of Janna's ringtone continued, and Daphne's heart raced.

With a deep swallow, she tiptoed along the side of the building, wondering why Janna was outside. Daphne stopped in her tracks as the answer dawned on her.

Of course. It all made sense now. Emily and Lynnette *were* conspiring together to play a trick, but so was Janna. They had planned the entire thing.

That had to be the answer. What else could it be?

Daphne continued on her path toward the back of the building. "Okay, you bitches. You can come out now."

No answer other than Janna's still-ringing phone.

"You can't hide anymore. I can hear your phone, Janna."

With every step, the ringtone grew louder, but Daphne didn't see any sign of her friends. *They're really playing into this, aren't they?*

She rounded the corner of the building, coming face to face with some large utility boxes. Janna's ringtone was as loud as it could be. Her friends had to be on the other side. Daphne stepped forward, creeping around the edge.

"Janna, you–" Daphne choked on the syllables. She froze in place, her stomach plummeting into her feet.

There, piled together on the ground, were her friends, deep crimson dripping from the slits across their throats. It slid down their pale, limp bodies, pooling around them as they stared lifelessly into the air.

And in Janna's hand was her phone.

Daphne opened her mouth to scream into the night, but it was quickly muffled by a large hand. She flinched, reaching up to grip her attacker's forearm and push it away. He wrapped his other arm around her torso and pulled her against him.

Daphne fought as hard as she could, wrenching her body in every direction as she screamed into the madman's palm.

When she flung her head back, she cracked her head against his and heard something clatter onto the pavement. Glancing down, she saw the sugar skull mask staring back at her. Her whole body shook uncontrollably as her blood turned to ice in her veins. She went slack; all the fight had been drained from her.

Sugar took advantage of her temporary paralysis, and gripping her tightly, he pinned her arms to her side. He tilted his head and placed a kiss on her neck.

Tears slid from Daphne's eyes. Her cries of terror were now nothing more than muffled whimpers beneath Sugar's palm. He dragged his lips up the side of her face to her ear, and Daphne caught a whiff of a familiar scent.

Cinnamon.

No wonder she had reveled in his touch. He gave her what she had been missing, because *he* was who she was missing. Her insides twisted, nausea roiling in her stomach.

"Thor…" His name bled through her lips on an icy breath.

"No more obstacles, babe."

Daphne winced at the words. His voice should have been comforting, but instead it filled her with dread.

With a soft caress of her earlobe with his lips, Thoren whispered, "I told you you'd be mine again."

# ABOUT THE AUTHOR

RC Lehan began her writing journey at the ripe old age of 35. Since then, she has dabbled in different genres, played with ranges of characters, and tested her skills with varying writing techniques. But she always gravitates back to the dark side. She enjoys telling stories with strong female characters who are handed the worst of circumstances. Things may get messy along the way, but it's always an adventure.

RC resides in Colorado with her husband and her two children. Writing is her passion, but she also enjoys any type of creation, be that painting, sculpting, or drawing. When she's not creating, she can be found playing Minecraft with her kiddos (against her will), watching movies with her husband, or reading if she's so lucky to have some alone time.

Right now, readers can find RC's first publication, The Light of Dawn, on Kindle Vella. More episodes to come! Otherwise, find her on social media:

IG: @rachel.c.author
Threads: @rachel.c.author
X: @AuthorLehan

# carnival prey

## Sarah Trala

*Memories are linked to our behavior in ways that are often ignored.*

*If you burn your hand on the stove, you know not to touch a hot burner again.*

*What happens if you've forgotten how painful that burn was?*

*If you've forgotten how long it took to heal?*

V iolet eyes, or reddish depending on the light—hell metimes they have the lightest blue shade I've ever seen—spy me at the same time I do them. I want to spend the rest of my life enjoying this feeling, where the whole world stops with just that one look. Is this love?

Translucent skin, the vein on River's neck a telltale sign their heart skips the same beat at spotting me, as mine does seeing them. An outfit made to impress is expected, but Halloween gives them a reason to be even more extra. Dressed like a modern-day vampire straight from a young adult novel, with frills and glitter, pressed slacks and polished dress shoes. Today, they've tossed on lavender highlighter, with ample shimmer so that even the flickering candles offer enough light to reflect and show off their high cheekbones.

"*Mommy*." They take my hand with a kiss, leaving behind an imprint of rosy pink from thin-lipped pucker. It's not my name, but rather than upset me, the spin on it, spoken with adoration, continues the reminder of our first date. An inside joke that only they can get away with. "Happy one year anniversary. I hope this place is alright."

"Of course, anywhere with you is more than alright." A tickle in the back of my head forces a twitch in my eye. Before, that tickle used to have a voice, one that screamed, begged me to believe this was all a lie. It's been a long while since then, the fight no longer worth giving it attention.

Our late lunch is done on purpose, even the location chosen out of convenience. That doesn't mean the crew of the Carnival Prey has spared any expense in making the mess hall tent any less spectacular. Tables fill the space, each one taken except the one I'm led to, hand in hand with my love. Small candelabras make up the entirety of the centerpieces, atop dark red velvet tablecloths. No chairs, as most diners don't stick around too long, and the extra weight in the trailers is unnecessary. In the middle is a circular bar, staffed by Spyder. One man, his six arms long enough to both mix drinks and grill meals at the same time. A birth anomaly he's expertly perfected in a fantastic field.

"How long until showtime?" This is my first Halloween working with the carnival—last year I was a guest. Tonight, I share the stage with River, introducing act after act with the traveling Carnival Prey. Then, after the show, I'll share their bed.

It was fate, a year ago, that my dating app matched me to River the night before Prey was set to run in McHattie. Our first date ended on a great note, but I woke to a cold bed. On my kitchen island, they'd left me a ticket and a journal. That ticket was my own personal invite to a one-night-only event that changed locations every year. Whereas the journal was meant to be a way for me to write down everything that happened so we could discuss it on date two. We never got around to looking through the journal; I can't even remember where it went, to be honest. I've filled a number of them since, so it's probably in the same trunk as the rest.

"We've got about an hour before the gates open. Another forty-five before seating is allowed at the center ring." Nervousness laces their tone. Who wouldn't be nervous with what they have planned? I saw the small, box-shaped object bulging in their pocket. Could it be earrings? Possibly, but I know better than that. "There's something I need to ask you first, before we eat."

"Yes." I'm sure they prepared a speech, but I don't need it. The answer is the same no matter what. Any fool would know that. River is mine, forever and always. "Of course I'll marry you."

Only, River looks confused instead of relieved.

Rather than the box, they grab something tucked into their waistband.

A black journal, with flaking gold-edged pages, the ribbon bookmark crinkled, unthreading, and stained with crusty dark red splotches. The peeling leather cover painted in matching gold calligraphy, with my name, *Mamie Summers*.

The mystery of the missing journal, solved.

"I was curious if you'd be willing to read to me about how we began."

"Oh." My nerves spike as they slide the journal to me across the table. In the back of my head, that tickle of a voice gets a little louder. Still, I can't make out the words, but I feel the insistence, the demand, to take it. Read it. Believe the words, no matter what they might say. However, I push it back to River instead. "There's no need. I already know. We matched on...you know I can't even remember the name of that app. But, we met up on Devil's Night, in Cheers & Beers. You decided to try and blend in, caked yourself in makeup and lies, but I saw right through the ruse. Made you wash it all off in the women's restroom and come back to my place. Strapped you up and we had fun until we passed out. Then I came here, enjoyed my time, and wound up in *your* bed. Never left. What else is there?"

"Humor me."

With shaking fingers, and their assistance, I bring the book back to me and open to the first page.

I KNOW, I KNOW. YOU WANTED ME TO WRITE ABOUT MY TIME AT THE CARNIVAL, BUT IT FEELS RIGHT TO START AT THE BEGINNING OF OUR STORY. SEEMS MORE FITTING, SINCE I HAVE A FEELING I'LL BE SEEING YOU MORE THAN JUST TONIGHT.

DEVIL'S NIGHT. A TIME WHERE BACK IN THE DAY, PEOPLE HOLED UP IN THEIR HOMES, AVOIDING THE STREETS, THE PRANKS, THE FIRES. NOW, IT'S MORE OF AN EXCUSE TO GO OUT DRINKING. USUALLY, I'D SPEND THE TIME ALONE, WITH A CUP OF BLACK COFFEE, A BOWL OF POPCORN, AND RERUNS OF AMERICAN HORROR STORY.

LAST NIGHT, I HAD PLANS WITH YOU, RIVER.

NELLY SHOWED ME PICTURES, OF COURSE, BUT HE REFUSED TO SHOW ME YOUR PROFILE. HELL, I DON'T EVEN KNOW WHAT YOU SAW ON MINE—NELLY NEVER LET ME LOOK AT THAT EITHER. SAID I'D WANT TO CHANGE EVERY DETAIL AND REJECT EACH PICK HE KNEW WOULD BE PERFECT. HE'S ALWAYS LOOKED OUT FOR ME, YOU'LL LIKE HIM. DON'T BE UPSET IF HE FLIRTS WITH YOU, HAHA, THAT'S JUST HOW HE IS. HE'S NOT TOO PICKY WITH WHO HE LETS IN HIS BED, ONLY WHO WILL BE IN IT A SECOND TIME.

"This sounds like me, but I don't know a Nelly." I flip through the pages, and everything is in my own handwriting. I remember writing them, but the words aren't quite right. I've never known a Nelly, then again I don't remember creating my profile on the app either. How odd. But, if he wasn't *my* friend, "Is Nelly a friend of yours?"

"No," River says. "Keep reading."

Thumbing back to the first page, my eyes catch where I left off.

I WAS LATE. ONE PART OF ME HOPED YOU WOULDN'T BE THERE, THAT YOU GOT BORED OR THOUGHT I'D STOOD YOU UP. I WANT TO SAY I WAS TOO BUSY PICKING OUT AN OUTFIT, BUT INSTEAD I DEBATED ON WHAT EXCUSE TO USE.

BEING SICK GOT ME OUT OF PAST BLIND DATES. OR THE GOOD CALLBACK OF SAYING I HAD CAR PROBLEMS. IT WOULDN'T HAVE BEEN HARD TO CONVINCE YOU, SEEING AS MY GRAND AM IS OLD ENOUGH TO LEGALLY VOTE AND RIDDLED WITH DEATH TRAP LEVELS OF RUST.

BUT, I WENT.

YOU WERE STANDING AT THE BAR, LEANING AWAY FROM THE OTHER PATRONS, IN YOUR OWN LITTLE WORLD AS THE OBNOX-IOUSLY LOUD BOOMBOX BLASTED COUNTRY MUSIC. POWDER BLUE STREAKED YOUR WHITE HAIR, THE STRUNG HALLOWEEN STRING LIGHTS BRINGING THE COLOR TO MY FULL ATTENTION. YOUR FACE SPLATTERED WITH FRECKLES THE SAME COLOR AS THE CHARCOAL THAT LINED YOUR EYES. LIPS STAINED A ROSY PINK, COVERED IN A GLOSS THAT REMINDED ME OF THE KIND PATRICIA USED TO WEAR IN MIDDLE SCHOOL (BEFORE SHE THOUGHT MAKEUP WAS A

PETRI DISH FILLED WITH DANGER). SHE'S COMING WITH US TO THE CARNIVAL, TOO. BEST WAY TO MAKE A GREAT IMPRESSION IS TO DOUSE YOURSELF IN HAND SANITIZER FIRST. ALTHOUGH, I MIGHT NOT GET THE CHANCE TO TELL YOU THAT BEFORE YOU SEE HER.

"Patricia?" Another name I don't know, along with a warning as if she were my best friend. None of this makes sense, I came alone to the carnival. There's pictures to prove it. From what I can see, there's tons of them, slotted between the pages.

No, I didn't take the photos myself, I had employees and other visitors take them for me. In front of the Ferris wheel, game alley, that children's coaster with the bright green dragon, ring of fire, and the many, many, tents filled with various oddities and exhibits. I was there for hours before making my way to the big tent, the main event, just as the sun set and created a stunning orange glow on the horizon.

That one, I *did* take myself. One of the last pictures the little Polaroid popped out before…I gave it back. Who did I give it back to?

My fingers press into the pages, about to riffle through to find that picture, that clue, but River stops me.

"Spoilers, *Mommy*. I want to hear your words in the proper order." They smile, hand pressing hard atop the book, but the smile twitches. They're hiding something from me. When I lean back, they match the movement. "Trust me."

YOU WERE SO OUT OF PLACE IN THE BUSY BAR. IT WAS A TERRIBLE IDEA TO MEET AT CHEERS & BEERS. ALL FLAIR, WITH A RUFFLED HIGH-NECKED BLOUSE, SEWN WITH SILVER THREAD, HELD SHUT BY PEARLESCENT BUTTONS, TUCKED NEATLY INTO SHINED LEATHER PANTS. NOT AT ALL BLENDING IN WITH THE PLAID AND TORN-UP JEANS OF THE GUYS SURROUNDING YOU.

A BAR FULL OF HICKS. FRIENDLY HICKS, SURE, BUT HICKS ALL THE SAME.

I thought the whole idea was a mistake and was ready to book it out the door and back to my car. There was no way I could hold a candle to you; I was far too plain. An off-the-shoulder peplum top and skinny jeans? Did I think it was 2010 again? Fairly certain even the chunky necklace I grabbed was from high school.

But you caught me before I could make it out the door. Inches from my exit. Mere feet from never meeting you in the first place.

"*MA'AM-IE*, I presume?"

So close, and I couldn't blame you for getting it wrong. I told you as much. It's what I say to everyone who says it wrong; nice-ish in tone, while still holding a bit of bite. Swallowing all the negative thoughts, I accepted my fate.

"The name is Mamie."

"Thank goodness, I've got a thing for *MOMMIES*." From anyone else, that line I've heard a thousand times over, due to the unfortunate name I'd been cursed with, would've been met with an offended insult.

INSTEAD, I STOOD FROZEN IN PLACE.

IT WAS SLIGHT, THE GAP BETWEEN THE EDGE OF YOUR PUPIL AND THE COLORED LENS SURROUNDING IT, BUT I NOTICED. YOUR PHOTO HAD YOU WITH DEEP BROWN EYES, THE SHADE OF BARK LATE IN THE FALL, BUT THAT WAS CLEARLY NOT THEIR TRUE HUE. BEING CLOSER, NEARLY NOSE-TO-NOSE, MORE STOOD OUT. THE STREAKY TANNER, HANDMADE FRECKLES, AND THE FACT YOUR HAIR HAD BEEN POWDERED THE SPECTACULAR SHADE OF BLUE—RATHER THAN DYED.

"SHIT, SORRY." EITHER YOU DIDN'T NOTICE MY INSPECTIONS, OR DIDN'T CARE. MAYBE YOU THOUGHT IT WAS DUE TO SOMETHING ELSE ENTIRELY. "THAT WAS A TERRIBLE OPENING LINE. CAN I TRY THAT AGAIN?"

"WHAT KIND OF BULLSHIT CATFISHING TRICK IS THIS?" ONE OF MY WORST ATTRIBUTES, ACTING BEFORE THINKING. MY LAST GIRL-FRIEND PACKED HER SHIT AND LEFT AFTER I TOLD HER THE PHO-TO SHE WAS USING AS A PROFILE PICTURE LOOKED LIKE SHE WAS SMELLING A MASSIVE DUMP. PROMISE, I DIDN'T SAY IT TO BE MEAN. SHE'S A STUNNING WOMAN—THE SHOT DIDN'T DO HER JUSTICE AND WAS BETTER OFF BURIED IN A BOX OF DIGITAL CAMERA FILES FROM 2007.

"WELL," IT WAS OBVIOUS YOU WERE EMBARRASSED, TRYING TO BRUSH THE MOMENT OFF WITH JOKES. "THAT BEATS MY MOMMY COMMENT."

"Is this a look you did to make yourself feel more confident?" Oh lord, the words wouldn't stop. I begged, internally, for someone to save me from the mouth diarrhea. Asked myself why it had to be so aggressive. But, I had to know the truth. "Or because you thought it would make me more comfortable to be seen with you?"

"Um, well." You spun a silver ring on your index finger, the diamond clearly fake based on the massive size of it. Another lie, I thought, while also counting to ten. Therapy has been useful for many things, like keeping my anger in check. My eyes shifted from one contact to the other, trying to figure out which one to stare at as you dug for an answer. It wouldn't have done well to push you, but my foot tapped in impatience. "I tend to get stares when I'm in public."

I grabbed your hand, nearly letting go when a small static electricity jolt zapped me, and dragged you into the women's room. A first date wouldn't be filled with falsities, and I knew no one there would even bat an eye in your direction. There were enough weirdos living in McHattie for them not to really care.

It was fairly clean, for a bar bathroom, and you stood awkwardly in the middle, watching me in the mirror as I pulled out a wad of paper towels.

"Sink. Now." My demands weren't questioned, you stepped forward those few feet and looked at me with wonder. "How much do you love this top?"

"It's new." A non-answer that made me roll my eyes.

"Not an answer. Try again."

"Enough to not be happy if it got ruined." Much better, a quick learner. Points towards a green flag, but there was more work to do before I even considered a second date.

"Take it off." One day, I might not be so demanding, however you took it in stride. Your long, painted nails, glittery from a fresh manicure, dove under the ruffles to undo the buttons. Busying myself by turning on the tap, I gave you a little bit of privacy in case you changed your mind, but no time was wasted sliding off your top.

"Is there anyone in here?"

"It's a little late to ask that." Another eye roll as I took your shirt, folding it neatly and setting it by the end table by the door. Returning to start my process, I noticed again

YOUR NERVOUSNESS, ARMS CROSSED OVER YOUR BARE CHEST. SO, I THREW YOU A BONE AND EASED BACK WHILE SOAKING THE TOWELS IN THE WARMING WATER. "NO, NO ONE IS HERE. EVEN IF THERE WERE, YOU'RE WITH ME, AND NO ONE WOULD DARE START SHIT ABOUT IT."

KILLING THE flow, I RIPPED off A STRIP, ADDED A DAB OF SOAP, AND GOT TO WORK SCRUBBING. LAYER UPON LAYER OF BUILT-UP MAKEUP RAN DOWN, THE WATER TRAILING DOWN YOUR NECK AND STREAKING THE FAKE TANNER. EVENTUALLY, YOUR ARMS DROPPED.

I TRIED NOT TO NOTICE YOUR MISSING NIPPLES AND U-SHAPED SCARS, BUT THE SIX PACK WAS HARDER TO IGNORE, AS WAS THE V HEADING DOWN BELOW YOUR BELTLINE. IT'S NO WONDER WE DIDN'T LAST LONG IN THAT BAR.

ONCE EVERY INCH OF MAKEUP HAD BEEN ERASED, I WENT BACK TO YOUR EYES. MY IRRITATION SPIKED AGAIN, DESPITE TRYING TO TAMP IT DOWN.

"THE CONTACTS; DO YOU NEED THEM TO SEE, OR ARE THEY JUST TO HIDE THEIR TRUE COLOR?"

"THEY'RE COSMETIC."

"TAKE THEM OUT." I DUG IN MY PURSE AND FOUND MY OWN CON-TACT CASE. BEFORE LEAVING, I'D PUT IN FRESH SOLUTION BECAUSE MINE TEND TO GET FOGGY BEFORE THE END OF THE NIGHT. MY GLASSES ARE HEAVY, AND UNCOMFORTABLE, MEANT STRICTLY TO WEAR BEFORE BED AND IN THE MORNING BEFORE I HAD MY TEA. "HERE, YOU CAN STORE THEM WITH THIS. I'VE GOT SPARES AT HOME, SO DON'T WORRY ABOUT GIVING IT BACK."

LEAVING YOU TO IT, I HEADED BACK TOWARDS THE DOOR FOR YOUR SHIRT. IT REALLY WAS STUNNING. THE STITCHING DOU-BLED ON EACH SEAM, WITH SILVER THREAD, SMOOTH RATHER THAN SCRATCHY. DESPITE BEING FOLDED, NONE OF THE WRINKLES HELD IN THE ULTRA-SOFT MATERIAL. EVEN THE BUTTONS HAD A THIN LAYER OF EPOXY ON THEM, PROTECTING THE COLORFUL PASTEL RAINBOW SWIRLS. IF I DIDN'T KNOW BETTER, IT WAS SOMETHING MOSSY WOULD MAKE, BUT THE PALETTE WAS WRONG. SHE PREFERS EARTH TONES ON HER CREATIONS.

"Who, the fuck, is Mossy?" I'm sick of these games. Gripping the book by the spine, I turn it, dumping the inserted photos onto the table. River quickly swipes them away, but I'm able to catch glimpses of each one as they flutter face down on the black tarp flooring. Rather than just me, there's multiple people there. Smiling faces I can't remember. My arms wrapped around them. "Is this some AI trickery? A big prank before you pop the question?"

Their fingers grip my chin, keeping my head up and staring at them instead of inspecting the photos like I want to. From the bar, Spyder stops, slowly setting down everything he holds.

"This isn't a trick." River begs me with their stare. How could it not be a trick? In the back of my head, that tickle is whispering, faint but I hear her insistence. *Keep reading.* Over and over, she says it. I don't move until River speaks again, just as softly pleading as the voice in my head, "Please, keep reading."

I STEPPED BACK TO ADMIRE MY WORK, YOUR SHIRT FOLDED OVER MY ARM, BUT FOUND MYSELF ADMIRING YOU MORE. THE DATE WAS SUPPOSED TO MAKE NELLY HAPPY, GET HIM OFF MY BACK ABOUT FINDING SOMEONE TO FUCK AND RELIEVE SOME TENSION. FUCKING YOU DIDN'T SEEM A HALF BAD IDEA.

"AM I ALLOWED TO GET DRESSED NOW?"

"I DON'T KNOW," I SAID, POINTLESSLY SHAKING OUT THE TOP, "I PREFER YOU SHIRTLESS."

GIVING IN, I HELD THE SHIRT OUT, DIRECTING YOU TO SLIP ONE ARM IN AT A TIME. YOU STOOD IN PLACE WHILE I CIRCLED TO YOUR FRONT AND TOOK MY TIME POPPING EACH BUTTON BACK INTO THE CORRESPONDING HOLE. WITH A FLUFF OF THE RUFFLES AS I FINISHED, I LOOKED UP INTO YOUR EYES, THE COLOR MESMERIZING ME.

"YOU'RE NEVER ALLOWED TO COVER THOSE AROUND ME." THE WHITES NEARLY SEE THROUGH, RED VEINS CLEARLY VISIBLE, AND SURROUNDING THE WIDE BLACK PUPILS ARE THE LIGHTEST BLUE SHADE I'VE EVER SEEN. IN THE RIGHT LIGHT, THEY'D BE A STUNNING VIOLET. "HOLY FUCK, YOU'RE BEAUTIFUL."

YOUR HAND SNAKED UP THE BACK OF MY TOP, SKIN-TO-SKIN, PULLING ME INTO YOU, SMASHING MY PUSHED-UP B-CUPS INTO YOUR CHEST. SMALL SPARKS IGNITED, AND IT WAS ALMOST TOO INTENSE.

MAYBE I NEED TO START ADDING VINEGAR TO THE WASH, OR POSSIBLY TIN FOIL TO THE DRYER. WOULD THAT CAUSE A fire? LOW HEAT WOULD PROBABLY BE BETTER, JUST TO BE ON THE SAFE SIDE. UNLESS YOU LIKE THE STATIC ELECTRICITY BUILD UP—I'VE HEARD SOME PEOPLE find IT KINKY. I KNOW I DO, YOU'VE PROVED THAT.

YOUR COOL LIPS PRESSED TO MINE. FRESH MINT INVADED MY SENSES, WITH A HINT OF VODKA. I MAY HAVE BEEN TOTALLY SOBER, BUT YOUR TOUCH MADE ME DRUNK, AND EVEN MORE IMPULSIVE.

"FUCK THIS BAR, LET'S GO BACK TO MY PLACE."

RIVER SEEMS LOST IN THOUGHT AS I READ THE LAST LINE. I DON'T BLAME THEM, IT WAS ONE I WOULDN'T FORGET. THEY'D WALKED TO THE BAR, SO I offERED TO DRIVE THEM TO MY APARTMENT. WE CHATTED ABOUT A FEW THINGS, BUT MOSTLY MY HAND ROAMED THEIR THIGH. EACH TIME I GOT TOO CLOSE TO THEIR ZIPPER, CURIOUS AS TO WHAT I WOULD find, THEY'D GENTLY REDIRECT THE ATTENTION AWAY.

FEAR TRICKLED INTO MY DROPPING GUT THAT THEY WERE GOING TO REJECT ME, GIVE ME ONE LAST KISS AND THEN CALL ANOTHER RIDE. I'D UNDERSTAND, HOLD OUT HOPE THERE WOULD BE AN offER FOR A SECOND DATE, BUT INSTEAD, WHEN WE CROSSED THE THRESHOLD INTO MY UNIT, THEY GRABBED ME BY THE BACK OF MY NECK AND PULLED ME INTO THEM AGAIN.

MY LIPS FOUND THEIRS, PARTING, ALLOWING THEIR TONGUE AC-
CESS. AND ACCESS THEY TOOK, BATTLING FOR DOMINANCE BE-
HIND MY TEETH, SEEMING TO SAVOR AND EXPLORE EVERY INCH.
MEMORIZING AND LISTENING TO MY RESPONSES. HOWEVER, I WAS
NEVER ONE TO SIT BACK, AND I GRABBED THEIR HAIR, TWISTING
THE STRANDS AROUND MY fiNGERS TO SEPARATE US. GIVING US
A MOMENT TO CATCH OUR BREATH, I THEN SET IN ON LEAVING
MY MARK ON THEIR NECK. GENTLY KISSING, TESTING THE WATERS,
BEFORE SUCKING, NIBBLING, AND LICKING MY WAY DOWN THEIR
COLLARBONE. RELEASING MY HOLD ON THEIR HAIR TO POP EACH
BUTTON AND MOVE DOWN THE CENTER OF THEIR CHEST.

ON MY KNEES, STARING UP INTO VIOLET EYES, THEY PLACED A HAND
OVER MINE TO STOP MY PROGRESS BEFORE UNZIPPING THEIR PANTS.
THEY HAD A CAUTION IN THEIR STARE, A SADNESS, A SECRET THEY
WERE TERRIfiED TO SHARE.

The same look they have now, across from the high-top table. River doesn't
talk, they don't need to, not after telling me twice already. Instead, a manicured
nail taps the pages of the book, on a continuation of the story I already know.

"I NEED TO WARN YOU ABOUT SOMETHING." A PHRASE I NEVER
THOUGHT I'D HEAR. ONE SPOKEN IN A HANDFUL OF MOVIES, TV
SHOWS, AND BOOKS, RIGHT BEFORE GIVING EARTH SHATTERING
NEWS WITH NO TIME TO PROCESS BY THE TIME SOME PIVOTAL
MOMENT HAPPENS. WORDS YOU TOLD ME, STANDING IN MY BED-
ROOM, SHIRTLESS, NUMEROUS HICKEYS DECORATING YOUR NECK.
FUN FACT: TURNS OUT IT DOESN'T TAKE MUCH SUCTION FOR THOSE
REDDISH-PURPLE MARKS TO SHOW ON YOUR FAIR SKIN. PRACTICE
MAKES PERFECT THOUGH, THAT BORDERLINE BETWEEN A SIMPLE

TASTE AND LASTING REMINDER THAT I'VE BEEN THERE. MAYBE YOU'LL GIVE ME THE CHANCE FOR A REPEAT.

"I'D ASK IF YOU HAVE A NIPPLE THAT'S INVERTED, BUT YOU DON'T HAVE ANY." NO, SEE, ONE OF MY PAST PARTNERS HAD THAT ISSUE, AND IT EMBARRASSED THE HELL OUT OF HER. I DIDN'T SEE THE PROBLEM—WITH A LITTLE ATTENTION, IT POPPED OUT JUST FINE...WELL MOST OF THE TIME. I'D TELL HER IT WAS ACTING SHY AND FOCUS ON A DIFFERENT SENSITIVE AREA.

"UM, NO. BEFORE WE GET TOO FAR INTO THIS, YOU NEED TO KNOW," YOU TOOK THE BIGGEST BREATH BEFORE CONTINUING, AND I PREPARED MYSELF FOR SOME MAJOR RED FLAG. "I HAVEN'T HAD MY BOTTOM SURGERY YET. SO, I DON'T HAVE A..."

THINKING BACK, I'M CURIOUS IF YOU TRAILED OFF BECAUSE YOU WERE NERVOUS, OR IF IT WAS BECAUSE I STRIPPED OFF MY SHIRT TO SHOW OFF THE MESH BALCONETTE BRA NELLY GAVE ME. THERE WAS NO HIDING *MY* NIPPLES, THOSE GIRLS WERE HARD AS DIAMONDS.

"DICK?" AS CUTE AS YOU WERE, MY PUSSY WAS CRAVING TO BE FILLED. I DIDN'T CARE IF IT WAS BY YOUR BLOOD-HARDENED FLESH, YOUR FINGERS, SILICONE, PLASTIC...SHIT, I WOULD'VE TAKEN WOOD. "DO YOU WANT ONE?"

"SOMEDAY, HOPEFULLY. I'M ON TRACK TO GET IT DONE, BUT—"

"Do you prefer long or short?" Impatience is my middle name, as you're sure to learn in due time. "Thick or thin? Does it have to be human shaped? Pretty sure there's some with knots and scales in here too."

I led you over to my favorite drawer while I listed off options. There's a lock, but I only ever engage it when Mossy's daughter comes over. Little Fern is an adorable toddler-sized shit that enjoys exploring every nook and cranny. She once ran out with my super-powered wand and pretended it was a microphone for her magical rendition of "Let It Go." Probably wasn't the best idea to hold a kid's birthday party at my place.

"I don't think I've ever seen this many outside of a sex shop." Best. Compliment. Ever. Inside is a collection ten years in the making, after bidding goodbye to my last boyfriend. I love the feel of cock, but I don't usually love the men attached to them. Some of my toys were flesh textured, others plastic, while the rest filled out between. Straight, curved, barbed, knotted, circumcised and uncut, tentacles and fist shaped. Where there was a need, there was an attachment to match. You weren't scared off though, more curious. "Which one is your favorite? We could start there?"

"How about I pick out a strap that fits," I told you, "and a tool you're comfortable handling. Who knows, maybe you'll find the perfect size for later to tell your doc."

Beneath my go-to drawer is another, filled with a variety of straps. When a partner sticks around for more than a few sessions, it's routine to take them to be properly fitted—it's also the first thing they throw at me when they leave. Out of the thirty or so, I chose a light blue one that perfectly matched your powdered hair. From there, I went back to the top drawer and grabbed one of my newer pieces, Miss Unicorn. She was an impulse buy during my last visit to Madam Scarlett and had Petri gagging over the speckles. "It looks like it comes pre-packed with STDs," she'd told me. Covered in glow-in-the-dark confetti, and ribbed, resembling a unicorn's horn. The blue pieces matched the strap, whereas the purple ones were nearly the same shade as your eyes, and the silicone lightweight so it wouldn't be too daunting to wield.

"To put it on, imagine you're about to go rock climbing or ziplining," I explained as I handed you the completed set. "Pretty much the same process."

Instead of stepping into it, you brought the horn to your nose and just stared. An eyebrow raise from me, and the words come out from your adorable pout.

"Never done that."

"Never? No girl scout trips to adventure campgrounds?" My question made you narrow your eyes, the violet nature popping even more in the white lights of the room. "What about hitting up Dick's and climbing their wall? No? Nothing?"

"I pretty much stay home, for the most part. Going out into public causes a stir, and we have everything we need in our community."

"Not everything, clearly." Curiosity spiked in me over your comment, but my horniness overtook it. I was ready to bounce on that beautifully handsome body, and if that meant dressing you myself, I was more than willing. "Strip."

Shock trickled through me while I watched you snap open your leather pants and ease them down. Your muscles etch down past your abs. A person who treats their body as a temple, I can respect that. Did you know that your red veins are visible through your skin—it's a map of the best points to devour.

I sank to my knees before you, opening the leg holes of the harness.

"Step in," I ordered, and one of your pedicured feet lifted, teetering for a moment before setting a steadying hand on

MY SHOULDER. SLIPPING IT TO YOUR CALF, I HELD IT WHILE YOU STEPPED INTO THE OTHER SIDE. AS I WORKED THE HARNESS UP YOUR BARE LEGS, MY TONGUE LICKED OVER YOUR SMOOTH SKIN. ONE OF THESE DAYS I'LL HAVE TO ASK YOU WHAT YOUR SKIN ROUTINE IS. MAINTAINING HOLD ON THE STRAPS, I SPUN AROUND TO YOUR BACKSIDE AND MOLDED MYSELF TO YOU. KISSING DOWN YOUR COLLARBONE, LICKING EACH MARKING FROM EARLIER, I GRABBED THE WAIST STRAPS AND TUGGED. ALTHOUGH YOU HISSED FROM SHOCK, YOU DIDN'T PULL AWAY. "GOOD, RIVER. THAT'S PERFECT. WE'RE ALMOST THERE."

"THIS FEELS GREAT." YOUR WORDS WERE FULL OF WONDER AND BROUGHT A SMILE TO MY FACE. FATE HAS A FUNNY WAY OF WORKING, AND I'M PRETTY SURE I WAS MEANT TO BUY THIS ATTACHMENT SPECIFICALLY FOR YOU. MAYBE I'LL BRING IT WITH ME AS A GIFT FOR YOU TONIGHT.

WHILE YOU WERE DISTRACTED WITH YOUR NEW APPENDAGE, I WRIGGLED OUT OF MY JEANS AND MADE MY WAY TO MY FOUR-POSTER BED. IS IT A LITTLE YOUNG FOR ME, WITH THE WHITE METAL POSTS AND FAINTLY PINK CURTAINS? SURE. BUT THE WATERPROOF WHITE-TUFTED COMFORTER AND PILLOW TOP MATTRESS ARE MADE FOR A SOLID NIGHT'S SLEEP.

AND LACK OF CLOTHING.

WHEN YOU FINALLY LOOKED UP, SPOTTED ME IN THE MATCHING LINGERIE SET, AND STARED AT ME LIKE THE WORLD HAD STOPPED

SPINNING, THAT'S WHEN I KNEW I'D MADE THE RIGHT CHOICE IN BRINGING YOU HOME. EVEN IF OUR SECOND DATE IS OUR LAST, AND WE NEVER SEE EACH OTHER AGAIN WHEN YOUR LOCATION CHANGES TO SOMEPLACE NEW, WE'LL HAVE THAT MOMENT.

CROOKING MY finger, I CALLED YOU OVER. STARS IN YOUR EYES, YOU OBEYED. IT WAS SO TEMPTING TO MAKE YOU CRAWL TO ME ON YOUR KNEES, SEE HOW FAR I COULD PUSH BEFORE YOU RAN FROM ME, BUT I PROMISED MYSELF THAT WOULD BE FOR ANOTHER TIME.

"ARE WE PUTTING YOU TO WORK, GIVING YOU TIME TO PLAY WITH YOUR NEW TOY?" I fingered THE THIN STRAP OF MY PANTIES, GIVING YOU A HINT OF THE ANSWER I HOPED YOU'D GIVE ME. "OR WOULD YOU RATHER I STRAP UP, MYSELF, AND POUND YOU INTO THESE SHEETS?"

"WHATEVER *MOMMY* WANTS."

FUCK, THAT SHOULDN'T HAVE MADE ME BUST OUT IN GOOSE-BUMPS, BUT IT DID. BLAME THE LACK OF SEX RECENTLY, OR THAT YOUR WILLINGNESS TO BE UNDER MY CONTROL DID SOMETHING TO SCRAMBLE MY BRAIN CHEMISTRY.

"WORSHIP ME."

Running your nails up my thighs, you slipped a finger under each side of my thong. I lifted, allowing you to slide the silk material over my ass, down my legs, and drop them to the floor. Peppering kisses from the crook of my knee upwards, until you reached the mound in dire need of attention, you then paused.

"What's wrong?"

"Nothing. It's just…" Can I say, the way your face reacts when you have something to tell me, is the cutest and most heart-breaking thing. All of your dreadful secrets so far had been so minor to me, that it didn't make me worried about this new concern. "Are you clean?"

"I took a shower before our date," Not what you were asking, I was just curious how you'd react. And boy, did you squirm. "I'm kidding. Breathe. My last test was a few months ago, and I was clean, but there's dams in the side table if you'd prefer one. And finger condoms to cover your nails."

My horny ass prepared as you stepped away, running my hand down to where you'd left. Parting my folds, I used my middle finger to rub soft circles over my clit, unsuccessfully stifling a moan. I hadn't even noticed you come back until you pressed down on my hand, adding pressure to my actions.

To my surprise, you didn't stop me. Setting the dam on my abdomen, you stepped between my legs, spreading me open, and slipped a single, gloved, digit into my opening. A few test moves, and you found the perfect spot, curling over and over until I was practically purring.

One finger wasn't enough and, as if reading my mind, you pressed in a second, then a third. Butting your palm against me, gently pushing me out of the way, and taking over completely so I could lean back to enjoy the buildup.

The buildup and rushing release as a fourth digit was added, stretching me with a blissful burn. My mind went blank, walls contracted, squeezing your hand, but the rhythm never faltered, thumb dragging out the sensation. Another grew before the first orgasm had a chance to settle. I tried to push your hand away, believing it too much, that I might die on the spot.

Tried and failed, wonderfully.

Stars burst, my scream echoed off the walls.

And your chest was soaked in more than sweat.

"Good pet," I whispered, trying to catch my breath. "Now, let's see how well you handle that dick."

Sweat trickles from River's hairline, leaving streaks in their dusted-on high-lighter. As much as I'd like to enjoy the recall from that first night, instead I'm stuck on details. These people that I keep mentioning, they're *my* friends. Friends with family of their own, who—somewhere in the back of my mind—were family to me as well.

Nelly, who gave me a lingerie set. Before today, I never even knew that name, but now I can see him. Darkened from too much tanning, covered in glitter, wearing a tube top and jeans that had more holes than material, waving the hangered set before me in the store.

"A perfect number to hide and reveal if they've proved themselves to you," he'd told me. "Any lover would drop to their knees and do whatever you asked."

And Pandora, better known as Mossy, with her daughter Fernanda. I was the maid of honor in her shotgun wedding senior year of high school. Carried her daughter down the aisle myself, tossing flower petals down the walkways between rows of pews towards the man who eventually left her for another woman.

How could I have forgotten Petri, the reason I kept those dental dams and gloves in supply. Condoms were standard, but it wasn't until she spent a good hour explaining why they were essential for safe play that I bought my first pack. The woman who kept what was effectively a mini suitcase of first aid supplies, and at least four bottles of hand sanitizer, with her at all times.

"Was it you?" Tears line my eyes, and I don't dare wipe them away. There's no possible way River took my friends away from me, somehow managed to scrub them clean and left what I now see were fragments of my past. "Please, tell me this is all some trick."

"I...I can't." They fidget with the same ring they wore that night a year ago. Is that where their power is stored? It seems impossible, something from a fable to tell children, but so is completely erasing more than a decade of my life. "Trick isn't the right word, and I'm sorry for this, but you need to read it for yourself. I can't *tell* you."

"Of course you can't, that would make everything too easy. Wouldn't it?" Slamming the book closed, I drop and flip over the Polaroids from the ground. Dozens of them, all from the carnival. My tears fall, acting as a magnifier over the smiling faces. The five of us with our faces shoved in a carnival cutout, pretending to be a clown, lion, strong-man, trapeze artist, and a ringmaster. Mossy holding Fern up to toss rings onto bottles. Nelly carrying a giant panda on his back, its arms tied around his neck via a pastel scrunchie. Petri glaring at the camera while wiping down a ride seat. Picture after picture, until one stands out.

Bringing it to my face, I see me. Only me. In front of the big tent. Right before I entered, alone, to meet River at the end of the night.

Where had everyone else gone?

"You need to read it." River kneels, meeting me at eye level. One hand has all the Polaroids in a clean stack; in the other is the journal. "If you want to know the truth, I can't tell you, but you can read it."

"*If* I want the truth? You act as though I have a choice in this," My voice cracks with hysterical laughter. "Ever since the day I met you, I haven't had a fucking choice in anything. We move from city to city, clean animal shit on the daily, have to deal with nasty customers and live in filth. I left behind a home, friends, a job, *my entire life*, because I didn't think I had any of it. Because I didn't know any better. You made me believe I was meant to be here, that it was *fate*."

"That was never my intention. It's just—"

"Let me guess; it's just how it is."

"You can find out for yourself, allow yourself to understand our ways," River lifts the journal as they speak, "but you have to read it."

"You said I had a choice?" Glaring at the journal, I can't help but ask. "If I don't want to read it, what other option is there?"

"You take these pictures, hide them somewhere safe." Between their manicured fingers, they fan out the photos. "Only bring them out when your memory falters again. Keep their memory fresh, but stay with me."

I need to know, don't I? As much vitriol as I hold for what the carnival has stolen from me, my time here has been shockingly enjoyable. There's never a dull moment, always something to do, people to talk to, and shows to watch. Plus, I'd be a ringmaster soon—well, co-ringmaster. Sharing center stage with

River, being the reason guest after guest leaves smiling. Leaves to go home, with their family and friends.

No, I couldn't do that. I need to know what happened to them. Nelly, Petri, Mossy and Fern, they don't deserve to be forgotten. What if they're in trouble? What if this past year they've been in their own version of memory loss? What if they're better off having forgotten me?

*They need you.*

*Find them.*

Snatching the journal, I turn to where I left off. Plopping onto the black tarp, dried mud crumbling under my ass and sticking to my bare legs, I dive back in.

EVERY WORD, EVERY MOMENT, GETS JOURNALED. I'VE DONE IT FOR WELL OVER A DECADE, MY first ONE GIVEN TO ME BY MY MOTHER A COUPLE WEEKS BEFORE SHE PASSED AWAY. IN A WAY, THE WORDS ARE FOR HER, EVEN IF SHE'LL NEVER READ THEM. MAYBE SHE HAS HER OWN COPY IN HEAVEN AND WAITS EACH NIGHT TO CATCH UP WITH ME. OR WAKES EACH MORNING TO ENJOY THE NEW ENTRIES WITH A CUP OF TEA, THE SAME flavor AS MINE.

GUESS IT'S GOOD YOU'VE GIVEN ME A NEW ONE, I CAN'T SEE HER BEING EXCITED ABOUT MY SEXCAPADES. NOW I CAN WRITE TO YOU, AT LEAST FOR NOW, UNTIL WE NEXT MEET.

THIS MORNING, I WOKE TO AN EMPTY BED AFTER FALLING ASLEEP WITH YOU WRAPPED IN MY ARMS. THAT FELT RIGHT, MY BODY MOLDED PERFECTLY TO YOURS, LIKE YOU WERE MEANT TO HAVE ALWAYS BEEN THERE. I ALMOST THOUGHT THE WHOLE NIGHT HAD BEEN A LONG DREAM, A FANTASY BEFORE MY ACTUAL BLIND DATE THAT I'D INEVITABLY BAIL ON.

But, no. Fresh cup of morning coffee in hand, I spotted this journal on the kitchen island, five tickets to your carnival sticking out from the inside. The best night of my life had indeed happened.

Everyone is excited as hell to join me. They hadn't known about the Carnival Prey either and should be here soon. I can't wait for you to meet my friends. We might not be related by blood, but they're family to me. Without them, I'm not sure where I'd be. They're all I have left in McHattie.

Whoever came up with your entrance signs needs a raise. Bright pinks and metallic gold, with shredded caution tape and frozen pieces of confetti? Brilliant. The lines, even split into four separate groups, still run all the way down the block.

MOSSY BROUGHT US A POLAROID CAMERA SHE FOUND IN THE CLOSET. WHILE DIGGING FOR MATERIAL TO MAKE NEW COSTUMES FOR HER AND FERN, SHE SPOTTED THE BOX UNDERNEATH THE DARK GOLD AND LIGHT-THYME-COLORED FABRICS. THEY MAKE A SPECTACULAR PAIR OF FAIRIES, THE LITTLE LILIES BRAIDED INTO FERN'S HAIR MATCHING THE ONES MOSSY HAS SEWN ACROSS HER BUST, BRINGING THE LOOK TOGETHER.

I WANT TO SAY THEY STAND OUT, BUT WE'RE A SOLID MIX OF ABSURD.

BESIDES OUR PAIR OF FAIRIES, NELLY HAS ON THE SHORTEST PAIR OF SHORTS I'VE EVER SEEN—THINK DIAPER MEETS MOM JEANS—ALONG WITH A CROPPED LIGHT PINK SWEATER VEST EMBELLISHED WITH A SPARKLING PASTEL RAINBOW ACROSS THE FRONT. ROUNDING OFF THE OUTFIT WITH A UNICORN HEADBAND, HE'S ABLE TO PLAY OFF HIS ATTENTION-GRABBING APPEARANCE AS A COSTUME.

PETRI EVEN BROUGHT HER OWN TWIST TO THE FESTIVITIES. HER SCRUBS FROM WORK ARE COVERED IN LIONS, CLOWNS, AND RING-MASTERS, HER CRAFTING FANNY PACK STUFFED FULL OF CIRCUS THEMED FIRST-AID ITEMS.

I'M COMING, RIVER.

BUT, FIRST, WE NEED SOME OF THOSE GOOD OLE FASHIONED CAR-NIVAL TREATS.

ANOTHER PROP TO YOUR CARNIVAL, THESE GAME PRIZES ARE ADORABLE. THE ONE FERN EYEBALLED FROM THE ENTRANCE IS COVERED IN SEQUINS WHERE IT WOULD NORMALLY BE BLACK FUR. SWIPE ONE WAY, AND IT'S BLUE. SWIPE THE OTHER, PINK. OUR ORIGINAL IDEA OF GRABBING SOME FOOD WENT OUT THE WINDOW—MUCH TO MY ANNOYANCE—AND WE FOUND OURSELVES RUNNING FOR THE RING TOSS STAND, CHASING THE SPIRITED KIDDO WITH THE ENERGY OF A THOUSAND BORDER COLLIE PUPPIES.

"PITS OF DISEASE," PETRI TOLD US AS SHE HANDED OVER A $10 BILL TO THE GAME ATTENDANT. "I'M WARNING YOU ALL NOW, WE'RE GOING TO GET SICK AND HAVE TO CALL OUT OF WORK."

"OH NO, A SICK DAY? WHATEVER WILL WE DO?" NELLY DRAMATICALLY SIGHED, REACHING FOR THE BUCKET OF RINGS. HE DIDN'T GET FAR BEFORE PETRI SMACKED HIS HAND. "OW, YOU TOO-TIGHTLY-TWISTED-BUNNED, CUN–"

"COUNTRY BUMPKIN!" TOSSING HER HAND OVER NELLY'S MOUTH, MOSSY SMILED AT FERN. "PETRI, WOULD YOU MIND CLEANING THE

RINGS FOR US THEN? THAT WAY FERN HAS TO PACE HERSELF BEFORE SHE WINS HERSELF THAT GIANT PANDA."

"PANDA! PANDA!"

"YES, DARLIN'. ARE YOU READY?" WITH AN EASE I KNOW WILL FADE IN A FEW MONTHS AS FERN GETS BIGGER, MOSSY SCOOPED UP HER DAUGHTER AND SET HER ON THE HALF-WALLED PLATFORM.

BEFORE SITTING DOWN TO WRITE THIS, I SNAPPED A SHOT OF THEM FOR YOU TO SEE. HOPEFULLY IT'S NOT AGAINST THE RULES FOR HER TO BE LEANING SO FAR OVER THE BOTTLENECKS, NOT THAT SHE'LL BE ABLE TO RING ANY OF THEM ANYWAY OH MY GOD SHE GOT ONE! SHE GOT THE PANDA!

RIVER!

SHE GOT THE PANDA!!

ALRIGHT, I'M OFF TO CHASE THE KIDDO AGAIN. SHE SPOTTED THE FUN HOUSE. WISH US LUCK! I'D HATE TO GET LOST AND MISS THE GRAND FINALE WITH YOU. IT'S ONLY GOING TO BE MYSELF, FERN, AND HER MAMA GOING THROUGH. THE PANDA IS TOO BIG, SO NELLY IS STAYING BEHIND WITH IT. AND, I'M SURE YOU GUESSED, PETRI THINKS THERE'S TOO MANY CORNERS FOR GERMS TO HIDE IN.

Your team continues to blow me out of the water.

I'm used to seeing the plexiglass maze at the start, but beginning with the spinning tunnel threw me off enough that it made it impossible to run through like I usually do. I made it, though!

Adding a stool at the end is a great spot for anyone needing a break, like me as I catch my breath. I wasn't sure if you'd sprinkle in a scare factor for Halloween, so the fairy lady has gotten most of my attention.

She'd be cute, if it weren't for her screaming.

If I didn't know better, she seems like a mom who's lost her child. Tears run down her face, hair a tangled mess from

PULLING ON THE BRAIDS, LILIES SCATTER THE FLOOR AROUND HER FEET. EVEN HER BENT-BACK NAILS LEAVE BEHIND BLOODY STREAKS AS SHE SCRAPES AT THE SCREEN YOU'RE PROJECTING HER IMAGE ON.

SOMETHING INSIDE OF ME WANTS TO BACKTRACK INTO THE MAZE TO HELP HER, BUT I SHOULD KEEP MOVING FOR THE NEXT GROUP THAT IS SURE TO COME SOON.

THOSE SHIFTER PLATES NEARLY KNOCKED ME ON MY ASS, AND I'M PRETTY SURE I HAVE A CONCUSSION FROM THE HANGING PUNCHING BAGS. HAHA.

THE ONLY PART THAT NEEDS A LITTLE WORK IS SECURITY. WHEN I HIT THE STAIRS TO THE NEXT LEVEL, I FOUND A TODDLER-SIZED GIRL CRYING. SHE WANTED HER MOM BUT COULDN'T DESCRIBE HER TO ME. CUTEST LITTLE THING, DRESSED IN A FAIRY COSTUME WITH LILIES BRAIDED INTO HER HAIR. IT'S A FAMILIAR GETUP, BUT I CAN'T SAY I PAY TOO MUCH ATTENTION TO THE POPULAR HALLOWEEN TRENDS ANYMORE.

WE'RE IN THE HALL OF MIRRORS NOW; THANKFULLY HER OWN REFLECTION DISTRACTED HER SO THAT THERE'S NO MORE TEARS.

MENTAL REMINDER TO MYSELF, AND I GUESS YOU, TO ASK HOW YOU MANAGED TO RIG UP THE EFFECTS IN HERE. SEEING HER REFLECTION NOT MIMIC HER MOTIONS, BUT RATHER REACT TO THEM IS SOMETHING NEW. THE KID WRINKLES HER NOSE, HER REFLECTION STICKS OUT ITS TONGUE. AS SHE POPS UP ONTO HER TIPPY TOES, IT CROUCHES. WHEN SHE REACHES OUT, HER HAND GOING PAST WHERE I WOULD THINK THE MIRROR IS, THE REFLECTION SEEMINGLY PULLS HER IN.

I'LL GIVE HER A FEW MORE MINUTES OF PEACE, BUT THEN I'LL HEAD DOWN WITH HER AND SEE IF WE CAN SPOT HER MOM. OTHERWISE, THERE'S GOING TO BE A DETOUR BACK TO THE MAIN GATE.

ALTHOUGH, I WONDER IF WE COULD LOOK FOR THE KID'S MOM FROM UP HERE—THE VIEW SHOWS ME NEARLY THE WHOLE LAYOUT. SHOULDN'T BE TOO HARD TO SPOT HER.

IN FACT, AH, THERE'S NELLY WITH PETRI. HE GOT LUCKY AS HELL TO WIN THAT PANDA, I'M SURE HIS LEANING HELPED GET THE RING OVER THE BOTTLENECK THOUGH. CLAIMED HE WAS TRYING TO SNEAK A PEEK AT THE GAME ATTENDANT, BUT I KNOW DAMN WELL HE SIMPLY WANTED AN EXCUSE TO CHEAT.

THEY'VE PROBABLY FIGURED I GOT LOST. IF I DON'T LEAVE SOON, THEY'LL WANDER OFF WITHOUT ME. I'LL SNAP A QUICK SHOT AND SLIP DOWN THE SLIDE. THERE HASN'T BEEN A SOUL IN THE HALL SINCE I GOT UP HERE AND SAT DOWN TO START WRITING.

LINE MANAGEMENT SEEMS TO COME SECOND NATURE TO THE RIDE OPERATORS. THEY TAKE THEIR TIME, YET WE'VE BEEN ABLE TO POP ON AND OFF A HANDFUL IN NO TIME.

I'VE ALWAYS WANTED TO RIDE ON THE FERRIS WHEEL. MCHATTIE HASN'T ALLOWED THEM IN A LONG TIME—ACTUALLY I'M SURPRISED YOU WERE ABLE TO GET THE PERMITS FOR THIS POP UP. WHEN I WAS A KID, WE'D GET A CARNIVAL EVERY YEAR FOR...WELL SOME EVENT OR ANOTHER. THEN THEY ALL STOPPED, WENT AWAY, ALONG WITH RUMORS OF MISSING TEENS AND POCKET MONEY.

PETRI HAS TO RIDE WITH ME, AS EACH CAR ONLY FITS TWO AND NELLY WANTS A FEW MINUTES ALONE WITH HIS PRIZE. "IT'S TIME FOR AN UPGRADE TO SOMETHING REAL," OR SO SHE WHISPERED TO ME UNDER HER BREATH.

Don't tell anyone, but I slipped the lady loading passengers a bill to stop us at the top...and as an apology for how long Petri is taking wiping down our seat. Of course I snapped a picture of it—can't have you missing out on anything.

Maybe I'll spot you while we're up there.

The sun is beginning to set.

It's almost our time.

Our second date.

A second of what might be many.

"You should really look at this view, Mamie. No, don't keep writing, you need to...HEY! ARE YOU WRITING WHAT I'M SAYING? Nuh-uh, missy. You stop that right now! Okay, fine, let's see you keep up with this. Salmonella. Listeria. Shigella. Streptuh...streptocock...streptokookoo. HA. Knock it off and look at this view."

Before us is something meant for paintings, to be hung in museums and admired by people paying admission prices. Fiery orange streaks through deep blue, turning an almost pinkish color. Wisps of clouds float past, like ghosts looking for their next haunt.

Below us, a Ferris wheel's car rocks.

"See, that's why I cleaned ours." Sorry for the wet spot—Petri just splattered the page with a glob of sanitizer. "People love to come up here and get handsy with each other instead of enjoying and appreciating what's right in front of them. Like you and that damn journal; didn't I already tell you to put that away?"

She did, but I can't help but keep watching the swinging metal cabin and writing down what I'm seeing. An itch in the back of my head pulls at me, directing me to be alarmed. But, what's so alarming about someone getting frisky, besides a little bit of white splatter.

OR, IN THIS CASE, RED.

A COLORFUL PANDA, WITH A PATCH OF SEQUINS—HALF FLIPPED PINK, THE OTHER PART BLUE—SPLATTERED IN DEEP CRIMSON PAINT. NOT MY CHOICE OF TOY, AND A BIT MORBID LOOKING, BUT CUTE ALL THE SAME.

THE PASSENGERS SEEM TO SETTLE AFTER THE PLUSHIE DROPS, AND THE WHEEL STARTS TO TURN AGAIN. GUESS MINE AND PETRI'S FEW MOMENTS OF PEACEFUL SUNSET ARE OVER, AND MY TIME TO MEET YOU COMES CLOSER.

I'M SURPRISED PETRI'S STUCK BY ME THIS WHOLE DAY. FULLY EX-PECTED HER TO BOW OUT ONCE SHE SAW THE SIZE OF THE CROWD, BUT THROUGH EVERY GAME, EXHIBIT, RIDE, AND PILE OF TRASH, SHE'S BEEN BY MY SIDE. YOU CAN TELL US WHICH ONE IS MORE EXCITED TO FINALLY MEET YOU—ME OR THE WOMAN WHO KNOWS SHE CAN SPLIT AS SOON AS I HAVE A BABYSITTER.

IT'S NOT THAT I GET INTO TROUBLE, OFTEN, IT'S JUST I TEND TO MAKE IMPULSIVE MOVES. MY WHOLE LIFE SHE'S THE ONE WHO PICKS ME UP, BRUSHES ME OFF, ADDRESSES THOSE WOUNDS, AND SENDS ME BACK OUT TO DO IT ALL AGAIN.

MY RIDE OR DIE.

MY ONE AND ONLY FRIEND.

GUESS WITH YOU, IT'LL MAKE US A ROUND THREE-PERSON CREW.

A QUICK PIT STOP TO GET AN ELEPHANT EAR, AND WE'LL GET TO THE BIG TENT FOR YOUR SHOW. IT'S ALL ANYONE CAN TALK ABOUT IN THIS BATHROOM, YOUR MAGNIFICENT PRODUCTION. STARING OVER AT PETRI, SCRUBBING HER HANDS FOR THE EIGHTH TIME SINCE WE WALKED PAST THE GATES, I WONDER IF SHE SEES THE SAME THING I SEE. HER HANDS HAVE BECOME BRIGHT RED, RAW, FAR PAST THE POINT OF PRUNED. SKIN THAT SHOULD BE A SOFT CREAM PEELS BACK FROM THE TIPS, CURLING UP TOWARD HER KNUCKLES.

YES, OF COURSE I CALLED OUT TO PETRI, TRIED TO PULL HER OUT OF HER OBSESSIVE CLEANING, BUT IT'S NOT WORKING. IF SHE KEEPS AT IT, I'M WORRIED I MIGHT SEE BONE SOON. NO ONE IN THE RESTROOM IS PAYING ANY MIND TO HER, EVEN AS THE WATER FROM THE MOTION-ACTIVATED FAUCET CHANGES FROM CLEAR TO CRIMSON.

I NEED TO GET HER HELP, NEED TO LEAVE HER—JUST FOR A MO-
MENT—AND SEE IF SOMEONE IN THE FOOD COURT CAN GET HER TO
STOP.

HOURS AGO, THESE PICNIC TABLES WERE FULL OF SMILING FACES,
BUT EVERYTHING SEEMS TO BE CLEARING OUT QUICKLY. AS I LEFT
THE RESTROOM WITH AN EMPTY BLADDER AND FRESHLY CLEANED
HANDS, ONE OF THE WORKERS IN A FOOD STALL WAVED ME OVER
TO PICK UP MY ORDER. DAMN, THE FOOD HERE IS GOOD.

JUST A FEW MINUTES MORE, TO FINISH MY LEMONADE, AND I'M ALL
YOURS. FUCK THE SNACKS, I'D RATHER A TASTE OF YOU ANYWAY.

THE TENT LOOKS SO MUCH SMALLER ON THE OUTSIDE VERSUS IN HERE.

EVEN SMALLER WHEN YOU FACTOR IN THERE'S NO ONE ELSE HERE FOR MY BIG, YET PRIVATE, SHOW.

DUSTINGS OF POPCORN LITTER THE STANDS. DISCARDED NAPKINS AND A STRAY BUNNY PLUSHIE THE ONLY SIGNS THERE HAD BEEN ANYONE IN HERE AT ALL. ONCE A FULL SEATING, A SOLD–OUT EVENT, SOMETHING THAT WILL STICK IN THE BRAINS OF A HUNDRED SOULS FOR YEARS TO COME, NOW WHITTLED DOWN TO AN EXPERI-ENCE FOR ONE.

I SNAGGED SOMEONE OUTSIDE TO TAKE A PICTURE OF ME ENTERING, WITH A POLAROID CAMERA THAT MANAGED TO MYSTERIOUSLY AP-PEAR IN MY BAG, BEFORE ONE MORE SHOT OF THE SUNSET. THEY ACCEPTED THE CAMERA FROM ME TO HAND OFF INTO THE LOST AND FOUND BIN.

YOUR CARNIVAL HAS BEEN AMAZING, BUT THERE'S SOMETHING MISSING.

ALL THESE EMPTY SEATS...

FOR YEARS, SINCE MY MOTHER MADE HER WAY ON A NEW ADVENTURE, I'VE BEEN TRYING TO fill THAT EMPTINESS. SOMEONE TO SPEND THE REST OF MY LIFE WITH, TO WAKE UP EACH MORNING EAGER TO SEE, AND FALL TO SLEEP DREAMING OF. FRIENDS WOULD'VE BEEN NICE TO HAVE, PROBABLY MAY HAVE MADE MY LIFE EASIER IN A LOT OF WAYS, LESS LONELY FOR SURE, BUT JUST LIKE WITH DATING, NOTHING EVER STUCK.

SO MANY FACES THAT CAME AND WENT, ALONG WITH LOST OPPORTUNITIES TO GET OUT AND SEE THE WORLD.

WITH YOU THOUGH, I HAVE THAT CHANCE. CARNIVALS GO ALL OVER, RIGHT? WE COULD LEAVE THIS SMALL TOWN BEHIND, WANDER INTO THE BIGGER CITIES. HAVE BIGGER LIVES.

BASED ON YOUR SMILE, FROM YOUR PERCH A FEW FEET AWAY FROM ME AS I WRITE THIS, I THINK YOU HAVE THE SAME IDEAS.

I'M SO GLAD I TOOK THAT CHANCE, FORCED MYSELF TO GO INTO THAT BAR, FOLLOWED MY HEART TO YOU. WHO KNOWS WHAT MAY HAVE HAPPENED IF I'D NEVER MET YOU.

"So, where are they?" I followed the rules, read the damn story, and I'm no closer to having my friends back. Fuck this journal, fuck this carnival! "WHERE ARE THEY, RIVER?"

"I…they…*Mommy*, I swear. I thought." They take the journal from me, rifling through the pages themself as if the secret to the universe was contained within it. "You write everything, *everything*, how could you not write the ending?"

"Excuse-the-fuck-me? I didn't write the ending?" None of this is my fault, none of it. River invited me to the Carnival Prey, not the other way around. So what, I forgot to write what happened after everyone went home and we decided to spend the next year together. My friends are *gone*, vanished without a trace or memory of having ever existed. "What kind of bullshit is this? You've had me for a goddamn *year*, trapped in this traveling lie, and somehow that's *my* fault?"

River, distracted by the book, doesn't notice my approach. It seems absurd, what I'm about to do, given that this day began with me thinking that the world revolved around this person. But all I can think of is wrapping my fingers around their neck. As hot as choking is at the right moment, this ain't it—my only goal is to wring out the truth.

A strong grip on my shoulder stops my progress, but I can't bring myself to look because it doesn't stop my words.

"Where." My fingers curl into fists. "Are." Blood rushes in my ears. "My friends?" River's mouth moves, but nothing comes from their lips. No clues. No hints. No answers. All while questions spiral in my head. Nelly, Petri, Mossy, and little Fern. What happened to them? Are they okay? Seconds, that feel like hours, pass before the question burning the most comes out. "Why would you take them from me?"

"We can't tell her, River." The hand loosens, comforting rather than holding me back. Sliding a side eye, I realize the bartender has joined our walk down memory lane. "We've accepted that part of the carnival. It's too late for us. But, if you love her the way I think you do, you have to try."

"What do you think I've been doing? Of course I love her—you, Mamie. I love you." From inside their pocket, they pull a velvet black box. I was right, they planned on proposing, not exactly the way I imagined, though. Instead of being excited, I'd rather throw it in their face. River sets the box down alongside the journal, staring at the two. "I did this because I wanted you, wanted to have a chance at knowing you, caring for you. How well can you really love someone, though, when vital parts of their life are missing. You're not *you* without your friends."

No more is a hand on my shoulder. I guess Spyder's comfort can only go so far when your mind is warring between two different realities. As far as I'm concerned, River and I are alone. Between us, my options are clear.

Stay with River and live a future with the carnival, or choose my friends and a past where I knew familial love. It's more than just that—everything in my bones knows I'm simplifying matters. Choosing River means leaving my friends to live out their own hells. Little Fern's face is now so clear in my mind, scrunched up, tear stained, searching for her mother. Her mother, who I'd seen moments before, trapped behind glass frantically trying to get to her only daughter. The Ferris wheel, it wasn't rocking from a couple teens messing around, it was Nelly, the falling panda covered in his blood. All the hand sanitizer in the world wouldn't have been enough for Petri. Oh god, Petri, I left her scrubbing away the flesh from her arms. How could I have just walked away? How can I walk away, again?

"I need to find them." My knees shake, threatening to send me tumbling to the ground. It's only my mind that keeps me standing, willing me to push forward as my heart screams to reunite with the people that have shaped me into the person I am. "But, how can I? They're gone."

"Maybe you can flip it." River looks defeated. All I can think is that they're not happy with my choice. Yet, they're still here, helping me. "The world has forgotten, but you broke through that and remembered. What if you forget the Carnival Prey?"

"Would that work?" I join River at the table, running the tips of my fingers over the journal. My pinky twitches towards the ring box, curiosity nearly winning out.

"It might. Or, you'll try and become a forgotten memory, too." Their breath hitches. I don't dare to look River in the eyes, knowing full well tears are brewing. Crying won't help matters, or so I tell myself as a lump forms in my throat. "If you leave me, it'll be for good."

"So, this is goodbye?" Forever is quickly becoming never. Can I really do this? "Guess this breakup is better than the guy that dropped me off on the side of the highway in the middle of rush hour. If past experience is any matter, I'm sure I'll be ignoring your future texts asking for your jewelry back."

"You were safe here, because you had me." They spin their ring, for what will probably be the last time I ever see. "The carnival is one thing to forget, I'm different. Someone important gave me this—I couldn't tell you who, even if I knew—and I think it's time to pass it along."

River twists the ring, pulling it over their knuckle, and reaches over the table for my hand. Impulsive be my middle name, I gave it to them, allowing the metal to slip onto my middle finger.

"Your friends aren't forgotten, not anymore." Their words hit a chord inside me, making me close my eyes to picture their smiling faces. "I'll be simply a face on an app you should've swiped left on."

"Have fun with your next prey." Harsh words I speak with a sad smile. They deserve to be happy, just not with me. Turning my back to them, I face the flap of the tent, imagining it's the door of the bar. The door I should've walked my ass out of a year ago and never returned to.

Slowly, the door becomes more tangible, the tent flap a foggy memory. A memory quickly fading as though it never happened. With a shove, I'm free, looking out into a nearly empty parking lot. My Grand Am the only vehicle. Rusty, old, but ready for one more trip.

Sunlight peeks over the trees as I crank the engine and pull out of the parking lot, leaving the bar in my rearview mirror.

This is where I belong.

In McHattie.

My home.

# ABOUT THE AUTHOR

*Sarah Trala was born in Michigan and raised in South Lyon. She self-published her first book, Small Town Murders, in 2022. Since then, her fictional town of McHattie has grown to include an expanded collection of characters, creatures, and trauma.*

*Writing is only one part of Sarah's life. During the day, and after hours for emergency cases, she has been a plumber since 2016. On top of that, she enjoys crocheting, building model kits, collecting knickknacks, spending time with friends & family, and finding new ways to expel her creative energy.*

*You can find more of her work inside the original Twisted Tales of Halloween Horror, on Kindle Vella with Too Vivid to Be True, and other various titles on Amazon. To catch the most recent updates, be sure to follow Sarah on her socials.*

*Instagram: AuthorSarahTrala*

*TikTok: SarahTralaWrites*

# THE PAPER MAN

## Dahlia Blackwell

*Come one, come all, to the carnival's thrall,*
*Where the man with the paper skin waits for your call.*
*Yellow eyes gleam in flickering light,*
*A grin that knows no wrong or right.*
*Step closer, dear child, to the night's parade,*
*Awaits your entrance to the macabre masquerade.*
*For once you're inside, the show will begin,*
*You'll find yourself lost in the world within.*

# CHaPTer one

I t was late October of 1961 when my eyes first caught sight of the red tent, its hue mirroring the fiery palette of the surrounding autumn landscape. The canvas structure filled Mr. Elsworth's empty field with the dazzling splash of the vibrant red canopy stretching out under the afternoon sun. The fair came through Richtor every fall, yet this ode to the big top tents of traveling carnivals was a part of the decor I had never seen, despite being born and raised in this tiny town. Leaves in their final, colorful deaths danced in the air near the tent as if in celebration of its presence. Its sudden appearance was as intriguing as it was out of place, holding promises of hidden wonders and secrets, striking a chord within my heart. I had always longed for a real-life adventure. It began a month prior to the arrival of the tent. At twenty-one, my life consisted mostly of keeping my head down and getting lost in the words on a page. I had never been the type to draw thoughtful, lingering gazes as people passed by me. I have been called, quite correctly, mousy. My hair, long and straight, resembled the unremarkable hue of oak bark, complementing my stature, which fell a bit short of average. I was unconcerned with my appearance. The characters in my stories would never know what I looked like anyway. Books have always been my refuge, their worlds a comfort against my solitude. Preferring them over social circles has inevitably placed me on the fringes, a reality that hit hard during my high school years. Once I had opened *Farewell, My Lovely* by Raymond Chandler at a basketball game, only to find that, as if by magic, an invisible divide had formed between me and everyone else. I had resigned myself to solitude, a silent observer ever just outside, until him. Alano.

It was as though he had stepped right out of the pages of one of my cherished novels, his presence as arresting as any character crafted from ink and imagination. Alano. His name alone was too sweet on my tongue to abbreviate to something as mundane as Al, though many did. They diminished its resonance, a disservice I could never bring myself to commit. I found him—or perhaps he found me—on an ordinary Thursday, amidst the historical heart of the campus. The university library, with its towering shelves laden with centuries of knowledge, had become my sanctuary. Alano approached with a grace that seemed at odds with the cluttered surroundings of the library tables. His white T-shirt highlighted the contours of his lean frame, his dark jeans that spoke of a practical elegance, and black canvas shoes with white toes. It was an apathy which I hesitate to express with something as trivial as "coolness," yet is exactly how I felt when I saw him. He was cool.

His hair, a dark wave pushed back as a nod to the rebels of the silver screen, framed a face that must have been sketched with an artist's loving precision. But it was his eyes that did me in. His eyes were a striking blue that captured my attention fully. They held a curiosity, an intensity that saw through the mask of my self-imposed isolation.

"Mind if I join you?" His voice carried an accent. The table, covered with my books and notes, suddenly felt embarrassingly chaotic. "Sure," I managed to say. I shut my book, uncertain if it was impolite to have it open while he spoke to me. I placed it atop my unstable stack.

He settled across from me. "You have a taste for good books," he noted, nodding towards the copy of *A Separate Peace* I was holding. "I should be studying for debate," I confessed, my voice a mix of defensiveness and relief.

"The last place I studied, I think the newest book was *Of Mice and Men*." His playful critique caught my attention. Knowing about Steinbeck felt personal, acknowledging a piece of myself most people overlooked.

"Mrs. Cleaver, the librarian here, is fierce when it comes to keeping new books in the budget." I replied with a note of admiration. "Ah, yes. I have met her. She's been quite helpful, actually. Found me a copy of Ray Bradbury I'd been seeking for ages."

"Really? Which Bradbury book?" My interest grew. I hadn't been a big fan of Bradbury, but I couldn't ignore his growing popularity. Now, with Alano's interest, I was keen to explore every piece Ray Bradbury had ever written.

"*Dark Carnival*," Alano said with a hint of mystery. His eyes sparkled, suggesting he knew well the stories it contained. I almost let slip that I hadn't read it, intrigued but aware of my own gaps in knowledge.

"I thought he was a science fiction writer, exploring the uncharted regions of space and things like that." I smiled, somewhat pleased with myself for making such a smooth transition. "Speaking of the unknown, how did you find your way to Richtor?" The words tumbled out, perhaps a tad more emphatically than intended, underscored by a curiosity that bordered on awe. In my emphasis on "you," I inadvertently highlighted his distinctiveness—a man who, with his exotic allure, elegant manner, and accent, seemed a world apart from the rustic charm of our surroundings. Whatever culture had birthed him, it was far from the woods that surrounded our little town.

He flashed an understanding smile, "You don't seem to fit in either. Perhaps we could be outcasts together?"

The bluntness of his observation, rather than alienating, was a gentle caress to a soul bruised by isolation. In a life where my companions were confined to the pages of books, where endings were as finite as the stories they concluded, the prospect of a real, tangible connection was both a novelty and a salve. "I think I would like that," I responded, my voice carrying a weight of earnestness and a flicker of hope.

He smiled, his teeth perfect in the library's light, causing a rush of emotions in me. His smile made me imagine scenarios where he'd close the gap between us for a bold kiss, deepening our connection without words.

"My name is Alano," he introduced himself with a formal air that belied the electric current running beneath our exchange.

"Carolyn," I responded, cursing the mundanity of it. In Richtor, "Carolyn" was as common as the oak trees lining the town's outskirts.

"Everyone has somewhere they feel they belong, even those who seem to stand out from the crowds." His eyes met mine with an earnestness that bridged the gap between mere observation and a shared, deeper understanding. "I'm glad to have found a place here."

I glanced around to see that several eyes were darting toward us, then returning to their own conversations. "I'm glad you feel that way. In this library, once you sit at a table with me, you're basically Sweden."

His laughter, warm and unguarded, echoed softly against the library's quietude. "I am okay with that," he affirmed, a smile playing on his lips. Then, with a gentle nudge towards the book that lay atop my stack, he quoted, "I felt that I was not, never had been and never would be a living part of this overpoweringly solid and deeply meaningful world around me."

The accuracy with which he cited the passage, one I had only read just this morning, was a thread pulling us closer. My response was a mirror of his laughter, a shared moment of joy that seemed, for an instant, to draw the entire library into our sphere of intimacy.

# CHapTer TWO

The ensuing month unfolded like a passage from one of the very novels we often discussed, swift and laden with a sense of inevitability that I had never anticipated. Our relationship transformed in ways that echoed the fervent hopes I harbored in secret. Our togetherness became a force of its own.

My desire for him was insatiable, a craving that pulsed with its own lifeblood. I gave myself to this hunger, to him, two weeks before the arrival of the tent. This awakened something within me—a wildfire that no reasoning could quell. I indulged myself without any restraint. I would sneak him into my dorm room most nights, or slip out to meet him under the stars.

It was one such night, as dawn marked the end of our passionate adventure, that we stumbled upon a sight as startling as it was enchanting. A red canvas tent standing in Mr. Elsworth's field. Alano pointed to it. "What if I fucked you in there later tonight?"

I mulled over the tent, its presence sending a ripple of unease through me. "Maybe another night," I murmured, trying to suppress the burgeoning anxiety. As I turned towards him, his expectant gaze met mine, dissolving my apprehensions instantly. Still, I was glad when he did not press the matter and instead took my hand. We walked away from the field, leaving its mystery for tomorrow, and headed back to my dorm.

Three days after its sudden emergence, the tent was swallowed by the carnival that blossomed around it, transforming Mr. Elsworth's field into a spectacle of lights, laughter, and the sweet scent of treats. There was an unspoken agreement between us: We were going to the carnival together. Our conversation effortlessly shifted to which rides we'd conquer together and the array of confections we'd indulge in. Without labels or formal declarations, without even the utterance of boyfriend or girlfriend, it was clear. I was irrevocably his, and he was mine, a truth more profound than any physical intimacy we'd shared.

# CHAPTER THREE

As Halloween night unfolded, Alano and I stood in line to grab tickets. I breathed deeply of the night's magic and mystery, carried upon a sweet breeze laden with remnants of caramel and hot oil. Booths formed mazes just beyond the ticket stand, their bright reds and whites standing out against the dark, while strings of yellow orbs stretched from pole to pole, creating constellations of light above us.

We paused by the carousel, its charm undeniable yet impractical for us. We sought to experience the rides together. Opting for the Ferris wheel, we boarded one of its many carriages with me instantly sliding onto his half of the seat. The structure moaned under its burden, lifting us skyward, joining others in a slow ascent to the top. A shriek of thrill, not far above, punctuated the air as another bucket swung with deliberate mischief. Alano, however, harbored no desire to frighten me. His intentions were of a gentler kind. Clasping my hand, he directed my gaze towards the silhouette of the mill, perched quietly beside the town's meandering river—a site familiar to us from nights less illuminated than this. "You can see the old mill," he noted, his voice a blend of nostalgia and discovery.

"Richtor almost looks beautiful from here," I mused, the view lending a new perspective to the familiar.

His reply came softly, charged with meaning. "From where I'm sitting, there's no more beautiful sight." The sincerity in his voice prompted me to turn towards him, only to meet his gaze already fixed upon me. The moment our eyes locked, the world outside our Ferris wheel carriage seemed to fade into insignificance. Our lips met, and I yielded to the pull between us—a desire so profound, it bordered on addiction. In his embrace, I found a hunger that demanded to be sated yet grew with each touch, each kiss. I understood the siren's call that led one to surrender entirely to their vice, driving sailors to their rocky doom. For in his presence, I wanted nothing else.

As the Ferris wheel completed its rotation, gently lowering us back to earth, a comedic whistle sounded from above and behind. I didn't need to look to know their distractions were far removed from the fervor that enveloped us. A fleeting pity for them surfaced within me; their moments paled in comparison to the intensity of ours. His tongue teased my lips apart, igniting a pulse of desire that quickened my heartbeat. My thoughts daringly ventured towards the possibility of escalating our intimacy right there. I wished the wheel had halted, granting us a secluded haven amidst the sky.

But fate had other plans. As the ride ceased its journey, we were the first to get off. His hand, extended to assist me, tightened its grip as I stepped out, leading me away from the illuminations of the Ferris wheel. A mutual, unspoken understanding propelled us forward, each step a shared search for seclusion, a space where our desires could unfurl unchecked.

Our search led us behind booths, into the temporary sanctuaries of carnival workers, yet each was flawed, lacking the privacy we craved. A fleeting horror gripped me as he veered near the portable toilets, but relief replaced it as he passed them without a second glance. Then, halting, a grin unfurled across his face.

"There?" His nod directed my gaze towards the fun house, its entrance an asymmetrical wonder, adorned with clown paintings and bathed in the same lights that canopied the carnival.

"Impossible. Too crowded," I countered.Instead of replying, he marched up to the ticket taker, pulling me along in tow. He leaned in, close enough that the rest of the assembled crowd could not hear him. "I'll give you twenty dollars to shut this down for fifteen minutes. Say some kid threw up in there and it's being cleaned."

The man looked down, noticing the bill that had appeared in Alano's hand though I had not even noticed him drawing it from his pocket. He nodded, plucking the bill from his hand. "Fifteen minutes kid, make 'em count."

Inside, the fun house unfolded in a kaleidoscope of colors, its floors wobbling beneath our feet, challenging our balance. Though the novelty of the setting tugged at my curiosity, I was driven by a deeper yearning. We navigated the twisting corridors, sometimes ducking, sometimes climbing, until we found ourselves encircled by mirrors. In this secluded chamber, he wrapped me in his embrace. I gave no hesitation as I surrendered to the moment.

My eagerness matched his, reaching for his shirt and drawing it up. I felt his hands tugging at my skirt, yanking it up to my hips. He lifted it, continuing to draw it off me completely, pulling the rest of my dress up and over my head. He wasted no time, dropping to his knees before me, ripping my panties down. "I want to taste you," he declared, pulling them free of my ankles.

He placed his warm hand on the back of my smooth calf, gently lifting my leg and spreading it apart from the other. As his tongue softly glided along the edge of my slit, I watched him, mirrored on every side. His hands moved upwards, caressing my thighs with an eager touch, pulling me closer to his mouth. I released the clasp of my bra, tossing it to the floor. Now I stood naked except for my shoes in the hall of mirrors, watching him from every conceivable angle as he pleasured me with his tongue.

I thrust my fingers into his hair, forcefully pulling him away. In the faint light, his chin glistened, adding a touch of allure. Without uttering a word, he rose, his mouth finding my neck.

Fumbling in the darkness, my hands searched for the button on his pants. Finally, I succeeded, pulling his jeans and boxer shorts down. His erect cock stood proudly, eager for its next venture.

Grasping it firmly, I ran my hand up and down, feeling its pulsating excitement against my palm. Overwhelmed with desire, I broke away from his kisses. I quickly dropped to my knees, using our clothes as a cushion. "Fuck me while you have the chance," I commanded.

A moment later, he entered me, sliding effortlessly in. I went down on one elbow, my other hand reaching below to rub my clit. I pressed, feeling the pleasure of it rush along my body. Sensation became the focus of my world. "Oh my God!" I said, vibrating with excitement as he repeatedly thrust in and out.

His movements were rhythmic and steady, allowing me to lose myself in pure bliss. I closed my eyes, not caring for the mirrors. The intensity built, and I could feel the wave of orgasm approaching. I bucked against him as he stiffened, his pace growing uneven. And then, unable to contain it any longer, a scream escaped my lips. Desperate to muffle the sound, I bit down on my arm. He continued to move, but now with a newfound control, each thrust deliberate and measured, prolonging the waves of pleasure.

He pulled out of me, looking around with uncertainty. His hand fell to his cock, still stiff and waiting. "You have no way to clean up if I..." he pumped a few more times, shuddering as he did so.

I turned to face him, pulling his dick toward me. It filled my mouth as I took it into the back of my throat. I sucked for a moment, then released it, giving it a few pumps with my fist. He bucked against it. "Oh," was all he said, then it was back in my mouth, pulsing as he came. The salty taste coated my tongue and throat as I swallowed the first burst. Then there was more. Three more times I had to swallow to take all of it. His cock was still somewhat stiff as he moaned with pleasure.For a moment I thought there might be a chance of another round, but he would need some time to reset. Some nights we spent hours in pursuit of as many orgasms as we could find. In many cases, he would continue serving my needs while he rejuvenated, but now we did not have that time. Instead I sucked until I was sure there was no more to be drawn out of him.

I opened my eyes and gasped. Over his shoulder, in the reflection cast from a mirror, I saw the pale white reflection of a man's face, watching us.

# CHAPTER FOUR

The figure's reflection loomed over us, an unnaturally tall specter dressed in unrelenting white, from his suit down to the eerie pallor of his skin. His hair, completely white, framed a face that seemed untouched by life's warmth, standing sharply against the red of his hat—a splash of color in an otherwise ghostly visage. For a fleeting second, visions of classic horror icons flashed through my mind, painting him as a modern-day vampire straight out of a bygone era. But when I turned to confront this apparition, trying to quell the scream that had built within me, I found nothing. The space was empty.

Alano's confusion was palpable, having lost the intensity of the moment before. "What?" His voice trailed off into bewildered murmurs as he tried to follow my panicked gaze.

"There was someone there," I insisted, pointing back at the mirrors. A chill ran down my spine.

He began to gather our clothes, pulling his pants up and handing me my bra. "I don't think there's anyone else here."

"I know what I saw," I snapped, irritation and fear intertwining within me.

"Maybe it was a ghost?" His suggestion came not with levity but with a sobering sincerity. As I faced him, prepared to rebuke, I was met with an earnest expression, his eyes devoid of any jest. Offering my dress, his demeanor suggested he had merely commented on the weather's unpredictability, not proposed the presence of something supernatural.

"I..." His unexpected suggestion left me at a loss. Ghosts were beyond my belief system, yet the undeniable reality was that the figure had been there, only to vanish into thin air. "I don't know," I admitted, finally.

He paused, the dress in his hand momentarily forgotten, and stepped closer to offer a kiss. The intimacy of the moment caught me off guard, reminding me of my vulnerability. Under different circumstances, this could have led to another passionate encounter, but the eerie experience in the fun house had unsettled me deeply. This was soft, more comforting than passionate, as if to anchor me back to reality, to reassure rather than to inflame.

Clothed once again, we emerged into the carnival's lively atmosphere. We drifted from game to game, laughing at our consistent failures to win any of the seemingly rigged challenges. Alano's indifference to the lack of prizes spoke volumes. His priority was simply sharing these moments with me, successes or not.

Indulging in ice cream cones and a funnel cake, we strolled through the carnival. The sugary treat resembled a miniature snowy scene, a whimsical thought that brought a smile to my face. Yet, as we walked, an unease lingered in my mind, a shadow that the festive lights couldn't dispel.

My attention was caught by a flickering light from the big red tent. Looking closer, I saw it had luxurious red velvet curtains at the entrance, held back by golden tassels. It was quiet and welcoming, unlike the other louder attractions. There were no signs or barkers.

Then, my gaze fixed on a chillingly familiar sight: a barrel painted in the carnival's theme of red and white, and atop it stood the man in the white suit with pale complexion and snow-white hair against the red of his top hat, silently waving in our direction. His skin was the color of paper, though the texture reminded me of ancient scrolls and flaking edges of papyrus. It peeled away in long slender cracks around his chin and ran up along his cheeks like paint on drywall that has been sundered by the settling of an ancient house.

"That's him," I whispered, a cold shiver running down my spine.

"The one on the barrel?" Alano queried, his tone reflecting skepticism, as if the man was just another part of the carnival's many curiosities.

"Yes. He was in the fun house," I managed to say, turning away to hide the flush of embarrassment—and fear—that colored my cheeks.

Alano, dangerously curious or foolishly brave, approached the figure despite my protests. The man welcomed us with dramatic, playful gestures, inviting us in with a cane and a beckoning hand. His actions seemed designed to tempt us inside.

"Alano, stop," I pleaded, my voice a mix of fear and resolve. The thought of confronting this man, after the peculiar and unsettling experience in the fun house, filled me with a profound discomfort. The uncertainty of how long he might have watched us, coupled with his silent disappearance, was too much. It rendered the incident not just bizarre, but deeply violating. I wondered if the fun house operator had shared our secret with the carnival staff.

Alano took a step towards the tent once more, his frustration barely concealed.

"Let's just go," I found myself pleading. I was afraid. The thought of leaving the carnival behind, of escaping the watchful gaze of this paper man, was the only path I wanted to take. "My roommate has gone home to spend Halloween taking her little sister trick or treating. We'll have the whole place to ourselves." My suggestion, veiled as it was, aimed to distract him, to pull his focus away from the tent and back to us.

"Don't you want to know what's inside?" His question, seemingly oblivious to my offer, held a genuine curiosity. Since its first appearance, the big red tent had called to him, a mystery that he felt compelled to unravel.

"No, I want to leave," I insisted. My body was trembling, knots formed in my stomach.

Alano paused, turning to face me fully for the first time since the confrontation began. "Look, it's not like we haven't risked being caught before. He's not trying to get us in trouble or anything," he reasoned. "I'm sorry he made you uncomfortable, but we're just human, right?" His attempt at consolation fell short, especially as he added, "He seems to get that there's nothing wrong with two people expressing their love."

The word "love" hung heavily between us, with implications we dared not voice until now. Yet, the moment was tainted. Alano's stance seemed to critique my reluctance, branding it as immaturity.

With a sigh, he extended his hand towards me. Despite my reservations, I found myself drawn once again into his orbit, following him towards the tent and the unknown that awaited us inside.

The paper man nodded and took off his hat to welcome us as we walked in. A large crowd waited, filling nearly every seat in the room. We sat down among the strangers, in the only two seats that remained. Just as we settled, the lights went out, then the stage lit up, starting the show we had unwittingly agreed to see.

# Chapter Five

The silence of anticipation was broken only by the solitary figure of the first performer, his footsteps echoing on the wooden stage as he made his entrance. He held a black leather bag, from which he produced three gleaming balls. The act of juggling, simple yet mesmerizing, captivated the audience as the balls danced in the air, their movement soon replaced by the more dangerous allure of knives. The music accompanying his performance was a departure from the carnival's usual fare, weaving a complex melody with flutes, fiddles, and the resonant beat of drums. It was strangely beautiful.

Next, a magician who looked a bit like Bela Lugosi as Dracula but older, with gray hair and a serious face, took the stage. He was curiously quiet. However, his assistant caught my attention. Her red dress, slit daringly high, sparkled with silver threads that created a show of their own. Her dark eyes and flowing curls added to her mysterious beauty as she smiled through each dangerous trick, always emerging unscathed and much more enchanting.

The show unfolded with a series of acts as varied as they were captivating: a fire dancer whose flames seemed to lick the air in sync with the music, a snake charmer who commanded silence and awe in equal measure, a strongman, a sword swallower, and finally, a gymnastic duo whose performance was a breathtaking display of agility and grace.

After the last act, the music stopped suddenly, leaving a heavy lack of sound. There was no clapping. The audience just stood up quietly, as if their muteness was part of the script. They wore a mix of fancy and normal clothes, some looking like they came from another time, but it was Halloween and people were often dressed extravagantly. The crowd was young, mostly in their twenties, a detail I noticed, wondering if it was my perspective since I was their age.

"You ready to go?" Alano's voice cut through my unease as he stood and took my hand. His face bore the glow of someone who had thoroughly enjoyed the performance, oblivious to the turmoil churning within me.

"Yes," I replied. I needed to get out of there.

As we made our exit, weaving through the crowd with a haste that belied my calm exterior, I noted the deliberate slowness of the others. Despite our delayed start, we were the first to reach the entrance, where the paper man held the curtain open, his silent gesture granting us passage back into the night.

The outside air hit me with a wave of nausea, the once-tempting aromas of the carnival now repulsive. The sound was overwhelming, the noise far too loud to have been silenced by the simple material that stretched between the poles holding the tent in place. The normalcy of it all was almost grotesque in contrast to the world inside the tent. My head spun as the smell of fried food and spilled beer assaulted my nostrils. I was certain, though, I had been unaware of these things just inside of the tent.

"Are you okay?" His question, simple yet weighted with concern, prompted a reassessment of my own condition. The ground seemed off kilter, swaying below me in disjoined rhythm.

I nodded, trying to quell the rising panic, to silence the instinctual fear that screamed within me. Was it an effect of the carnival's strangeness, or something more?

"It's okay," Alano murmured, his arm encircling me, offering a semblance of safety in his embrace. I swallowed the lump in my throat, drawing comfort from Alano's warmth as I pressed my face into his shoulder.

As we moved to leave the carnival, I found myself compelled to look back toward the tent one last time. The scene that met my eyes was one of utter desolation. The tent stood abandoned, its lights extinguished. The velvet curtains that hung from the entryway were replaced with faded canvas flaps. The elegant facade was now stripped back to reveal the ugly, decrepit shell it encased, as if it had been forgotten in this field for months, or even years, as the sun bleached the color away. Though, it remained unnoticed by those who moved beyond it.

I tugged at Alano's arm, directing his attention back to the now silent tent. "Ghosts," he uttered.

"That's not possible," I countered, my rational mind grappling with the surreal evidence of my own eyes.

"At least they put on a good show," he quipped. He was attempting to lighten the mood with humor, though the levity felt out of place.

I struggled to respond, his attempt at jest leaving me further entangled in my thoughts. "Ghosts," I finally echoed, the word feeling foreign yet fitting.

"In my culture, ghosts are nothing to fear. They are echoes of the past, nothing more," Alano explained.

"Can we hurry, please," I urged, feeling a desperate need to distance ourselves from the place and its phantom inhabitants.

"If you like," he conceded, casting one last glance at the tent as if bidding farewell to an old friend. "Thank you for a wonderful performance," he addressed the empty air, his words a benediction to the night's unseen actors.

The gesture sent shivers down my spine. "Yes, thank you," I found myself saying.

As we walked away, Alano's curiosity resurfaced. "So, which was your favorite?" he asked, his tone lighter.

I hesitated, my mind replaying the performances. "The magician's assistant," I finally said, thinking of her image of grace amidst the chaos. "She was lovely."

Alano's turn brought his face close to mine, signaling a kiss. Despite my lack of desire, I didn't resist, hoping this gesture might lead him to accompany me home. After the night's unsettling events, the prospect of solitude seemed excruciatingly daunting. I needed the assurance of company, any company, to stave off the lingering horrors.

As our lips met, a brief moment of normalcy passed, but then it suddenly felt wrong. The kiss became too intense, feeling like it was taking my breath away. I opened my eyes. It wasn't Alano kissing me, but the paper man.

Panic surged as I found myself unable to scream, my voice stolen by the suction, his face, a nightmare of jagged teeth set in inflamed gums and a grotesquely swollen tongue. His yellow irises gazing at me from bloodshot eyes were the last things I remember before darkness claimed me.

I was being consumed, not in body, but in soul, rendered utterly powerless in the face of this predator.

# CHAPTER SIX

As consciousness gripped me anew, I found myself back within the confines of the tent, a place transformed and unrecognizable. I sat with my back against the front of the stage. Gone were the chairs that had been arranged before the stage, replaced now by a chilling discovery. The ground was strewn with bodies, an unfathomable collection of lives halted mid-breath, their final moments frozen in time. My attempt to scream was thwarted; a futile gasp of air was the only exclamation of my horror.

Rising, I was met with a macabre scene of others awakening, their movements sluggish, as if the concept of life was foreign to them. My voice failed me again. The sight that unfolded was grotesque beyond words. Skeletons clad in the remnants of flesh rose from the dirt in halting movements. They drew themselves into a line and shambled toward the stage.

A glance downward revealed a shocking truth. I was wearing the red dress of the magician's assistant, my skin a ghastly echo, tinted to her shade instead of my own. I touched the hair that fell around my face, feeling a curly texture so different from mine. I pulled it in front of me, the shade darker than it should have been. The absence of blood in my veins painted a web of gray just beneath my skin. It was a horrifying picture, one that no scream could encapsulate, for I had no voice with which to express my terror.

The others ignored me, drawn to the stage by a single focus. As they stepped onto it, they miraculously seemed to come to life, their bodies filling with vitality in an eerie display of revival. Exposed bone became covered with aged skin. Jaws that hung loosely from tenebrous remnants of cheek rose to rejoin the skulls, the holes in the skin sewing back together more with every step toward the stage. The strong man's right eye was absent, but strands of viscous red tissue grew over the hole. It pulsed, seeming to breathe in the dark socket. Finally he blinked and a bloodshot eyeball appeared from the sinuous material.

They started performing with a precision born of endless practice, a haunting show for an empty audience.

The magician's gaze found mine, laden with expectation. He stared at me as if he were confused, not by his predicament, but by my own actions, my sluggishness.

Stepping over a body beside me, I stumbled upon Alano, or rather, what was left of him. The recognition struck a chilling chord within me. His casual attire, now a ghostly reminder of the day we first met, lay in tatters against his skeletal remains, affixed to his form by the black vitriol his organs had liquified into over an unknowable span of time. The voids where his eyes once sparkled with life now stared back at me, empty and accusing above the slits that marked the location upon which his nose had resided in life. It was a sight so grotesque that it threatened to unravel the last vestiges of my sanity.

Compelled by an unknown force, I moved towards the magician, the sole entity in this macabre gathering who seemed to acknowledge my existence. As I stepped onto the stage, a bizarre sense of life coursed through me, though I never felt my heart beating, or drew air into my lungs properly.

I pointed towards Alano, my gesture a plea for understanding, for acknowledgment of the loss so cruelly displayed before us. The magician's reaction was unexpected, a display of grief so profound yet so mute, it pierced the confusion that had taken hold of me. His silent sorrow, his body wracked with sobs that no sound accompanied, mirrored the scream of despair that I could not voice.

The rest stayed absorbed in their endless practice, unaffected by the unfolding tragedy. Their obliviousness cast a chill on the scene. Surrounded by their indifference, I felt utterly alone with the magician.

His lower lip quivered as fresh sobs overtook him. He buried his face in his hands hiding his pain from me, or maybe unable to look at me, I could not say for sure. I don't know how long we stayed there, but before he stood up, he took one last glance my way. He closed his eyes slowly.

At that moment, I understood my fate. The paper man had forced me into the body of the magician's assistant, erasing her essence and cutting off her bond with the magician. Their last act together had been their unknowing goodbye, my insertion ending a collaboration that was more than just performance.

I tried to reach out to the magician, looking for comfort or maybe clarity. He acknowledged me for a second before getting back to his work.

I crept to the edge of the stage, gazing down at the dirt floor beneath. In a moment of desperation, I squatted down, stretching my arm to the ground. I traced "What happened to me?" with my finger.

My efforts to communicate, to make them see and understand the surreal nightmare we were trapped in, fell short. My gestures faded into the void of their focus. I was a stranger in a body not my own, surrounded by the ghosts of lives that had once been vibrant and full. I was alone.

I was a spectator to the eerie detachment of the others. Their movements were mechanical, devoid of the warmth and charisma showcased before an audience. In that instant, my soul, a concept I had always regarded with skepticism, was engulfed in despair, torn between the urge to flee and an overwhelming desire to collapse in sorrow.

I looked back at the undisturbed dirt, where my question had been traced. Just as harrowing as the sight of piled corpses, and the paper man's gaze, was the erasure of my message. The ground bore no evidence of my touch. My words had vanished as if swallowed by the very earth.

A scream built within me, a sound for the terror fracturing my spirit. I longed for release from this purgatory, for the peace of oblivion or the promise of an afterlife. We were left to haunt the fringes of existence, mute and disconnected.

I whirled on my heel to where the magician kept his swords, the same ones that had been stabbed into the cabinet where the entity that had inhabited the body I now occupied had stood, awaiting their deadly sting. I was so ensnared by my own terror that I was incapable of hesitation. I pressed the sword against my chest and dove from the horrible stage.

As I plunged beyond the edge of the lights that lined the stage, I felt the energy vacate the emaciated husk of a body I now inhabited. I came down on the tip of the sword, the weight of the corpse pushing the blade in where there was no heart to stop. The sword passed bloodlessly through, scraping against bone with an awful scratch. I felt none of it. Even the impact when the body touched the ground was inconsequential.

I tried to rise, finding no strength in me to do so. Instead I lay in the dirt, impaled upon the sword, struggling to wail or cry or experience anything except for the silent, inscrutable terror. Death was not an escape, for it no longer cared to claim me. The assistant's body felt unnaturally heavy and utterly immobile. The magic that pulsed from the stage lost its power as I had leapt from it. Now, there was only a trace amount to animate the shell my consciousness was housed in. I tried to rise, but I could not. The best I could manage was to roll over on my side, pushing my hips back to inch closer to the stage. It took a few moments before I could reorganize the scant muscles of my new body and make another push toward the stage. I could hear others moving behind me, uninterested in my plight as they went about their routine. No one was coming to help. I pushed again, uncoiling my legs, feeling them reconstitute somewhat as they drew closer to the source of magic. It took three more attempts at coiling and expanding, like an impaled inchworm sliding sideways, before I felt the foot strike the wood of the stage. The magic rushed through the body, allowing me to rise and rest against the platform. I placed my hand around the hilt of the sword, pulling in an attempt to retract the blade. It was buried to the crosspiece between my ribs. The weight of my body had pushed it directly through the back, slicing through the skin near to the straps of the assistant's dress. I pulled with great effort in a second attempt to remove the sword, but the blade did not come free. The sensation was curious and mind-numbing. I expected pain, yet there was none. The blade grated along my ribs, the sensation much like a fork being scraped across my teeth. I had to twist the blade back and forth to fully retract it from my torso, creating a slight opening. There was no blood. There was only the place where the sword once was. Before I thought better of it, I moved my fingers to the opening, inserting one inside. My mind reeled at the surreal experience of feeling inside of my own chest.

Returning to the stage after what felt like an eternity, I stepped into a world where existence was defined by the act, by the performance, rather than by any acknowledgment of each other. Each performer was adrift in their own existence, lost to their practice, save for the magician. His gaze held a depth of sorrow that broke the boundaries of communication between us.

As I stood beside him, an inexplicable wave of knowledge washed over me. It was as if the mysteries of our craft, of the illusions we wove together, were suddenly laid bare before me. I understood the intricacies of each trick, the delicate balance of deception and distraction that made the impossible seem real. The box, which had once symbolized a mortal threat, now revealed its secrets to me, its dangers rendered moot by my newfound understanding.

I moved in harmony with the magician, knowing exactly how to enhance the illusion and merge our actions into a single, magical performance.

The magician's gaze met mine again. His grief was a mirror to my own confusion and longing for answers.

"I'm sorry for your loss." I formed the words as clearly as I could with my lips, exaggerating the shape of every syllable.

His mysterious reply made things even more intriguing. He said, "Colah gepo unbarra," in a way that sounded important, even though the words were unfam iliar.He showed me something about his hat, calling it "colah," hinting at some meaning I couldn't quite catch. He was patient, pointing between the hat and the untouched dirt, repeating the phrase as if it spoke of deeper truths.Through his actions, the magician tried to show the gravity of our situation. His gestures and the way he mimicked speaking, especially when pointing out our inability to truly understand each other. The phrase "colah gepo unbarra," repeated with resignation, symbolized our mutual confusion and disconnection.

Understanding the nature of our prison was unsettling. It wasn't built of walls, but of altered perceptions. A place where we were close yet forever disconnected. Our attempts to communicate, whether through speech, movement, or silent appeals, were all in vain.

I felt an intense urge to vomit, but the body, no longer mine, refused even the smallest comfort of a physical response. Resisting our fate was pointless.

# CHAPTER SEVEN

I never grew tired or felt the desire for food. There was only the stage and our craft to pass the time without distractions. I contemplated escape, but the horrible knowledge of the stage's power and the lack of animation the body would endure compelled me to stay. I would watch for an opening. Perhaps, eventually, there would be an avenue of escape. In the meantime, I practiced, ingraining the routine into my muscles and my mind.

The transformation in the room was as sudden as it was grotesque. The once lifeless bodies that lined the floor stirred, rising and filling just as we had when we crossed onto the stage. I watched as Alano's body reconstituted itself. The black ooze that had pooled around his corpse flowed back into him, forming eyes, a tongue, and other organs I could not see. The shapes filled the sockets where they had once belonged and then color gradually returned to them. Then his clothing seemed to mend around him, making him look the way he had the moment he had approached me in the library. The haunts parted, lining the wall to clear the space in the center. There was a strange pop as the chairs that I had sat in with him sprang into existence where they had not existed a moment prior. The ghouls filed into the rows, occupying the chairs with eerie promptness. The room looked exactly as it had the night of my damning arrival.

As they took their places, the paper man entered the room. His eyes locked onto mine, his smile revealing swollen red gums and sharp teeth beneath his alabaster lips. With a satisfaction only a tormentor could possess, he surveyed his dominion before exiting the tent.

The others moved from the stage, stepping to the small alcoves on the sides. We waited, only myself moving among the others. Their glares were laden with disdain for my fidgeting. The stage was set, the velvet curtains—which I had not noticed, but perhaps had been conjured along with the chairs—parted to signal the beginning of an ordeal I had not anticipated.

I watched as I was led, or rather, my former body was led, into the heart of the tent. A sense of violation overwhelmed me. Someone had changed my hair, bleached to a passable shade of blonde that might have fooled me if the body had not once been mine. The makeup was done impeccably, better than I had ever done it in my life. I began to shake, wanting to scream at whatever soul was inside. I wanted my body returned home to my parents, so that they could stop the search I knew they had out for me.

Attached to my body's arm was a man around the same age as me, with green eyes and shaggy brown hair that fell to his shoulders. He looked around the tent as he entered, noticing a pair of seats conveniently open for them.

I watched as they both sat down in the seats beside Alano, an added insult to the injustice that had been done to me.

The world began to tilt. The magician's assistant's body gave no impression that it was preparing to retch, but my consciousness willed it to. I wanted the meat sack that housed my mind to react the way I demanded. But this was not my body. I was a passenger in it, given only permission to perform for the audience. My true body, where I had learned to walk, talk, and dance, was no longer mine. It was being operated by something else. Something, I suspected, that was the same consciousness that had been inside Alano when I had fallen for him.

The lights went out, then the one in the center blazed to life. The juggler stepped forward, taking his place upon the stage.

I felt myself shaking when our turn arrived—my fear was so great that I could not stop it. We walked out, my body understanding where to position itself. I let it lead me at first, but a growing sense of righteous fury rose as we performed our routine. I turned and looked directly at the shaggy boy.

I tried to scream, "Run!" But as I attempted to voice my warning, an invisible force sealed these lips, a reminder of the imprisonment that extended beyond mere physical confines. My face looked back at me from the chair sitting next to him. It curled into a rictus smile, the eyes shone yellow in the irises, the whites turning that unnerving blood red they had been when the paper man had replaced Alano. I knew if my mouth had opened it would be filled with gapped, jagged sharp teeth and inflamed gums.

I watched without control as the magician and I performed. The moment we were off the stage, the assistant's body collapsed into the dirt, facing the back canvas wall of the tent. The world swam before my eyes as they unfocused, and the next phase of my horrifying existence began.

# CHAPTER EIGHT

From the place where the corpse lay, all that was visible was the wall of the tent. A small gap between the ground and the wall spread just wide enough to allow a glimpse of the outside world.

Scant strands of browning grass crowded up to the edge of the tent. I could not move. I could not blink. I could only lay motionless, unable to sleep or disassociate from the corpse I inhabited as days stretched into an endless expanse. My rebellion against the paper man's grim designs had led to this perpetual limbo. It was a bitter pill, my punishment for daring to disrupt his malevolent harvest.

I watched a caterpillar crawl along the grass just beyond the gap. It did not come inside but carried on with its life toward its evolution into a beautiful moth. I remembered having read somewhere that a fall caterpillar would always mature into those lovely night creatures, though I had no way of knowing if it were true. My own metamorphosis had confined me to this unholy chrysalis of a decaying corpse. I wondered if the caterpillar could even sense I was there.

Was the tent still in the same field it had been in when Alano and I entered it? If not, where had we been moved to? I imagined a field, with a circular barren spot that housed an invisible house of the dead. I thought of people walking along green fields and finding a circle of dirt where grass refused to grow and seeing nothing standing upon it, our tangential existence barely beyond their perception, existing in an alternate spiritual realm layered upon their own, where our ghosts lay dormant in these hollow puppets until our master called upon our services.

Despair ravaged me from the inside. Still I lay unmoving, waiting for the paper man to summon me again. I could not stop the thoughts. They raced through me, moving through theories. I had become convinced that we all existed to serve his purpose. I wondered if there had been more than one of him, working together to lure victims into this tent. I could not shake the feeling that it was all one entity, and that he had swallowed me when I had kissed Alano the final time.

Throughout the winter I felt my mind fracturing. I yearned for something to change within the body, but it did not. I could only lie there, watching the snow fall, melt, and then fall again through the little gap where day and night cycled perpetually.

I entertained many theories about what had happened to me but returned repeatedly to the thought that my soul had been consumed by the paper man. I had been put into the body of the magician's assistant, but what had happened to the original owner?

Maybe it had finally been devoured when I had assumed the mantle. The thought of the blissful release of non-consciousness became so compelling that I grew to crave it in a way I had never craved Alano. Death, a true death, assumed the guise of a lover whose arms were open and waiting for me. I reached out but fell short no matter how much I willed myself to push toward it.

Spring's arrival, signaled by the soft drumming of rain on canvas and earth, brought no change to my condition. Summer's heat bore down upon the world beyond the tent, and still, the corpse I inhabited did not stir.

It was not until the leaves began their annual descent, blocking my view through the narrow gap, that I heard a stirring behind me. I tried to move the body that had not responded to my input for a year, finding it reluctant, but capable of movement. I rose. Relief flooded over me as the joy of being able to move overtook the abject terror that I constantly lived in.

I considered my new reality, finally accepting this body as my own. The seasons spent awake felt already distant, but horrifyingly real. I had rationalized that my consciousness for all that time had been a punishment. I must perform, seamlessly integrating into the paper man's spectacle. I would not risk his ire and another stint in the conscious death state I had endured.

The juggler attempted an escape, panic etched on his face. His collapse near the tent's entrance was met with indifference, a collective silence born of fear and self-preservation. We were all too aware of the cost of defiance.

Rehearsals resumed with a somber regularity, a procession of the damned rehearsing for an audience of dead bodies. I saw Alano, his body residing in the same place it had been. Beside him was the remains of a young girl. My former body, now just a corpse, lay near his. The shaggy boy was nowhere to be seen, but I already imagined that his body would appear near my own after our next show.

I wondered who the real Alano was among the performers. Could he be the snake charmer, the strong man, or perhaps one of the acrobats? I would never know, and even if I did, the man I had fallen in love with was not Alano's true spirit.

Now, somewhere beyond this tent, a shaggy boy was convincing another soul to follow him into this carnival of corpses. Once our show was completed, he would ask his date what their favorite part had been. Just as I had said the magician's assistant was mine, and, I assume, the shaggy boy had said the juggler was his.

Some time afterward, the shaggy boy who had come with my body to the previous show, entered with his hair cut and styled back. Hanging onto his arm was a dark-haired girl with gray eyes, all curves and dark colors. She smiled as she took in the sight of the tent. The shaggy boy flashed the paper man's vicious grin.

The juggler took the stage, his eyes wide. He ran forward, opening his mouth as if he were about to shout. Then his eyes glazed over. I looked into the crowd and saw the shaggy boy. His eyes were the unsettling yellow that had replaced Alano's when I kissed him the final time, the same eyes that had fixed on me from my own face when I had tried to warn the shaggy boy to run.

The juggler performed his routine in silence with mechanical precision. I knew what punishment awaited him. He had no personality to his routine. He was being forced to do it.

When he exited, it was our turn. I tried to catch the girl's eye, smiling and winking as I paraded myself around for her attention. I understood the game. It was her or me, and after a year of wakeful death, I had no intention of it remaining me. Whatever awaited after this, it could not conceivably be worse than this existence.

When we left the stage, the juggler lay facing the edge of the tent, looking out at the sliver of the world where the gap formed between the tent and the dirt. His eyes no longer blinked.

# CHAPTER NINE

I don't know how long the paper man has been doing this, but there are hundreds of people that crowd the tent now each time the corpses rise. The attire has progressed along the years as many different people have joined us. He seems to favor those who look like the ones that were here when I arrived. I see them in the crowd every year. So many look as if they just disembarked a boat from Ireland. I wonder if that is where he is from.

I'll never know, because he does not speak to any of us. I have come to understand his nature in my years serving in his macabre sideshow. He uses the body of the one he switches to in order to lure his next victim in. He selects the outcasts, the ones like me, memorizing quotes that endear him to our kind or portraying himself as a kindred spirit. Everything is so that on the night of Halloween, when the festival occurs and the townsfolk gather, he will be able to manipulate them into going into his tent.

I don't know what awaits my consciousness when someone selects the magician's assistant, though I try with every show to compel their eyes and ensnare their attention. After we perform, a great weariness comes over me. I feel compelled, much as I did the one time I tried to disrupt the show, to walk off the front of the stage. The magic fades away before the body I inhabit can hit the ground.

Each new soul tries to escape and has their period of punishment. After each show, it seems someone is facing the gap in the tent where I spent a year awake.

One year is usually enough to break them of their desire to disrupt the show, it seems. Though, there was a fire breather that spent three years facing the back of the tent. I suspected he was trying to set the whole place ablaze. He never succeeded and finally broke as the isolation wore him down.

I wish I could ask if the others dream during the dead time. I do. I remember the nights with Alano. In my dreams he is who the paper man pretended he was. There's a house, a small child with curling hair bouncing about their shoulders. They giggle as Alano pushes them in a tire swing. I've lived a lifetime in the spaces between our shows, where I can almost forget what has happened to me. It feels so real, but even when dreaming I know it is a lie.

It is a story I tell myself, like the books I can never touch again.

Another show has started, the juggler has left the stage. When we woke up, one of the twin acrobats had been swapped. That was the first time I have seen either of them being picked. The man who had clearly selected her, his spirit now trapped in the body of the acrobat, walked in the tent a few minutes ago with a young woman attached to his arm. He looks different, of course, but it is most certainly him. The paper man always changes his victims when he takes over their body.

The magician swapped out two shows ago. He has switched four, or maybe five, times. I can't honestly say that I know. This one is very good at what he does. I suspect the soul inside him had a genuine fondness for the craft and that's why it selected the magician. He is the only one of us I have ever seen smile during his performance.

This show's victim sits in the same spot they do every time. She's watching me. Her eyes follow every move I make, oblivious to the magician's tricks, despite his obvious flair. There is a desire there, a lust I've seen before in some of the men, but they never pick the assistant.

This show is for her, every move I make, every subtle touch of my fingertips trailing down my skin, drawing her attention to the curves of my body. As the magician closes me into my box, my eyes lock with hers, the door being the only thing that breaks our gaze.

The show ends. One acrobat lays beside the back of the stage, facing the exterior wall.

My dream starts even before I have felt the magic slip away. Alano is here, inside the tent. He walks into my view and looks down at me. He's as beautiful as the morning sun breaking over misty mountains. I glance beside me, where the corpse that once belonged to Alano, before his soul joined our damned sideshow, should be, but it is gone. I want to believe that he's really here, but I know he is not.

The paper man wears his skin as he looks down at me. He doesn't speak, though I long to hear Alano's voice one more time, even if it was all just the evil machinations of this demented being. He stoops down and lifts my hand. I allow myself to rise, only then seeing what is directly behind him.

This year's victim lays face up in the dirt, her final wide-eyed moment of terror frozen on her face.

Alano follows my sight, then nods. I understand his meaning. She chose me.

His hand rises away from mine and finds the curve of my cheek. His fingertips brush against the hollow of my neck, cupping the curve of my jaw as he reaches behind me. I offer no hesitation. After my time in this hell, I welcome his touch. It doesn't matter that it was all a lie. Lies sometimes are better than reality. Our lips meet and he pulls me to him.

I close my eyes, not wanting to open them and see the paper man. I don't want to know what is really happening, and he doesn't force me to see. For the briefest of moments I'm back with the boy that took me to the carnival. I remember the dreams, lives stolen and only glimpsed in fragments.

There's a curious sensation of sinking as I drown in the darkness of the release I've longed for. In my final moment, I'm grateful that his face is the last thing I saw, the final tether severed from a life that was stolen from me.

# ABOUT THE AUTHOR

*Dahlia Blackwell writes dark fantasy stories where romance often leads into unexpected and dangerous territory. Her work focuses on complex relationships with morally ambiguous characters where the villains get the spotlight over the heroes. Her stories feature otherworldly creatures and explore the darker sides of desire, power, and connection. Her debut short story is just the beginning, with a full trilogy planned for release in early 2025. Fans of dark fantasy with heavy romance, especially those who root for the bad guy, will feel right at home in her writing.*

*When Dahlia isn't writing, she's traveling with her pups, meeting new people, and gathering inspiration for her next project.*

# krewe De Désir

Krystyna Lee & Elizabeth Fey

"You are afraid to die?"


"Yes, everyone is."


"But to die as lovers may—to die together, so that they may live together.
Girls are caterpillars when they live in the world, to be finally butterflies
when the summer comes; but in the meantime there are grubs and
larvae, don't you see—each with their peculiar propensities, necessities
and structures."


-Joseph Sheridan Le Fanu, Carmilla

H ot, humid air slammed into Michelle's face as she and Josie walked out of the airport terminal into the muggy New Orleans breeze. She couldn't help but cough from the thick air. Josie laughed.

"Come on! It's not that bad!" she giggled while pulling her long, red hair into a messy bun, sweat already visibly forming at the nape of her neck. Michelle sucked in one long, deep breath and held back the urge to choke. Eventually, it became easier to breathe in the swamp air.

Vibrant jazz music played over the loudspeakers above the doors trying uselessly to drown out the impatient sounds of honking cars and men shouting at one another within the arrival lane. Michelle watched and focused on the scene erupting to distract her from the sweltering air causing a thin layer of moisture to cover her bronze skin.

"I can't believe it's *this* hot! It's the end of October! Does this place just never cool down?" Michelle groaned as she piled her dark hair on top of her head. A local man walking by paused upon hearing her. Tawny skin stretched and crinkled as he smiled, appearing like worn leather. He was wearing a green polo shirt and khaki cut-off shorts that seemed two sizes too big. His shoes were shabby and tattered. But the thing that caught Michelle's attention the most were his eyes. They were the color of amber.

"*Mon cherie*…it's New Orleans. If you ain't sweating your balls off, you freezing them off!" The golden-eyed man smiled and continued to look between each of the girls before finishing his statement, his tone switching to sullen and severe.

"You girls be careful now, ya hear? Halloween time is wonderful, but sometimes it brings out…monsters…beings looking for lost souls. They take them to their palaces of sin and those lost souls will be sacrificed…for the creatures' darkest desires." He cast those saffron eyes from Michelle to Josie, and back again with every pause in his speech. The base of Josie's neck tingled. A tingling that told her to run screaming from the man, from the city altogether. Chills streaked down her back causing an involuntary shudder. Michelle looked at her and took in a shaky, nervous breath.

"May God be with you," and with that, he resumed his walk down the sidewalk. Both girls watched him shuffle away until he turned the corner; only then did they look at each other. Josie burst into nervous laughter.

"What the hell was that? I mean, I know New Orleans has some weird people, but I wasn't expecting them to show up as soon as we left the airport," Josie snorted as she pulled out her phone and began typing, her scarlet nails clicking rapidly. Michelle looked over Josie's shoulder. Josie peered towards Michelle and smiled before raising the phone in front of them.

"Smile!" She beamed into the camera. Michelle followed suit, both girls wearing radiant smiles. Josie looked over the photo with a critical glare. Her nose began to scrunch up as if she smelled decomposing garbage.

"Okay, nope. You need to fix your hair. It's way too messy. You look like you just woke up." Josie pulled Michelle's hair out of the tangled mass of charcoal curls she had just made.

"Well, we just got off a four-hour flight," Michelle retorted, side-eyeing Josie. She winced as Josie's fingers snagged in her hair. Josie let out a frustrated sigh.

"Well, our followers don't need to know that!" She continued while pulling half of Michelle's hair up into a quick updo.

"What followers," Michelle sighed, thinking of the measly hundred people who are actually interested in what they are doing during the day. Josie stopped to glare daggers at Michelle.

"We could grow faster and get sponsorships if you tried harder to not look like a slob," she snapped. Michelle sighed and relented, allowing her to finish. After she was done, Josie bounced up and down in excitement as she prepared the camera for the second attempt. Three more pictures later, Josie was finally satisfied. Putting her phone away, she bounded ahead, dragging Michelle behind her. The girls abandoned the exuberant saxophones and trumpets of the airport to catch a taxi waiting to take them deep into the heart of New Orleans: the French Quarter.

Michelle looked out the window as the driver took them past streets of fast-food chains, suburban houses decorated with pumpkins and twelve-foot skeletons, and department stores covered in black and orange decor. Everything appeared…ordinary. None of the mystique that she was expecting. No French buildings, no brick-lined streets, no performers on every corner singing and playing jovial Cajun tunes. She began to feel a pit forming in her stomach. A voice began berating her for letting Josie talk her into this mess. Into spending hundreds of dollars to fly to New Orleans during one of the busiest seasons of the year; all for a failing attempt at being "travel influencers." If it was just going to be a normal American Halloween, they could have saved their money and stayed home in Montana. Just as the anxiety began to consume her, Josie began smacking Michelle's arm excitedly, waking her from her racing thoughts.

"We're here! We're here!" Josie kept chanting while hitting Michelle's arm hard enough that she knew there would be a bruise later. Finally freeing her arm, Michelle stared out the window and all she saw was beauty. Two-story Creole houses were lined up side-by-side in all different colors: blue, white, yellow, and green. People were leaning against wrought iron railings that were enveloping wide balconies. People danced along brick-lined streets to music played by an old man on a trumpet while a kid near him banged out a beat on an improvised drum made of an upside-down bucket. Michelle watched a woman walk by holding a giant lime green plastic cup the size of her arm. Josie leaned over and pressed herself into Michelle's back to gawk at the woman.

"That must be the famous Hand Grenade drink! Oh, we have to get that! We can record ourselves trying it and post it online," Josie rambled her various ideas into Michelle's ear while she tried to return to gazing out the window. Eventually, the taxi came to a stop outside a giant building. The building was alabaster white with an immense spire at the top. It cast a grand shadow that covered the brink pavilion in front, reaching the edge of a gated garden. Multiple vendor stalls were scattered across the pavilion. Women wearing dresses with plunging necklines and corsets that pushed their breasts up to the customer's eyeline were seated in front of decks of cards. Men wearing top hats with damasked vests and dress pants were speaking with spirited gestures to plainly dressed people, selling them various charms. Michelle looked at the driver.

"Where are we?" she asked. The bleary-eyed driver turned to look at her. His tired look let her know that he currently thought she was dumber than a sack of rocks. "Jackson Square," he said curtly. He pointed a knotted finger towards the pale building, "And that is Saint Louis Cathedral." Michelle returned to stare in awe at the cathedral towering above her. She could hear some conversation between Josie and the cab driver but she was uninterested. The sun gleamed off the tremendous building in such a brilliant light that she had to cover her eyes.

The girls climbed out and walked towards the cathedral as their driver pulled away. Jackson Square was crowded. People pressing into each other, shouting *excuse me's* before pushing past. The smell of sweat and body odor burned Josie's nostrils. She tried to pull her phone from her pocket, but everyone's bodies were pressing too close together. It became quite evident to the girls that the crowds surrounding them were other tourists, all stopping short to take an endless sea of selfies. Once they squeezed out of the crowd, Josie leaned onto a black iron gate outside a garden and huffed.

"How are we ever supposed to compete with this? There are so many tourists and I bet *so* many are influencers. We won't stand out at all!" She slumped further down the iron gate to the garden. The smell of magnolias cut through the air, reprieving Michelle from the overarching scent of sweat, vodka, and rum that pervaded the air. Josie looked out at the passing crowd, her blue eyes beginning to well up with frustrated tears. Michelle sighed and went to hug her friend, pulling her into a tight embrace. Josie buried her face in Michelle's thick curls to help quell her tears.

"Listen, everyone knows that Halloween is a very busy time here. There are bound to be countless tourists. So let's look for a less popular activity, okay?" Michelle pulled Josie back to look her in the eye, "No bars, no grenades, something completely different!" Michelle gave Josie the most reassuring smile she could muster, hoping that Josie was more confident in her plan than she was. Josie nodded slowly, thinking. Then she snapped her head up to Michelle's, a sharp glint in her eyes.

"I got it," she exclaimed, her excitement growing as she continued, "New Orleans is a party capital, and it also has a bunch of secret speakeasies and private parties. If we can get invited to one of these then we can post something unique and stand out from all these other people!" Josie brushed her shoulder up against Michelle, a devilish grin spreading across her lips.

"We'll be exclusive!" she put on a haughty voice. Michelle let out a snort as Josie jumped back and began her plan to gain them access to New Orleans' hidden underbelly. "I heard that there is a secret voodoo carnival somewhere in the city! We can try to find that!" But first, the girls walked to their hotel to prepare for the Halloween night festivities.

Lively jazz music flowed down Bourbon Street as drunk tourists skipped and stumbled along. Michelle watched people file past in various outfits; fairies, pirates, ghosts, demons, and various "slutty" animals, including an alligator. She even saw one or two "sexy nuns" with vampire fangs running from bar to bar. She stood at the corner outside their fifth bar, twisting her hair back and forth anxiously. She could sense prying eyes on her exposed skin, others undressing her with merely their gaze, but her costume fell short compared to Josie's.

Josie stood out from the crowd, wearing a green bodysuit and fishnet tights with silk leaves sewn on to contrast against her lush, auburn hair. The bodysuit was laced

down her back, stopping at the base of her spine, revealing smooth, white skin. Black knee-high boots made her legs look miles long. Josie made a killer Poison Ivy. Michelle, on the other hand, tried to show less skin but Josie was insistent on being at least a little provocative. Michelle donned a white silk dress that fell to just about mid-thigh. The sweetheart neckline brought just enough attention to her chest without being obvious. At the base of her spine, a fluffy white bunny tail protruded from the dress. To match, she donned white lace bunny ears and fingerless gloves. She completed it with a pair of black thigh-high boots.

Josie said they had to dress up to stand out, but all Michelle sensed was lustful stares from drunk frat boys. The cost of standing out was too much attention. One tried to grab her ass but she beat him away with her purse. Sighing, she looked back into the bar to find Josie's slim form in the crowd.

Her back was to Michelle as she tried to sweet talk the bartender. She crossed her arms just right to push her cleavage up. The front was cut low, leaving little to the imagination. Josie knew how to get attention. Male, female, nonbinary, Josie knew her way around them all. Michelle watched the bartender shrug and turn away. He was immune to her charm. Josie turned around and walked out of the bar defeated, not noticing all the eyes following longingly after her as she swayed from the building. Once outside, Josie laid her head on Michelle's bare shoulder, filling her nostrils with the sweet smell of vanilla. Josie let out a huff.

"This isn't as easy as I thought it would be," she moaned. Michelle stroked her friend's hair, trying to offer her some comfort. People continued to walk by,

occasionally bumping into the girls. Someone slammed into Michelle hard enough to knock her off balance and send both girls stumbling.

"Hey!" Michelle snapped, spinning around. A tall, slim figure slowly turned around. She was wearing black and red leather pants that hugged her curves. As the girl turned, Michelle saw that she was also wearing a matching top with a plunging neckline and a temporary tattoo that read "Daddy's Lil Monster." Harley Quinn. Her eyes were a brilliant green that popped against her red eyeshadow. Her black lips broke into a smile exposing dazzlingly white teeth. She tossed her long blonde hair over her shoulders. The tips were dyed blue and pink.

"Sorry, I didn't mean to," she spoke in a warm, silky voice with the slow drawl of a Cajun accent. "Crowds this time of year, it's bound to happen." Josie took in a quick gulp of air, unable to take her eyes off of the mesmerizing woman. Light from the overhead lanterns created gold specks to dance across the deep green of her eyes. The woman took a step towards them and stretched out a slender hand with long fingers.

"My name's Angelique," she offered smoothly, saying her name in the French pronunciation. Michelle froze as the world went on without her, staring at the outstretched hand. The spell was only broken when Josie's hand snapped past to give Angelique a curt shake.

"Josie. And this is Michelle," Josie gave her friend a questioning look. Michelle blinked a few times before the world reformed around her. She quickly took up Angelique's extended hand. Her skin was cold to the touch as if she just took an ice bath. Michelle's breath instinctively stuck in her throat. Angelique retracted her arm, looking haughtily between the two girls.

"So I take it you ladies are here for the Halloween season?" Angelique asked, eyeing them up and down. Michelle nodded while Josie sighed. "Yeah, but we want to see more than just the regular tourist stuff. We're travel bloggers and the city hasn't given us anything special," Josie said, exasperated. Michelle nervously glanced at Angelique, hoping Josie didn't insult her. Angelique looked amused by Josie's statement.

"You are looking for where the locals go, away from the tourists? To the real party?" Her slow alluring voice drew them in.

She leaned closely toward Josie's face, so close that Josie could smell a sweet scent on her breath. The smell was both mysterious and reminiscent. Josie couldn't quite place a name to the smell. Her mind growing foggy, she was mesmerized by Angelique's emerald green eyes. She was so close that Josie could see a speck of red in the center, creating a piercing, vibrant effect. The room seemed to shake and spin as Angelique leaned even closer.

"The place where all the devils and freaks come out to play?" Angelique whispered, keeping her eyes on Josie's. They were finally getting somewhere. Angelique smiled and offered her hand out. "I know just the place. Come with me. Y'all can be my special guests," Josie quickly took Angelique's hand and bounded off after her; Michelle had to jog to keep up. The women walked further into the city, leaving behind the lively music and bright neon lights.

After some time the three reached a tall wooden fence with a wooden gate. The gate had ornamental designs of filigree and fleurs-de-lys covering it. There were also depictions of pomegranates, apples, and figs littered throughout. Angelique grabbed a metal handle in the shape of a gardenia and turned. The door silently opened, revealing a hidden world. There were multiple people in various costumes and states of undress running around and laughing. The girls walked in, past some people bobbing for apples. One couple had seemed to take over an old bounce house, the man in the process of undressing his partner. Streamers in red, gold, and black were slung haphazardly across the trees. Clowns dressed in bright yellow and red walked by, large, unchanging smiles painted onto their faces. Another group was watching a contortionist back bending until her head touched the ground behind her.

Everywhere people were carrying around cups and glasses filled with a deep red drink. Michelle's eyes eventually reached the circus' big top. Faded stripes of red and yellow enclosed the entire back portion of the alley, muffling the sounds from inside. Slight smells of alcohol, sweat, and something sweet emanated from the tent flap. Michelle looked around at the carnival surrounding her. The alley didn't appear large enough to hold it. Angelique saw Michelle's confusion and laughed before leading the girls to the entrance of the big top.

Standing beside it was a tall man. He had thick black hair that grazed his neck. A few pieces were left loose to frame his face while the rest was pulled loosely back with a black satin ribbon. He was wearing a flowing white button-down shirt with black slacks that emphasized his slim waist and long legs. His shirt was unbuttoned, save for two of the buttons right on his chest, leaving the rest of the top to blow open with the wind, showcasing milky white abdominal muscles. A lacy black mask covered the space around his eyes. The hypnotic feeling began to wash over Michelle. The same one that came over Josie when she met Angelique. The man turned to look at them all as they approached. His eyes were the color of steel. A smile played at the corner of his mouth.

Angelique walked ahead, still holding Josie's hand. She smiled at the man. "Samuel! I brought friends!" She exclaimed. Samuel quickly passed over Josie, his eyes settling on Michelle. A shiver raced down her spine. He stared at her through his mask with his piercing silver eyes. Finally, Michelle's mouth remembered how to function. "Hey, I'm Michelle," she muttered nervously. She looked towards Josie, but she seemed engrossed in a private conversation with Angelique. Their faces were close to one another as Josie quietly laughed. Michelle watched as Angelique's fingers softly stroked up Josie's spine, dancing delicately over the laces from the bottom of the bodysuit up to the nape of her neck. Michelle could see Josie's face begin to flush, but she seemed to enjoy Angelique's attention, leaning more into her. Michelle focused back on Samuel. He seemed to be looking her over, calculating. Whatever he was trying to decide, he made up his mind. He placed his hand on the tent flap and looked Michelle over once more. "Why don't you come on in and we can have a drink?" Samuel suggested. He pulled the canvas aside and gazed at her warmly. Something about his striking eyes compelled Michelle to step forward to take a closer look. The smell hit her first. Warm hops and earthy licorice, layered with sweat and the sweet stench of sex. Out of the darkness, shapes began to emerge. Then bodies. The heat in the tent, she realized, was due to the activities going on. People slicked with

sweat and various other bodily fluids laid together on vast beds, intertwined on couches scattered around the ring, or barely even getting undressed to satiate their desires while they waited at the bar. Sex. Everywhere and between everyone. Men, women, and people who either didn't have or didn't want a gender. All were present here. Cocks and tits were out and free. Moaning and heavy breathing surrounded Michelle; she had never seen so many at once.

Michelle gasped and took a step back in shock. Her hand covered her mouth in surprise. Samuel curled up a strong eyebrow and smirked. Michelle coughed and played it off, wiping some sweat off her forehead. She turned to see if Josie was seeing the same thing she was. Angelique pulled Josie towards the tent but slowed so that Josie could whisper in Michelle's ear.

"I think Angelique's into me!" She squealed before being pulled away by the object of her affection.

"Josie?" Michelle tried to respond but Angelique was too quick.

The pair of girls had already slipped inside and got lost in the throng of people. Josie and Angelique managed to find an empty couch and sit down. The pair were entwined both in deep conversation and physically. Josie leaned towards the alluring woman and Angelique had her legs in Josie's lap. Angelique gently caressed Josie along her neck and collarbone. Her skin began to tingle under Angelique's fingertips and she felt herself becoming wet with desire. She brought her hand up to Angelique's waist, touching her cold skin to pull her even closer. Angelique obliged, shifting into a straddle. Josie's breath caught in her throat as Angelique lowered herself onto Josie, looking deep into her eyes. Josie watched as Angelique's pupils dilated, and her breathing began to shudder.

"Shall we?" Samuel urged again, breaking Michelle from the scene in front of her. His steely eyes bore into her and the strange compulsion to follow him took over. He led her into the tent and up to the bar. He spoke to the bartender in a hushed tone. Once the drink order was in, he turned back to Michelle.

"Do you often come to places like this?" Michelle asked while clearing her throat, trying desperately to keep her eyes off the pair of men at the other end of the bar, one taking the other's cock deep down his throat.

Michelle had watched her fair share of porn and Josie was adventurous enough to where she shouldn't have been so shocked to be in a place like this. Josie always wanted to go to an orgy. Michelle just never thought she'd end up at one with her.

"Only during Halloween," Samuel responded. His smooth voice slid down her spine and she shivered despite the heat. "Angelique prefers this scene more than I do." He looked her up and down, "You make a precious little bunny."

Michelle's face flushed at the comment. Her hands smoothed over the silk dress and tugged the hem as if trying to cover more skin.

"And who...or what, are you supposed to be?" She scanned his outfit but found herself drawing a blank.

"Do I have to wear a costume to have fun? Besides, eons ago Halloween had a different meaning," he explained, reaching up to carefully tighten the mask on his face. "It didn't used to be about beer, candy, and provocative costumes."

"I'll bite," she ventured, "What was it about?"

"It is a day that the veil between the worlds of the living and the dead is the thinnest. It allowed spirits of the dead to cross back over into the living world. Centuries ago this was a sacred day. To ward them off, people wore costumes or masks to make sure they couldn't be recognized. If a spirit recognized you then you would be followed until they snatched your soul and dragged you back with them." Samuel narrated his story slowly, his voice dropping low and sultry. He inched closer to her until she could see the pores on his perfect skin. "'Tis a childish notion, to dress up and beg strangers for candy. I don't fancy partaking in the cheap costumes, so a mask will have to do."

"You seem comfortable here," Michelle commented as the bartender handed over their drinks. Samuel accepted the two glasses of wine, one white and one a deep red, the same drink she saw outside. Samuel offered the glass of white to her. "I never would have expected this kind of drink at this kind of party. Not to mention in a circus tent of all places. I guess I was expecting more of a beer menu."

"I've been to enough of these. They don't phase me any longer." Samuel took a generous sip of his wine and licked his rose-colored lips. Her eyes darted to them as she took a sip of her wine. The chilled, sparkling, white drink slid down her throat and she sighed dreamily. Samuel leaned in close to her, enough that she could see red specks within his silver eyes. "So what is a beautiful woman like you doing in a sinful town like this?"

"Josie has this crazy notion that we should be travel influencers, and therefore we need to go to exciting places and do exciting things so that we'll hit it big and go

viral." She explained, "We've been friends since college so naturally I was her victim of choice for this project."

"You don't think you'll be successful?" Samuel's siren-like eyes looked her up and down as she spoke. She watched his gaze slip down to linger on her cleavage, then her throat, then her lips. The angles of his cheeks and jawline looked like they were carved from marble. He had a single freckle just under his right eye and Michelle suddenly wanted to kiss it.

"I have my doubts, but at the very least it's fun. I get to spend time with my best friend, go on these crazy adventures, and meet beautiful people." The bold words were out of her mouth before she could cross-check them with the common sense department in her brain. She took another sip of wine before speaking again. "And of course, you are one of those beautiful people."

"You think I'm beautiful?"

"I hardly think it's a matter of opinion," Michelle continued, unable to believe the words coming from her mouth. What was in this wine? "It's a fact."

"I could say the same thing about you," Samuel tilted his head as he lifted a hand to brush a strand of hair out of her face. Despite Samuel's cold fingers, she couldn't ignore the warmth that pooled within her at the simple gesture. The heat under the tent sweltered and Michelle craved his icy touch.

"You think *I* am beautiful?" Michelle's eyelashes fluttered at his words and she found herself leaning towards him. She couldn't help the disbelief fluttering in her chest, but she swallowed it down.

"I *know* you are."

Samuel leaned towards her in return, gently setting his drink on the bar to get it out of the way. Michelle took another sip of her drink and let a drop remain shimmering on her lips. She hoped it would be enough to entice him. A sweet smirk lit up his face as he leaned closer. Michelle gasped slightly when his head quietly slid past hers to bury in her neck. His black hair tickled her skin. He inhaled deeply.

An arm wrapped around her waist and pulled her flush against him. She gasped at the unexpected contact. His chest, firm and cold, pressed against hers and her breasts swelled out of her dress. His free hand slipped along the other side of her neck to angle her the way he wanted. His cool mouth pressed against her skin, right under her ear, and she sucked in a breath.

"It's hard not to get caught up in the arousal of it all." He sighed against her skin. His plush lips grazed her skin and she had to bite her lip to keep from letting a moan slip loose. "If you don't want this, then you need to tell me now. Your answer will determine the trajectory of the entire evening, my dear."

"Want this?" Michelle's punched-out gasp made him chuckle darkly. When he pulled away to look her in the eyes, she gasped again to see that his pupils were completely blown out. His pale skin looked tinted with red blush, but was that his skin or the light from the tent?

"Want *me*. Your face gives you away, my sweet. Do you want to join the festivities…or not?" Samuel tilted his head towards the rest of the tent. Michelle's eyes wandered as she took in the sight before her. Writhing bodies moaning in pleasure, loud kissing messy with saliva, skin slapping on skin. Through her clouded gaze, she could just make out Josie on the couch, her lips entwined with Angelique's, tongues meeting and fighting for dominance. Angelique pulled Josie towards her, leaning back on the couch so Josie hovered above her. Samuel's intoxicating smell of fresh wood and wine washed over her, bringing her back into the present moment. A wave of arousal swept through her and her thighs clenched. Was it Samuel or the sensual scenes in front of her? Perhaps it was both.

"I…" Michelle turned back to look at Samuel, whose face had darkened with an expression she hadn't seen in a long time. Pure desire flickered in his eyes. Her core throbbed so deeply that she thought she might die.

"You want me, beautiful." Samuel whispered in her ear, "You want me so desperately. I will give you what you want if you will give me what I want."

"Yes…I want you." Michelle echoed him. Her voice sounded far away. "What do you want?"

"I want your soul, your essence to drip down my chin, to make you scream my name as you hurdle into ecstasy…into the dark."

"Yes," Michelle muttered mindlessly. Her mind swirled as she imagined him between her legs. Nothing else seemed to matter. Only Samuel.

"Come with me."

Samuel slid his hand down her arm and took the glass of wine from her. He gently returned it to the bar before grasping her hand. His long, slim fingers slipped in between the spaces in hers. Michelle let him guide her through the crowd as he searched for an empty space. Most flat surfaces were taken, but once Samuel saw a spot he wanted, he made sure he had it.

"Find somewhere else." Samuel snarled at a lively couple who looked like they were only just getting started. The girl shrieked and giggled as she dashed from the bed and her partner followed.

Samuel guided Michelle to sit down on the edge of the bed. The silk sheets were cool on her skin, and she was grateful for the reprieve from the unwavering heat. He maintained eye contact as he lowered onto his knees in front of her. His hands trailed up her calf until his fingers found the zipper on her boot. He slowly dragged it down, revealing more of her smooth caramel skin to his hungry eyes. His silver eyes cooled her skin like steel. Once her first boot was off, Samuel moved on to the second.

"You're so beautiful." Samuel carefully set her shoes aside and leaned up to gently cup her jaw. Next, he pulled the bunny ear headband off of her head. He tossed it somewhere else, never to be seen again. "You won't need that anymore."

"Touch me..." Michelle's knees parted on their own, giving Samuel the perfect view up her skirt. His eyes darted down to the apex of her legs and he licked his lips. Before Michelle could realize it, Samuel's cold hands gently cupped her cheeks once more. He looked her in the eyes, his piercing gaze holding her in place. His eyes slipped from her eyes to her lips, then back up. Michelle hardly had to think before she leaned down to kiss him.

Her arms circled his neck and her lips pressed onto his plush ones. Samuel responded immediately, parting his lips and licking into her mouth. His tongue tasted of wine and something sweet and utterly intoxicating. Michelle's tongue swirled with his, trying to get every single taste of him that she could. Her heart pounded in her chest and her breathing deepened as she melted into the kiss. The moans and gasps from the other couples faded into nothingness.

Samuel slightly pulled away only to land another kiss on her cheek, then another on her jaw. His mouth trailed from her lips down to her neck. His mouth closed on a sensitive spot, right under her ear, and Michelle let out a moan. He sucked lightly on the spot, nipping and licking to elicit more noises from her. Her blood raced, pounding through her so loudly that she could hear it. Her fingers curled into the hair at the back of his neck and she pulled him into her.

He kissed down her neck to her shoulder. His fingers played with the strap of her dress. He pushed it aside so he could kiss along her shoulder and suck on her collarbone.

Gently, his hands found purchase on her knees and spread them apart so that he could fit his body between them. He leaned into her, slowly pushing her back onto the silk sheets. Michelle sighed as Samuel kissed down her torso and pushed her white dress up her legs to bunch around her waist. Samuel sucked a hickey onto her stomach before finally lowering to be level with her core.

Michelle's face flushed at the thought of her plain, white, cotton underwear, but Samuel didn't seem to mind one bit. In fact, he barely paid them any attention as he peeled them off her and tossed them over his shoulder. His thumbs gently rested on the outer lips of her pussy as he spread her open. He blew a small stream of cold air right onto the wetness and Michelle jumped at the action.

"Look at you, dirty girl," Samuel smirked, "Getting all wet over the idea of fucking a stranger, huh?"

"Not just any stranger." Michelle reminded him, choking back a moan when his cold lips landed a kiss on her inner thigh. He sucked on her skin deeply, surely leaving a bruise to remember him by. "You."

"All for me then?" He chuckled, "Good, I don't want to share you with anyone else. You're mine now."

Samuel wasted no more time and dove in to lick a stripe up the length of her cunt. His lips and tongue went to work, mapping each and every inch of her. From her opening to the hood of her clit, Samuel swirled his tongue expertly through her folds. Michelle's eyes dropped shut and she moaned freely as the pleasure coursed through her veins. She pushed her hips up into his mouth more and Samuel placed a hand on her stomach to keep her still.

His lips closed around her clit and he sucked harshly. Michelle cried out and her back arched as Samuel focused his attention on that one spot. His tongue moved in expert figure eights or some kind of shape. Michelle couldn't tell, but she also didn't care. Pure pleasure sparked through her veins and her core began to clench. She whined desperately for more and she could feel Samuel smirk against her.

The wet sounds of Samuel devouring her made her cheeks flush with embarrassment, but they didn't deter him in the slightest. Her cries got more and more higher pitched the tighter Samuel wound the coil in her stomach. His heavenly tongue swirled on her clit in a sinful way that would make the angels blush.

"Samuel, I—" Michelle's broken cry fell on eager ears.

Samuel doubled down on his efforts, drinking her essence just like he promised. Her juices, sweet as nectar, spilled out of her and down his chin. Her candied musk invaded his nostrils and he wanted more. His eyes slid shut as he worked her toward the orgasm of the century. Her thighs began to quiver and close in around his head. He didn't bother to stop her as she suffocated him in her pussy. What a way to die. If only he actually *could* die that way.

Her orgasm practically took her by surprise. The coil within her snapped and she moaned so loudly that she was worried people outside the tent would be able to hear her. Her pussy quivered and spasmed as Samuel worked her through the most intense orgasm of her entire life. Her thighs tensed around his head. She had never cum so quickly or so hard before. Her hand reached down and buried itself in his lush black locks to hold him against her. She moaned his name as he urged her through wave after wave after wave.

After what must have been at least two minutes, Michelle's muscles relaxed and she released him. Samuel took this as his sign to place his last few soft kitten licks on her clit before pulling away completely. Michelle's chest heaved as she fought for breath. Samuel crawled up the bed and hovered over her, flashing her a smile that made her want to do sinful things to him. Just like he promised her before, his face was covered in a thin sheen of her wetness. He made a show of sticking his tongue out and licking the last drops of her off him.

"Sweet girl, you taste divine." Samuel nuzzled into her neck, giving her a few minutes to come down from her mind-blowing orgasm. "You're making me want to keep you around. How am I supposed to live without tasting you again?"

"Don't go falling in love with a stranger now." Michelle chuckled, reaching up to run her fingers through his hair.

"Oh, my delicious little thing, I want to make you mine," Samuel's teeth grazed her jugular and Michelle moaned, tilting her head to give him more room. "I want to ruin you for everyone else, make you crave and desire me even when we're apart."

"Make me yours," Michelle whispered.

She reached for the buttons and zipper on his pants. His face remained buried in her neck as she fumbled with the mechanisms and worked on freeing him. The bites against her neck grew longer and more insistent. His teeth sunk into her skin so hard that she wondered if he drew blood, and when she finally palmed the hard muscle she was after, her head flew even higher into the clouds.

"Mmm, so good." Samuel moaned into her ear, rocking his hips into her hand a little more. "You're going to take me so well, sweet girl. I need to feel you around me. Are you going to let me have you?"

"Yes, I want to feel you inside me." Michelle breathed, unsure of where her confidence was coming from. However, of all the times for it to be showing its face, she was glad that it was now.

"Hands and knees for me, beautiful." Samuel grinned.

Michelle wasted no time in rolling onto her stomach and rising onto her hands and knees. Samuel's large, cool hands found her waist and maneuvered her so that she was facing the couch where Josie and Angelique were occupied. Michelle couldn't see much except for Josie, spread out on the couch and Angelique settled between her legs. Josie's head fell back against the armrest closest to Michelle and her eyes were closed in bliss as Angelique did the same thing that Samuel had just done to Michelle.

Josie's moans stood out, high-pitched and whiny as Angelique worked her toward an orgasm. Josie's green bodysuit had been torn off her and laid in scraps on the floor next to the couch. Angelique had one hand dipped between Josie's legs and the other grasping onto one of Josie's perfect breasts for dear life, her manicured thumb circling her sensitive pink nipple. Angelique leaned over, her lips closing around Josie's clit as Josie's eyes lolled open in pleasure. She shot a grin at Michelle before a moan of ecstasy escaped her lips. They'd clearly made the right vacation choice.

Who would have thought that Halloween in New Orleans would be the place to go for a good night out?

Samuel positioned himself behind her and used his knee to kick her legs apart for him. His large hands gripped her ass, and a moment later, another stream of cool air hit her slick pussy and she jolted. Samuel chuckled a little, moving one hand from her ass to grip his cock and line it up at her entrance. "Wait," Michelle choked out, "What about protection or—"

"I couldn't get you pregnant even if I wanted to, little bunny. My kind isn't capable of that," he promised.

Before Michelle could ask what he meant, the head of his cock prodded her drenched hole, and she was sure that it would slip right in with no resistance. All thoughts left her body except for one. Her core ached and had only one desire. To be filled.

Samuel slipped the head of his cock into her and his head fell back. He moaned deeply as she sucked him in deeper, her silky walls clamping on him like a vice.

Michelle gasped at the intrusion but rocked her hips back a little to take him in a little more. Her body was *more* than ready to accept him into her. Samuel moaned and groaned beautifully as he pushed deeper inside her, and she wasn't sure that anything could make this moment any more perfect.

A blood-curdling scream tore through the symphony of ecstasy around them, tearing Michelle from her pleasure.

Looking up, she saw Josie pushing Angelique away from her and collapsing onto the ground with a sickening crack, like the breaking of bone. Blood was running down her exposed thigh from a massive bite wound near her pussy. Scratches and bite marks covered Josie's stomach and breasts; there was so much blood that Michelle was having trouble taking it all in. Finally, she saw the large gaping hole in Josie's crooked neck where blood was slowing to a trickle from her jugular. Michelle cried out as she looked up at Angelique. She stood naked before Josie's body, covered in her blood. Her nails were elongated into razor-sharp claws. Her face contorted, creating an ugly snarl, almost like the face of a grotesque bat. Her eyes were now purely red, filled with bloodlust. She laughed at Michelle before returning to Josie's mutilated body, running her tongue up from thigh to neck, drinking in as much blood as she could.

Michelle cried out in fear, pulling away from Samuel she turned to look at him for help. But the face that greeted her was not the one that had been kissing her moments before. His eyes were blood red like Angelique's. His face contorted into an expression of rage and hunger. He parted his thin cracking lips to expose two elongated, sharp fangs, and let out a short laugh before pushing Michelle down onto the bed. She screamed as she tried to push him off. His grip was strong, but she flung herself to the side, rolling off the couch and landing with a painful thud near Josie's mutilated corpse. She felt her fingers land on something sticky and moist. Bringing her hand to her face, Michelle saw blood. Josie's blood. Scrambling to her feet, Michelle looked around in shock.

Gone was the twisting of bodies together in pleasure. In its place was an orgy of carnage. Blood was everywhere. People biting into and tearing the flesh from their previous lovers with a sickening rip.

No, not people. Real-life vampires. As she got to her feet and stepped away, the smell of iron invaded Michelle's nostrils and turned her stomach inside out. Finally tearing her eyes from the bloodbath, Michelle ran as hard as she could, her lungs burning hot. She didn't care when her body protested. She needed to get out, to escape and find the police. The tent flap was right in front of her. She focused on her salvation as she heard the vampires growl and cry out. The loudest sound of all was Samuel. He was laughing—a cruel laugh.

Finally, Michelle threw the tent flap open and screamed. The bloodshed continued outside. The barrel originally filled with water and apples was now filled with ripped fingers and teeth floating in the crimson water. An eyeball rolled over and stared at Michelle, its dilated pupil forever frozen in terror. More vampires were outside, pulling people apart limb by limb, laughing as the victims screamed in agony. Others were hungrily licking the blood falling to the ground as if they had never tasted something so delicious.

Michelle froze, her legs unable to take another step as fear overtook her. A hand grabbed her wrist and pulled her arm up behind her back so quickly that her shoulder dislocated with a nauseating pop. She cried out in pain and was released to clutch at her limp arm. Angelique walked into view, and even naked and covered in Josie's blood, she was breathtaking. Every soft curve on her body was glistening red underneath the lights from inside the tent. Angelique cackled as she leaned over, her scrunched-up face reminding Michelle of the pictures of vampire bats she had seen on the internet. Now she saw the real reason they had that name. A human with a vampire bat face was looking dead into Michelle's eyes. As Angelique spoke, the lilting, Cajun accent came beautifully out of her upturned mouth.

"Now sugar, where do you think you are off to in such a hurry? The fun has just begun," she laughed darkly as Michelle struggled to escape, her limp arm dangling pathetically in Angelique's grip.

A new body pressed up against Michelle. One that had made her warm and wet only a moment before now made her blood run ice cold. Samuel ran his sharpened nail up Michelle's spine, starting at the base. He left a trail of blood streaming down her back as he tore her open and licked his work clean. Hot tears ran down Michelle's face as she trembled, as she felt his tongue on her again. Finally, Samuel reached Michelle's neck. Wrapping his hand around her throat, he leaned forward to whisper into her ear. Again, electricity coursed through her body as he spoke.

"Mmm, I could have kept you, my sweet bunny. Tasted you for the rest of eternity," he breathed into her neck, causing the skin to goosebump. Michelle took in a shaky breath. "Too bad you couldn't behave."

"Please," was all she could cry out. Her whole body trembled. Samuel smiled against her neck. He took in a long, deep breath, filling his senses with her smell, before opening his mouth. Samuel bit down hard, his fangs piercing into her jugular. Michelle tried to cry out, but all she managed to do was choke on her blood. Her lungs burned as each blood-coated bronchi restricted the flow of oxygen. She tried to cough and clear them, but Samuel tightened his grip, cutting off the last of Michelle's air. She jerked for a final time, her body fighting to live, before her legs gave out. Michelle's vision darkened as she listened to the moans of pleasure from Samuel and the cackling of Angelique.

# ABOUT THE AUTHORS

Krystyna Lee is an indie horror author out of Saint Louis, MO. She grew up in New Orleans and likes to blend her Midwestern and Southern experiences into her writing. While she prefers to write horror and fantasy, this story is her first foray into the romance genre. She does so with the help and encouragement of Elizabeth Fay. Krystyna is currently working on a YA dark fantasy trilogy set in pre-Christian Ireland. Krewe De Désir is her second story to be published in the Halloween Horror Anthology series by Sisterhood of the Black Pen.

When not working on her writings, Krystyna attends school with the intent of becoming a trauma nurse (who knows how this could affect her horror descriptions!) and runs a dark history and true crime podcast called Macabre Matters that is about to start its 3rd season! She enjoys painting, sewing, and playing horror video games with her brother. When it is time to relax, Krystyna cuddles up with her two fur babies, Geordi and Freya, to watch British competition shows.

*If you would like to keep up with Krystyna (or just to see the many photos of her cats) you can follow her on Instagram @bookmachta or follow her podcast @macabremattersofficial for updates on the newest spooky season!*

*Elizabeth (Lizzy) is a writer originally from Saint Louis, Missouri, currently pursuing a master's degree in Korean Studies at Yonsei University in Seoul, South Korea. Elizabeth primarily writes K-pop fanfiction and romance but is also working on a large-scale historical thriller that has been a passion project for some time.*

*A storyteller at heart, Elizabeth has been weaving tales for as long as she can remember. Writing is her way of giving life to the characters and worlds that have always lived in her imagination. In addition to creative writing, she thrives in academic settings and has numerous ideas for dissertations and thesis projects that keep her intellectual curiosity engaged.*

*While living in Korea, Elizabeth remains close to her family back in the U.S., including her parents, siblings, and beloved five nieces and nephews. She proudly identifies as a "Choka Pabo," a Korean term that affectionately describes her deep love and slight obsession with her nieces and nephews.*

*Despite a busy schedule with university, Elizabeth finds time to enjoy relaxing activities like playing video games such as Animal Crossing and Stardew Valley. She also has a passion for scrapbooking, traveling, and immersing herself in anything related to Korean language and culture, which she holds close to her heart.*

*You can find Elizabeth on Instagram at @chogiwa6192, where she occasionally shares snippets of her life and interests.*

# LOST and FOUND

Lizzie Strong

*Once upon a time, I was told about Baba Yaga, a horrific legendary character to keep children in line. My brother and cousins often would grimace and pull away, acting like she were some grotesque hag to be feared. The idea of ending up in her cauldron enough to keep them from wandering off of the straight and narrow. But, when the boys were gone, and the coffee was still warm, I would be told by the older women of my family about the witch of the woods. A guide to lost women who needed help. More than just her hut on chicken legs, but a place one could look for when the world has swallowed them whole. Who better to help you find your way than the witch sitting on the crossroads between life and death? A complex story as she was a beacon to women who would seek her out…and a vengeful spirit to the men who would hunt her down. Pray she's merciful, lest ye end up in her cauldron pot.*

# CHAPTER ONE

T he carnival was in town. I stared at the flyer that tumble-weeded itself into my hands from the gravel driveway. Bright colors, bold letters, and a buttload of glitter. *Who let a preschooler decorate this?* There was some weird, childish glee in my belly as I studied every inch of it. The edges were crinkled, and dust coated the thick poster paper. It probably rolled across the tiny town at the edge of a mountain in the middle of nowhere…and ended up here. I stared in wonder. *A carnival!*

I don't think I'd ever been to a carnival. If I had, how would I even know? Anything beyond the last five years was a foggy blur. Like I'm standing in a graveyard of memories, hazy smoke in every direction, and no idea where to even begin to dig. Every time I tried to summon the dead, it only crumbled apart.

I existed as a poltergeist of a woman, bound in flesh, lost. All I had was a husband who loved me and the memory of a car speeding toward me.

I heard the shred of paper before I realized I'd clutched it tight. I punctured it with a fingernail. With a surprised gasp, I plucked it from under my perfectly sculpted nails. Bradley liked them as little sharp ovals, soft nude colors, with a hint of glitter. I redid them every week just to show him. I hoped one day when I went to show him my nails, and he praised me for my precise technique…that maybe I would feel something for him.

The rumbling of an engine up the driveway ripped my attention away from my nails. Bradley's forest green, trail blazing vehicle came around the bend of trees at the end of our driveway. I used to imagine one day my heart would flutter and I'd remember being the doting wife. How would I know? Everything from before was a blank oblivion.

*Maybe the carnival will spark something?* The giddiness returned as I trembled down to my flats. *A carnival! Here?*

"What cha got there, babe?" Bradley chuckled sweetly as he popped out of the driver's seat.

"It's a carnival! They're hosting a carnival here!" I waved it vigorously back and forth.

"Really?" He scoffed, shaking his head. "I thought this town was above such gimmicks. Besides, where are they going to host it? There's no room!"

He had a point—our town wasn't even on most maps. If someone drove too fast, they'd miss the highway exit to our sleepy *little slice of heaven.* We moved here after my accident. He said it was for work, but I knew it was so he could look after me. I was in intensive care for a year, getting my body back in order. I should feel bad for making my husband leave his big city, corporate position to move to a small, middle of the woods cabin while I recovered…but I didn't. Not in the slightest.

*Did that make me a terrible wife?* Bradley was the sole breadwinner, drove us everywhere, cooked me dinner, and would stay up late into the night to tell me stories of us.

*The least you could do is play into his fantasy.* And so, I did. I played the happy wife. I painted my nails, brewed him coffee in the morning, and faked orgasms for him just so he'd get a glimpse of the woman he married. It would break his heart if he knew that I stayed awake at night, staring at him. *Give me one glimpse. Just one.* Anything, I'd take anything. But all I saw behind my eyelids were headlights racing toward me.

"Honey?"

"Huh?" I jumped in my skin, correcting my gaze to him. He loomed over me with confusion plastered to his rugged features. Bradley was six feet tall with dirty-blond hair. I liked the dark, murky brown of his eyes. His beard was deep brown and grew in wiry. But he'd grown into the mountain man aesthetic. *I didn't…mind it.* It wasn't a fantasy of mine, but it made him happy. What did I care? *I didn't even think of him naked.*

"I asked you where you even got that?" He pointed a judgmental finger at the flyer clutched to my chest.

"I found it—or it found me, to be quite honest," I shrugged, flashing him my best smile. "Please, can we go? I don't know if I've ever been."

"Trust me, carnivals are just cheap cash grabs for lowlifes. They're not any place I want my sweet wife anywhere near. What if you catch tetanus?" he reached for the flyer. Normally, I'd give in. What did I care about a carnival? *What can flashing lights and greasy popcorn really do for me?*

And yet…*I want to go.* The feeling overwhelmed me as I wrenched my prized possession out of his reach. "Please, Bradley, I want to go."

"Why?" He huffed.

"What if it's good for me? I'm always cooped up in this cabin. I'll start to talk to walls next! Please," I jutted out my bottom lip in the biggest puppy dog pout.

"It's a bad idea. All those flashing lights and loud sounds, what if it inspires some, I don't know, PTSD flashback? And what do you mean cooped up? We're here to keep *you* safe."

There was a sour note to his accusation. My face reflexively pinched as I spat back at him.

"We're here because *you* want to *keep* me here!"

My face fell, heart racing as something dark crossed his face. For no reason, I felt a cold chill run down my spine. I shivered in response to my outburst. Despite the crisp autumn leaves around us and the taste of fall in the air, it wasn't cold…yet. But the stare he gave froze me to the bone.

"We're here so that I can take care of you," he warned, like a rabid dog growling.

"Bradley," I softened. *He does so much for me.* His forehead relaxed as he studied my face. I stepped into his space, putting a tender hand to his chest. *He takes care of me.* "I'm sorry. I know you're protective of me, but I'm fine now and, you know, the doctors said going out and experiencing things is good for my memory. Don't you want me to remember us? I do! I want to remember falling in love with you. Didn't you tell me once we went to a festival or something together? What if this reminds me of you?"

His lips curled into a smile, his arms wrapping around me. "Oh, baby, I want that too! We went to a festival once, yeah!"

*Crack.* Something in me, like a glass window with a tiny pebble tossed against it, cracked. I heard it loud in my ears. I wrapped my arms around him, hugging him tight. *Scraaaaaatch.* Like fingernails against cracked glass.

*Bradley never once told me a story about a festival…he hates loud music and large gatherings of people.* I replayed the words, over and over as he rubbed my back. I let him kiss my cheek. *He lied. I lied.*

"We can go to the carnival, but just for an hour. Okay? And let's not get on any rides, don't want to crack you open more," he chortled in my ear. I nodded, grinning for him broadly. As he brushed past me into the cabin, my feet grew roots, cementing me to the porch. *He's allowed to remember things wrong. He remembers everything I can't! He got it wrong.*

Maybe the carnival would jog my memory of where we really went.

# CHAPTER TWO

Bradley held my hand as we wove through the gravelly parking space outside the carnival. It was everything I wanted. The stench of popcorn, hot and salty, filled the air. A small crowd of people were lured like moths to its flame. I squeezed onto Bradley's arm, nearly throttling him with excitement. My cheeks ached from smiling. Massive red neon lights flashed as we walked under the metal archway. The sun had barely set behind us and the night was illuminated in glorious color. Clowns rushed around in lupine packs, honking before running away from clumps of people. Vendors called out over the tinkling music. I forced my husband to stop just inside to merely soak it up.

It was magical. *It felt like home.* Glitter filled the air. I could taste sugar in the light autumn breeze. A creaking metal wheel rose into the night sky, full of hollering children.

"Oh, Bradley, this is…" I trailed off as a scent, so familiar it tugged on my heart, teased my nose. My lips trembled as the words failed to form. It was pink champagne! That scent! An image like a commercial played behind my eyelids. A pink crystal glass in the shape of a champagne bottle with a fake cork for the top sat upon a delicate vanity with flowers carved into the mirror frame. But when I turned to see the reflection, all I could see was the crack. A tiny pebble protruding from the center, fracturing me into four views.

"Babe?" Bradley booped me on the nose. "You okay?"

"Huh?" I laughed sheepishly. The back of my neck prickled with goosebumps. *Who…who was wearing that?* I searched the crowded carnival. The scent was gone, covered up by the stench of bodies and wet metal. "I thought I smelled something."

"Lots of scents here, that's for sure. What I'm smelling is popcorn." He tugged me to the left.

We rounded the Ferris wheel, following the promise of delicious, buttery kernels. I gasped with delight as a pack of clowns rushed up to us. One of them honked a horn in my face. I tensed up, lurching backward with my eyes snapped closed.

Headlights, bright and burning, filled everything from edge to edge. But…they were going in reverse. I tensed up, wrapped around my own steering wheel. Slowly I pulled back, opening my eyes. *Snow.* There was snow on the windshield, and I smelled of Pink Champagne. It was fresh on my clothes.

The clowns giggled, ripping me from the image as they rushed away from us.

"Rude! I hate clowns," Bradley huffed. He shifted to cup my face, studying me. "You okay?"

"Yeah," I panted for air, waving him off sweetly. "I think…I think maybe that unlocked my mutual hatred of clowns."

Bradley chuckled, pulling me toward him. I was putty in his palm. *My puppeteer pulling my strings.* His kiss was soft against my lips. Normally I close my eyes when he kisses me, but the fear of seeing those headlights again forced them open. Bradley's brow knitted together, pulling away, once again studying me intently.

"Babe?"

"What?" I smiled up at him innocently.

He gave me a once over. I leaned further into him, hugging his arm to my chest. With a shake of his head and another chuckle, he moved on. "It's nothing."

*Crack.* His kiss felt like nothing. It never had. *It never will.*

*Scraaaaaatch.* I blinked rapidly, laughing it off. "Sorry, it's just a lot to take in. I'm basically seeing a carnival for the first time in person and not on TV! Or…something."

*He's my husband. I loved him enough to marry him.* I tightened my squeeze around his arm as we found a popcorn vendor cart. The warm, strong, dependable arms of a man who held me when I cried at night. The soft embrace of the person who took care of me when there was no one else. Not…a stranger, but my husband…right? *I married him, so he had to mean something to me.*

And then the biting whisper in my ear turned my blood to ice. As if someone's lips were pressed to the shell of my ear. I whipped around, prepared to see the clowns again with their horrible horns. But there were none. Just a raspy voice, snickering in my eardrum. *Who says? Him?*

"Bradley," I murmured, twisting back to him. He offered me a bag of popcorn. I took a fluffy kernel, popping it into my mouth. Butter exploded on my tongue. He cocked his head in that golden retriever flop when he wanted me to continue. I let out a cute giggle to cover up my emptiness. "Why did we get married?"

"What?" He choked on his popcorn.

"I mean, why did you marry me?" I blushed with embarrassment. "We talk all the time about what we did and where we went but…why did we get married? What made you look at me one day and know I was the one?"

He softened, twisting his arm to loop it out of my grip and around my waist. "Oh, baby, I knew from the moment I met you that you and I were going to be together forever. We met in this coffee shop. I went there every day to get some brew before going to work. You stopped in a few times to get some coffee before class. I, of course, noticed the totally beautiful woman who happened to get the same order as me. Then, we both reached for the same latte and, you know, I looked in your eyes for the first time and just knew. I'd have proposed right then and there if I knew you'd say yes."

His face grew pink with affection, a twinkle in his eyes.

I sighed dreamily, taking another piece of popcorn. "I wish I knew what I thought when I first saw you."

*Please, just one memory. Just one to prove to myself…that this is me.* When one wakes up without a single memory, it's hard not to always hold a healthy sliver of doubt. There was some part of me that never trusted a word he said. But I wanted it to be true! Please, be true. *Because if it wasn't…*

"I suppose you probably thought something similar, baby. I mean…every time we got coffee at the same time, I know you were trying to be subtle about it but…I kept catching you glancing at me." He pulled away, stealing some popcorn.

I tried my best. Clenching my eyes shut, I returned to the graveyard of my mind. *Dig! Please! Dig!* But nothing turned up. Just a bunch of empty graves and hollow feelings. I sighed, taking another clump of popcorn. At least it tasted good.

# CHAPTER THREE

Like a clawed finger, beckoning me from the shadows, Pink Champagne brushed my nose once more. It forced me to snap my head around. The scent gave me a clue to my past, and I was desperate to follow it this time. We were standing at one of the many game tents when I whipped around in time to catch the retreating form of a woman. Long chestnut hair, wavy and bouncy, fell to her hips. It swung with every step as she offered pink vials to people. I lurched toward her but was tugged backward by Bradley. He'd been seconds away from winning a goldfish in a bag when she passed us.

I gasped, spinning to face him. "Who was that?"

"Who was who?" He put down the ping pong ball, glancing around with worry etched on his face.

I directed my question to the stripe-vested attendant next to the round table full of glass bowls. He froze like a deer in headlights as I slapped my palms against the booth front. "Who was that woman? The one selling the vials?"

"What's it worth to ya?" The guy with the fake mustache glued to his face wiggled his drawn-on eyebrows at me.

I rolled my eyes. *Of course.* "You want me to win my answer?"

He shrugged, sauntering up to the front of the booth. Bradley blurted out, "Babe, I thought you wanted me to get the goldfish?"

"That woman's wearing a perfume I used to wear!" I flapped my arm toward where she disappeared.

Bradley squinted at me in the way that people who haven't connected the dots but don't want to admit they're lost do. I huffed, returning my attention to the game vendor. My right hand extended, I wiggled my fingers. "How many balls?"

"Pfft," the vendor giggled, flopping himself into the front of the booth. "For you? Get one in, I'll tell you her name. For two, I'll tell you what she sells here. For three, I'll tell you where to find her. For five? I'll circle her tent on our little map brochure thingy!"

"Five balls it is!" I snatched five red rubber balls from in front of my husband and lined up my shots.

*I used to be good at this.*

The words turned my veins to concrete, my heart slowing down to a hard *thump...thump...thump.*

*I used to be good at this?*

Bradley never told me I had special talents. I'd only found out I had a steady hand when I painted my fingers and toes. If we'd been to a festival before, like he lied about, then wouldn't he have told me I was good at carnival games?

*It's all about a steady hand and a little bit of spite.* The raspy whisper crawled up the back of my neck again. Everything felt like television static. I stood there, arm raised, buzzing echoing in my skull. Then, without hesitation, I flicked my wrist and a red ball sank into the middle bowl.

"Ay! Atta girl! Betcha can't do it again!" The vendor teased, shimmying at me suggestively.

"Babe?" Bradley whimpered as he eyed me. I snatched up another ball.

*No...no, I learned to do this long before him.* I flicked my wrist again. Second ball, top right corner, outer ring of bowls. The vendor cheered again. *I learned to do this as a child...yes, that's right.* A wicked smile curled on my lips. Third ball, bottom left corner, evened out the table, circled the lip before sinking in. The vendor hooted, leaping in the air like a cartoon character. *Bradley wouldn't have known I knew how to do this...*I got the bowl next to the right of the center bowl with my fourth ball. *Because my mother used to bring me to the permanent carnival in my town.*

I gasped, nearly toppling over the top of the vendor table as I sank my final and fifth ball into a bowl. I didn't even see which bowl. All I felt was my world as a tilt-a-whirl. My stomach fell into my heels. My eyes swam in my skull. My body disconnected from me.

*That's right...there was a carnival...we lived near Circus City. There was always a carnival, every weekend. Mom worked there part time and I got to go all the time.*

I choked on my tongue as I gripped the top of the table separating me from the dancing vendor. Bradley wrapped an arm around me, rubbing my side. "Babe? You okay?"

I shook my head as I tried to rein it in. *Sick, I'm going to be sick.* I rushed to grab ahold of the rustic lemonade we bought to counteract the salty popcorn, washing down the feeling with the sweet liquid with hopes I wouldn't spew my stomach contents out. *If he thinks I'm sick, we'll go home. I can't go home yet.* Not until I find her—not until I have answers. I can be sick later.

The vendor plopped down a bag with a sad goldfish inside. I shook my head, croaking,

"The woman, who is she?"

"Oh! That's—" His voice cut out as the static took over. I had to force my brain to focus on him, watching his lips move to hear him. "She's our potion maker. Makes love potions, memory potions, the works. She's at the back side of the carnival, here." He pulled out a brochure with the same glossy texture as the carnival flyer. My fingers brushed it and I felt back in control of my body. With a big circle, he marked the potion maker on my map.

I wheeled back from the vendor's tent, taking deep breaths. Bradley waited till I was standing fully again, his hand constantly rubbing my back. "Maybe we should go home?"

"What? No! That was..." but the words didn't form on my tongue. *Go home? I just got back a slice of me.* "I was starting to remember things."

"Like what?" He arched a brow.

"When I was little, my mom *worked* at a carnival. We used to go every weekend. I got really good at the games." And I saw it in flashes. With every spin of the Ferris wheel over our heads, the images flooded back. A whoosh of air, the stench of popcorn, I was a six-year-old girl again. Pigtails, overalls, holding a bag of popcorn and talking with the lemonade vendor. The clowns would come and steal me to cart around the carnival on top of their tiny metal contraption.

*Crack.* I saw myself in a house of mirrors, staring at a reflection in pieces. I was not the little girl anymore. Instead, an adult, tapping against the glass. It began to spider out with every crack. *Tap, tap.* The glass would shiver as I spoke, but I couldn't hear me. Instead, part of me left the haunted house of mirrors, leaving me stuck in my shattered prison.

"Oh," Bradley whispered, tugging me in close. I wrapped my arms around him, the warmth of his embrace a soothing balm against the bone rattling cold of the unknown. "I didn't know that—I'm so sorry."

*Something changed…something stopped me from telling him. Why wouldn't I have told my husband that fact?*

"Come on, sweetie, let's go home."

"No," I croaked, tugging us in the opposite direction.

"No?" He eyed me with those big, murky brown eyes.

"Please," I begged.

He sighed. "I can see it's important to you."

*HONK!* We both shrieked as a gaggle of clowns cackled, scurrying around us like roaches. They took their aggressive horns with them. With a sheepish smile to Bradley, I tugged him again as playfully as I could. "Besides, I mean, I won that info on the potion maker. We should at the very least go see her? Right?"

*Memory potions…*

"It's probably just some fruit juice with edible glitter, baby," He snorted, shaking his head in disbelief.

"Or they could be real! I mean, the vendor says she makes the works. Including love potions!" I defended with a huff.

He scratched at his beard for a long moment. "But those love potions? What if…what if they're an aphrodisiac? Huh?"

His eyes widened, glancing down at me. *Typical.* A dark, ugly feeling spread in me at the thought of him hot and heavy over me. How his fingers would spread across my body and palm my nipples desperately. His lips made my skin crawl as he kissed my forehead. "And if it is just sparkling fruit juice, we can just…pretend."

"*You like it when I pretend,*" I whispered under my breath, the disgust nearly choking me.

"What?" He blinked, pulling away to glance at my face.

"Huh?" I laughed it off, "I said you'd like that, huh? Maybe we could roleplay in the woods. My rugged mountain man."

His cheeks burst into a bright pink. My stomach churned with acid as he tugged me in for a kiss. This time, when our lips brushed, all I could see were headlights. Bright and all encompassing, a horn blaring in my ear. I tensed up in anticipation for the collision. When I peeled my eyes open, I found myself still in his hands, dead lips pressed to his, and I felt nothing.

*I feel nothing for him.*

# CHAPTER FOUR

We rounded the Ferris wheel, stopping at the merry-go-round. Pink Champagne brushed my nose once more. My feet planted in the muddy, well-trodden earth. A dozen horses in varying stages of disrepair bounced up and down on metal poles as they went around and around and around. My potion maker stepped onto the ride, taking an extended dollar bill from someone and handing them a potion. I saw her clearer. A round face with a button nose. Tan skin with a sprinkling of freckles over every inch. She was accented by plum skirts and a cream blouse, the old school kind that I saw on historical television. Bradley stumbled backward, blinking rapidly as I wrenched him to a complete stop. I jabbed a finger at the magical, twinkling ride.

"A merry-go-round!"

Bradley grimaced, eyeing it from the side. "Really?"

"It's that or the Ferris wheel," I retorted, staring him directly in the eye.

I didn't want the Ferris wheel. I wanted to follow the potion maker onto the merry-go-round. Every time I followed her scent, I unlocked something. Desperation clung to me. *I want to know more.* If I followed her onto the merry-go-round, I didn't know what I would unlock. But maybe it would actually be the thing that explained how I ended up married to a man I didn't tell things to…how I ended up lying to the man who cared for me so deeply.

*Was I ever in love with him? Was I the cruel wife who married a man for money? Or power? Who was I other than the daughter of a carnival worker from Circus City?*

Bradley didn't get a chance to answer. I ripped him across the soggy earth toward the ride before my potion maker could disappear again. It slowed to a stop, creaking as the horses all came to a halt. A clump of people left, my potion maker not among them. I stepped onto the platform, wandering the rows of metal horses. Gone. *Drats!*

Bradley made a huff of disapproval, but I ignored it in exchange for mounting a horse toward the center. I swung my leg over its saddle, settling in the dip of its back. Cold metal bit through my jeans. Bradley stood beside me, looking around.

"All riders, please choose a seat!"

I glanced at him, "Hop on that one."

"But what if you fall off this one?" He squirmed, giving me a once over.

"I'm not seven," I snorted, nodding my chin at the horse in the next row. "Grab that one."

He hesitated, clearly considering standing by me.

The ride operator called over our heads once more, "All riders, please choose a seat!" A gaggle of children snorted and pointed at Bradley from the rows ahead of us. He scowled at them before mounting his own horse. While I was straddling a purple unicorn with pink flowers, he was riding a blue horse with green sprinkles.

The ride jerked forward, groaning as it started up again. It was a sharp snap upward before my horse shuddered back down, easing into a steady rhythm. One hand on the pole and one on the reins, my hips rocking with the movement.

Something hummed in my ear. The speakers, full of prickly static, struggled to play a tune as we picked up speed. My eyes fluttered closed as I let the ride set the pace. Up, then down, up, then down, it lulled me away from the merry-go-round.

*"That's it baby…"*

I opened my eyes, looking down at Bradley. Naked, covered in a layer of sweat, panting for air. His eyes were rolled back in his head, hands on my hips. He thrust into me with all his might, a nearly painful, sharp pattern that only ever resulted in his orgasm. Bradley clawed at my hips, yanking me down onto him clumsily. Up and down, up and down, I did my best to try and set a pace, but he took over. His pelvis slammed into mine, his cock slapping against my walls uselessly.

Once again…I would be taking care of my own orgasm while he snored away.

*But it wasn't always like that…I used to set the pace.*

It wasn't Bradley under me. Up and down, up and down, soft, strategic rocks of my hips, guiding the stiff cock where I wanted it. Hands roamed my sides, lips on my neck. I curled my toes into the sheets, whimpering a name that escaped me. Someone circled my clit, listening to my desperate directions. *Softer…right there…bite me.* There were two people ravishing me, letting me set the pace. A softer cock pressed into my backside, effortlessly slipping deep inside me. I was finally able to open my eyes.

The potion maker lay beneath me, a pink strap-on effortlessly fucking into me. Some faceless lover nipped at my neck as he rutted up into me. Only ever at my pace. Only ever doing as I asked. *They listened.*

A tingle ran up my spine as I could smell the perfume again. Pink Champagne, so pretty and soft, it came off her skin as my potion maker reached for my face. *Kiss me.* Our lips met with a clash as my world spun. Faster and faster, their combined heavy panting with my sharp inhale. I drowned in their desire. Up and down, in and out, I was in control of my passion. *I always enjoyed more than one.*

My core clamped down and a wash of something foreign crashed over me. I gasped, my fingers wrapping around a cold bar. The ride shuddered to a stop.

*Was…no…that wasn't.*

But it was, as I looked down at my lap. My jeans were darkened around the seam, growing darker by the second. My cheeks flushed as I ripped myself off it before Bradley could see. My legs wobbled. Bradley rushed to my side, his large palms burning against my hips as I tried not to squeak.

I had never fantasized about my husband. Not once.

But I just fantasized about a woman I didn't know and a stranger I couldn't name. I felt them inside me, on me, against my burning flesh.

*I used to love sex.*

The hot embarrassment of coming on a child's ride was swiftly replaced with confusion.

I'd never liked sex with Bradley. It was a chore. Something I did to make him happy. *He clearly loved and desired me…*I always imagined it would eventually spark something. *I loved him, I must have loved having sex with him.*

*Crack.* My attention snapped up to the hands holding me to the mirrored core of the merry-go-round. Fractured. In a thousand pieces, I stared at my reflection through hundreds of shards of glass. Bradley stood there, looming over me with worry.

But in one reflection, he wasn't soft. He wasn't worried. His face was pinched in fury. Eyes narrowed to slits, his mouth curled in a snarl, his hands wrapped around my throat. I wrenched away from him in an instant, whirling to face him. The cold unicorn pressed into my back as I forced space between us. He jerked, clutching invisible pearls. "Babe? What...what did you remember now?"

"You...and..." I couldn't form the words. My tongue flopped like a trout on land in my mouth.

*Who told you that you like having sex with him?...Him?*

I trembled as I side-stepped my unicorn. Bradley watched me with wide eyes. "Babe?"

"Have we...have we ever had a threesome?" I blurted out, unable to do more than hold onto the horse for support.

"Riders wanting to ride again, please choose a seat!"

I didn't feel safe. The thought struck me with a weird, tingling sensation. Despite everything, I'd always felt safe around Bradley. *Was that because he **was** safe or because he convinced me he was safe?* My mind turned into a beehive, thrumming with life. Angry wings buzzed around my skull, and stingers bit into the soft flesh of my brain.

"Riders wanting to ride again, please choose a seat!"

I jerked onto my horse. Bradley scoffed, taking his horse once more. He glared at me with an ugly purse of his lips. "Why would we have one of those?"

I stammered. *Because I loved having threesomes, foursomes, allsomes.* For the first time in five years, I stared at my husband, completely baffled. *I loved large parties full of people and blindfolds and women who did **exactly** what I told them to do.*

"Just...a goofy thought," I murmured, ripping my attention from him. The angry look on his face struck me like a hard slap. My husband didn't like carnivals, didn't know anything about my childhood, and didn't know how to please me.

"Well, let that goofy thought go. I'm not into sharing."

*Scraaaatch.* But this time, it was my own fingernails clawing down the shimmering pole of my unicorn. I swiveled my head toward him. There was no smile, no sheepish laugh, no apologetic look. "And if I was?"

He straightened, studying my face with shock. "What are you talking about?"

"What if I remembered having threesomes? Huh? What if I told you I liked sleeping with women and men and everyone who liked to share, especially if they asked nicely?" The words flew out of my mouth with a snap of my teeth.

His knuckles paled as he gripped his pole. Arms shaking, his voice wobbled, "You got over that phase in college, honey."

"Did I?" I cocked my head to the side. "I don't remember that."

He lurched toward me, but the ride stopped. Bradley toppled to the ground and there was a crack. I gasped. Rushing off my own unicorn, I helped scoop him off the silvery floor. Flashes of him holding me while he rubbed creams into my legs, kissing me on the forehead when I got fevers, spoon feeding me soup returned to my head. *This man took care of me when I was wounded! He held me when I sobbed! He cooked me dinner...*

All the usual excuses tasted sour on the back of my tongue as I tenderly prodded at his face. Blood dribbled out of his nose in fat globs.

"I'm so sorry, I didn't mean to shock you, I was just thinking," all the words clambered out of my mouth all at once. He stared at me with that pitiful, puppy dog look as he touched his nose. Bradley hissed, recoiling from me. I knelt there on the merry-go-round floor, dizzy and in shock.

My husband retreated from me, headed for the exit. I scrambled after him...pushing off the now skinny, scale-covered, fowl shaped legs of my ride.

# CHAPTER FIVE

"Babe, I just don't know where this is coming from," Bradley huffed, whirling to face me as we stopped at another food vendor for napkins. He dabbed at his nose tenderly. "Ow."

"I just…I'm just remembering things about myself." I flapped my arms out to the side. "Am I not allowed to be curious about my past? You remember *everything!* But I had a whole life before you, a whole personality. Is it wrong to want to explore who I was?"

"But I love who you *are!*" He pouted, waving at me with his free hand. The other continued to dab and clean up the blood.

"But I'm not anyone!" I roared.

"You're my wife!" He bellowed back.

*Your wife is a ghost…she isn't real.*

The raspy voice tickled the back of my ears.

"You love me? For who I am right now? So if I never remembered anything, you'd still be happy?" I rocked back on my heels. My sneakers dug into the sludge of mud in front of the cart.

"I've always loved you, baby. You're perfect for me! And sure, I'd love you to remember how we met and how happy we were together, but we're happy together now! Why should that have to change?"

*Liar.*

I swallowed the confession. *We're not happy now*…Bradley was happy. I was empty. I was a poltergeist. I was a hollow vessel for him.

And I did all of this to keep him happy.

*Why? Why do you care about his happiness?* The raspy voice growled, filling my chest with dark, sticky rage. It lashed out, touching every organ, and filled me to the brim. My hands trembled as it grew like a disease. With every dab of his napkin to his nose, the darkness took over.

"Let's go see the potion maker and go home." I stormed past him. Bradley whined, reaching for me, but I stayed out of reach. Instead, I busied my hands with the map. I tugged it out of my pockets and worked the brochure open in front of me.

"Babe, we can just go—"

"What about your love potion?" I snarled, ripping around in the muck.

He froze, staring down at me with bewilderment.

I didn't attempt to smile at him. Something foreign and ugly crawled out of my mouth, "I think we should get one. Maybe it'll help me remember why I married you."

"Don't take that tone with me," he huffed, stuffing his bloodied napkin in a trash can. I swallowed, even shocked at myself. Yet, it kept pouring out of me like someone else had control of my vocal cords.

"What tone? I thought you liked me as I was." *Who was this?* I couldn't go home. Not yet. *I'm so close.*

"Yes! My happy, bubbly wife who likes to snuggle with me on the couch and hear about my day. Not…"

Something sharp bit into my chest. Rage I'd never felt before filled the ghostly cavity.

"Not what?" I stepped toward him, my fists clenching at my sides.

His eyes narrowed on my hands first before darting back up to my face. There was something brewing beneath the surface for him too. We just needed *a little push.* "We're going home. You've had enough."

Hysteria cracked through me as I tossed my hands out to the side. *This is me.* I was a shattered mirror. *I'm angry with him.* Maybe the bubbly wife who liked to snuggle was the lie…*I'm not leaving!* The true me began to slither out of the cracked glass.

*Scraaaaatch.* A shiver ran down my spine. I laughed, hunched over in the middle as I stared him directly in the eyes. "I don't think I have! I mean, I remembered stuff about my childhood! I remember my years as a slut in college! How will I ever know how we got here if we don't continue, right? I mean, how did a poor girl from a circus town who was a rampaging, threesome-having slut in college end up with you? Huh? I can't wait to hear how you remember taking a chance on me! Come on! I bet that love potion will make me remember!"

He lunged for me, but I booked it for the tent. Around the bend of the carnival, weaving through vendor carts, Bradley called for me, the sound of his boots slapping against the wet mud echoing off the attractions around us. My flats caught in the muck. I left them behind. My map of the carnival flapped beside me as I pumped my arms. Cold, stinging slime stuck to the bottom of my feet.

*I ran from him once. But in much better footwear.*

I gasped for air as a floodlight went off directly in my eyes. My arms immediately flew up before me, tensing…preparing for collision. Light engulfed me. The scent of Pink Champagne burned my nose. A heart-stopping horn blared in my ears.

*Crunch.*

"What the fuck is wrong with you?"

My arms slithered back down; the map clenched in my rattling fists. I stared at one of the ride attendants turning off their head lamp as they ducked out from under another ride. They were crunching on popcorn in the most obnoxious way possible.

*Crunch.*

I turned slowly, toes curling around the icy mud as Bradley stormed up to me. He waved my soiled flats in my face.

"First you demand we come to this stupid carnival, then you lose it at every turn, and now you run from me? I thought you wanted to be here? Not a great way to show your appreciation for the husband who *took care of you for years*." He dropped the flats into the soggy earth.

"You did…didn't you," I breathed, staring up into his face. My body wasn't mine. The poltergeist of his wife took over, digging her razor-sharp claws into my muscles.

*Tap, tap.*

I was on the other side of the cracked mirrors, trying to tell me something.

*Tap, tap.*

Something was wrong.

*Tap, tap.*

He took care of me for years.

*Tap, tap.*

He held me tight as we slept.

*Tap, tap.*

He never *wanted* me to go anywhere in fear of what might happen.

"Yeah?" He scanned my face with confusion. *Tap, tap.* It was Bradley on the other side of my fractured glass tap-taping. He stared at me through frosted shards, mouthing something I couldn't comprehend. *Tap, tap.* "I did."

"When my feet were so crushed from wearing heels while driving that it took me a whole year to recover." *Crack. Crunch. Scraaaatch.* My body ached like the pressure of a thousand cars laid on top of me. "You took us out to that cabin so I didn't have to work. And you took a small job in our small town, leaving your big, important job to take care of us. You did all of this for me. All to take. Care. Of. Me."

His face set hard as stone. "What are you getting at?"

*No...please no...He wouldn't. He didn't. He's my husband! He loves me! He takes care of me! He wants what's best for me.*

*Who says? Him?*

I opened my mouth to speak when a woosh of fabric redirected my attention. My potion maker stepped out from a large, cabin-shaped tent. A cauldron with a massive wooden spoon was burned into a wooden sign. She was gorgeous, with sparkling hazel eyes. Extending a hand to me, she beckoned me forward. "I know that sound...that's the sound of a marriage in need of a love potion."

"No, we don't need anything other than to go home." Bradley reached for me, but I was already out of his reach. I stumbled, bare footed, into the warm embrace of my potion maker. *She's so familiar.* Her bell sleeves wrapped around me like a blanket draped over my shoulders. *I know that face.*

"Come now, sweet thing, we'll get you sorted out. One of my love potions, and you'll be more in love than ever before." She wheeled me through the giant flap of fabric. "Girls only. You understand, right?"

I didn't listen for his protest or acceptance. *He won't stay outside even if he knew it was good for him!* All I heard was the cacophony of sounds. *Tap, crunch, scraaaatch, crack.* It echoed in the chamber of my skull as I stumbled over a hardwood floor. *Something's not right.* But I couldn't voice the words. Something barged in behind me, but when I turned, it was just me and the potion maker. It took a few moments for my brain to even register I wasn't barefoot in the mud anymore. I glanced down and my brain went quiet except for one thought…*I know that face.*

"Who are you?" I whispered, barely able to form anything louder than a rasp.

"Why, I'm your potion maker, silly," she winked at me, hugging me to her side. "I'm here to help you."

"Do I know you?" I murmured. The floor creaked and groaned as we walked across it. *Like a cabin floor, deep in the woods.* They shifted, like the tent itself were settling.

"I'm sure it'll come back to you," her purr was dangerous and tempting as it drew me further in.

Warmth seeped into my bones as my gaze numbly wandered my surroundings. Inside, it didn't look like a tent anymore, with its solid wooden walls and exposed rafters. *Like she painted over the real world with a fantasy.* I squinted at them in curiosity. Ingredients, dried and hanging from splitting twine, dangled above me—definitely not chicken bones hung from rotting twine or twigs twisted up in hair. The walls held up an array of pots, pans, and kitchen utensils, not skulls. Surrounding us were counter after counter with cutting boards and empty vials. I stopped at the center, finding a crackling fire under a fat-bellied cauldron. It glistened, stealing my worries away as fire danced around it. *Something's not right.* For a second…I thought I saw someone in the pot. When I tried to focus on the flicker, she stepped in front of it.

"Now, let's talk about this love potion, huh?"

"Right," I breathed, standing up straight. It was strange to feel so disconnected and safe at the same time. I'd spent all evening feeling like a porcelain doll on the precipice of disaster. Yet, here, I was warm. Safe. Found. I let out a heavy breath that made the weight on my shoulders crumble. "The reason I'm in here."

My potion maker slithered closer. She raised a singular brow. "Sweet thing…what's the matter?"

Everything poured out all at once like I was a faucet stuck at overflow. "Something's wrong. I feel wrong. You seem familiar, and this place, it's right out of my memories. But I don't…I don't know you, do I? What if I don't remember anything else? I want to know who I was. Why am I here? Who am I?"

The anxious, angry wasps inside my brain returned with a vengeance. I played every scenario in my mind, spiraling down an unending drain. She waited for me to run out of breath before she smiled. A tender smile that slowed down my rapid heartbeat. "Sweet, little thing, what kind of potion *do you want?*"

"What do I want?" I parroted with a sniffle as I stood up straight. "I want something to help me remember. Because I feel so lost."

"I know you do," she cooed, rounding the cauldron once more. Guiding me away from it, she cupped my cheeks with silky palms that eased the angry buzzing away. I saw it again, just behind her back. Someone was clawing their way out of the pot. Something was shoving them in it. A gangly shadow using a large wooden spoon. Shove. Shove. Shove. Down into the cauldron it went with a heavy splash. *Someone else was in the tent with us.* My potion maker ripped my attention back with a crooked smile. "It's my job to help lost things...like yourself."

"How?" I whimpered. I tried to catch a glimpse of who it was, but it was curiosity, not worry. *Who else would barge into the tent where they weren't welcome. Weren't wanted!*

*He's always chased things he couldn't have, and when he was told no, he grew petulant.*

The potion maker chuckled, stealing my attention back. "We start with a base, huh? All good things start with a base. What is your base, my sweet thing?"

We stood by one of the counters as bowls of ingredients appeared before me. It hit me before I even saw all of it. A wide, childish grin crawled on my face. "Popcorn."

*But it's not popcorn.* It was fingers. In between the breaths it took for her to snatch them, I saw it. Human fingers. They curled around mine. Something was trying to tug them out of my grip. Blood made them slick. They were familiar and firm. A golden wedding band caught my eyes. If I focused on it, I could almost hear a scream.

"Ahh, yes. The more butter, the better," she cooed. With a slam of her fist against the counter, the playful image of popcorn returned. The kernels flew through the air. A tea kettle shrieked behind me as the popcorn fell into my open hands.

"My mother used to always buy me a bag. Every time we went to the carnival. And she'd pour all the butter she could squeeze on it. To the point the bag would be so soggy, I'd have to get a second just to keep it from falling open," I giggled, stealing a bite. A hard-as-bone kernel clicked against my teeth. I moaned with delight as butter exploded on my tongue. *Sticky, warm, bitter, the taste of iron.* Yet, when I looked down at my handful of popcorn, I couldn't see any blood. My potion maker guided me to the cauldron. My fingers, covered in red—*No!*—Oiled by the butter, glistened in the amber light as I sprinkled it inside. A cloud poofed from the cauldron, filling the air with a child's giggle.

*My giggle.*

"Now, what else?" She motioned to the other counter.

"A teddy bear!" I cried out, scrambling to the opposite side. The biggest, fluffiest, cheesiest teddy bear in creation sat just for me with a big, red bow around its neck. I scooped up the fluffy toy and found something soggy and wet. Flesh slapped against me as it was tugged free from bone. A jagged knife tore it free of the other pieces. Then her soft hand brushed across my back and the bear was in my hands. *Not someone's leg.* I squeezed it tight enough to leave bruises. "I always won them and gave them to kids who cried at the carnivals. I got so good at the games, it was unfair to keep them all to myself."

My potion maker beckoned me with curled fingers. I followed her, a lost lamb stumbling back to the cauldron. My teddy bear turned the potion pink, lifting a cloud of perfume into the air. I inhaled it deeply. "Pink Champagne."

"You remember?" She purred teasingly in my ear.

"I wore it every day. It was my signature scent. I found it in a drugstore near our house and wore it everywhere. Even in college."

A shredded foot was plopped into my hand—*NO!* A cold, hard crystal champagne bottle was placed in my hand. I blinked, seeing the sawed-off foot once more before clearing the blurry image from my mind. The sound of something carving through bone was replaced with the tinkling of bells. Glancing down at the vial, I twisted it back and forth. *Oh, look how it glistens.* I was mesmerized. Heavy and familiar, I brought it to my nose. It burned at first, taking a sharp whiff. A metallic taste coated my tongue before the lingering, sweet smell filled my lungs once more.

I popped the cork off it and poured it into my cauldron.

Soft murmurs, the sounds of bodies pressing together in a dark nightclub filled the air. Low, at first, then growing louder, I heard myself moan. It wasn't coming from my body, but the cauldron.

"Do you remember college? Oh, such good years for you. Exploring your needs, your desires, your wants…do you remember, sweet thing?"

I twisted away from my bubbling brew to my potion maker. *A dark thing stood in her place, gangly and drawn taut with glowing embers for eyes.* I stumbled into her embrace, dripping red. I walked her back into the counter, replacing the shadows with her body. Her hands cupped my cheeks seconds before our lips crashed together.

*I want to feel like myself again. I want to remember what it's like.*

Our teeth clinked as I ground my body against her. My fingers curled around her thick hair, pulling her into kiss after kiss until we panted against each other's slick lips. I swallowed her air. She tasted of delight and sharp liquor. I groaned against her, peeling her apron from her waist. Tugging and peeling until I could feel her silky skin in my palms. *Blood, I peeled back so much there was just gushing crimson onto my hands.* I gasped; her breasts filled my palms. The pad of my thumb traced her nipples, devouring her mewls of delight.

"I remember," I murmured against her open mouth. She smirked, twisting us until my back was against the counter. Something splashed the back of my shirt. She wrenched the fabric up and over my head. I tossed my hair over my shoulder. It slapped my flesh, stuck to me as it soaked in something. Viscera tangled with my hair. Something tugged at it, weak…*He tried to touch me one last time.* My hands were too busy peeling my jeans off my hips. Her right hand dove immediately between us, cupping my cunt. I broke our kiss with a gasp. My hips bucked for her as she traced my slit.

"Sweet thing, you remember?"

"I remember," I nodded vigorously as flashes of bodies returned. I babbled as her forefinger circled my clit dangerously slow. "I remember joining a club in college. The owners showed me everything. Answered every question. I remember fucking her sister. I remember it was the best thing I'd ever tried. She used to make me scream her name with that pink dildo."

And the image from the merry-go-round, it wasn't my potion maker any-more. It was Elywin. Her long blonde hair she kept in a high-ponytail till I tugged it. Her purple painted lips, the way her eyeliner dripped down her cheeks as I made her come to the point of tears. She invited me to her house, into her bed, into her love. One of her boyfriends, Vince, he called me cute words while she made me tell her everything I wanted.

"You liked living in her world." My potion maker grounded me with a bite to my lower lip. Hands that didn't belong to her or me slithered around me, cupping my breasts and my throat; they teased my burning flesh. I whimpered as my potion maker dove two fingers deep inside me. I bucked for her, over and over and over. Her thumb kept my clit on a knife's edge. My eyes rolled back in my head. Lips covered my skin like goosebumps, leaving traces of past lovers on my flesh.

I was in Elywin's office, letting her re-arrange my insides with whatever she wanted, draped over her desk like a tablecloth. She kissed me till I was drunk. *Coffee? On Wednesday, let's go to your favorite shop.*

I cried out as teeth sank into my flesh around my jugular.

"I was in love with her!" I confessed.

It broke me. My walls clamped around her, milking her delicate fingers as she drove me into oblivion. I sobbed as delight and relief washed over me in vicious waves. It ran cold shivers down my spine. My legs trembled. My potion maker smiled at me as she kissed down my chest, lavishing both nipples with tender kisses till her lips brushed my cunt. Her tongue swiped across my sensitive skin. My knees buckled, but strong hands held me up.

She caught my eyes, locking our gazes as she tended to my buzzing clit with a soothing tongue. Gentle circles that eased the tension in my body. *Just how Elywin used to...*a dreamy sigh fell off my lips as she kissed the insides of both my thighs. Then, in all her naked beauty, she sauntered from me. I was draped backward against a countertop, drenched in something, but my attention was glued to her. She winked at me before leaning over my brew. Dipping her glistening fingers into it, another puff of smoke exploded out of the cauldron.

*"I love you...you know that right? I love you and I want to spend the rest of my life with you..."*

My heart lurched as tears poured down my cheeks.

"I think your potion's almost ready, sweet thing. Come here. It just needs one last thing," my potion maker purred, beckoning me once more with curling fingers. I stumbled out of the collection of fingers and hands. *His hands.* My limbs were heavy. I nearly tumbled into the bubbling brew. She scooped me up by the sides, enveloping me in her warm arms once more. Her silky skin against my back, she whispered in my ear. A raspy whisper that brushed the shell of my ear. "A splash…of coffee."

My eyes shot open as I stared into the cauldron. Bradley was there, at the coffee shop. Our fingers brushed over a latte. I laughed sheepishly, letting him take it. But while he stood there, staring at me, I turned to greet Elywin as she came into the shop.

"His face…" I murmured, leaning closer to the brew. "It was always familiar. He always got the same drink as me."

Bradley took up the two lattes placed at the end of the bar of my favorite coffee shop. My potion maker growled in my ear, "The one you went to every time you waited for her to get off of work."

"She was a professor at the local college," I inhaled sharply, the scent of roasted coffee filling my nose.

"But that day was different? Why?"

"No," I whimpered, shaking my head.

"Sweet thing, why was that day different?" She urged, pushing me till my hands met the burning lip of the cauldron.

I cried out over the brew, my tears splashing into its belly. "Because she asked me to marry her!"

I was ripped back from the cauldron by my hair. The flesh around my palms sizzled as I flailed backward. I wasn't naked. The room wasn't a warm cabin of wooden walls with dangling ingredients. I was in a dark, cold, empty tent. My potion maker, made of shadows and glowing eyes loomed over a cold cauldron. Blood and sinew and bones were strewn across everywhere…and I was still holding the knife.

"How's that for a love potion, huh?" She cackled, a mouth full of swirling teeth glistening in the inky black. I trembled, my legs slipping backward. My bare feet squelched in the thick muck beneath me. "Go on! Give your *husband* that brew! I bet it fixes everything."

I shrieked as she bound over the cauldron. Whipping around on my wet noodle legs, I flew through the heavy fabric of her tent out into the crisp, night air. Under a full moon with no other stars in the sky, I came to a screeching halt. An abandoned clearing of broken metal and desolation. Not a single soul around. No honking horns or stench of popcorn or the whining of rides. Empty. Hollow. My heart thundered in my chest as I glanced from left to right. *I imagined all of it.*

"No…"

An old, decaying sign flickered like a lightbulb once in an archway. I stumbled toward it, like a moth to the flame. *Crack.* One of the lightbulbs in the arch shattered. Glass like snow fluttered around the arch. *Scraaaaaaatch.* My gaze followed the flashing arch downward until I spotted the cauldron. Cold but full. *Tap, tap.* My potion maker grinned over the top of the cauldron, her long shadowy fingers tapping against the lip of it. I followed her fingers down into its depth. Blood pooled like congealed tallow at the top of a soup pot. My possessed body reached into it, a vial for my potion in hand. I filled it with the viscous, ruby brew. As I pulled back, a face snapped up from the concoction. I shrieked, stumbling backward into the rigid legs of a dead Ferris wheel.

Pieces of Bradley floated to the top of the cauldron. Skin peeled away from the bones, his fingers were like popcorn, exploded around the knuckles and puffy. His arms were bruised with rings of purple and black as if they were squeezed tight between clamps. Everything but his head was ripped apart and chopped into pieces. My arms suddenly ached from the effort I spent carving him up, pretending like it wasn't him on her countertops. *Clinging to her illusions for as long as she let me, not ready to face the truth.* For some reason…I'd kept his head intact.

*So, he could see me as I left him there…lost in the middle of the woods.*

"Sweet thing."

I whirled around with a gasp at the feel of her breath on my ear.

My potion maker, now made of shadows and yellow eyes curled her fingers from the edge of the woods. It took all the might in my body to trample over the tall grass that brushed my arms. I trudged through muck and avoided broken pieces of a carnival long abandoned. When I stood at the edge of the woods, she slithered away. She turned into an old crone, using a massive wooden spoon as a walking stick. I followed her into the thick treeline. I barely caught it in the dark, but a cabin shifted on chicken legs, keeping nearby, never close enough I could study it. My potion maker slunk away, guiding me like a cold oil lantern through the night. With nothing but the moon at my back and my bare toes to keep me grounded, I wordlessly wound through the forest.

My attention fell to my hands, trembling as they unclenched. There was no pain or burnt flesh. No vial made of my *husband's* parts. It wasn't a potion at all but a flyer. Much like the map of the carnival and the flyer covered in glitter, a thick glossy paper I'd nearly punctured with my fingernails. I eased my grip inch by inch till I saw the missing poster in totality.

My face stared back at me. A sweet face. Chestnut hair, thick and wavy, went down to my lower back. Round cheeks and button nose, bright green eyes with freckles covering every inch of me. I wore a cream blouse tucked into the purple skirt I bought specifically to go to a Renaissance Festival with Elywin, Vince, and the others from the club. *My potion maker had been wearing my face all this time.*

Missing.

Stolen from her hospital bed. Suffers from amnesia. Was in a terrible car crash.

"He stole me," I breathed as the last piece of my memory returned. Bradley confronted me in front of that coffee shop on a snowy Wednesday after Elywin proposed. I ran, wearing nothing but heels and a little black dress. My car spun out on the road as I floored it away.

I didn't even realize he'd followed me until I looked up through my frosted, cracked windshield to see him tapping. *Are you all right? Baby! I'm so sorry! I'm gonna get you out.* But I screamed, thrashing in my damaged vehicle he ran off the road. *Tap, tap.* He told me to stop screaming.

*Scraaaatch.* I clawed against my window, desperately trying to get out. *Crunch.* Bradley stomped on the windshield as I thrashed about.

And finally, *crack*…I woke up in the hospital after that with no memory of the crash or my name. *And he'd always been so sweet and kind, no one suspected a thing.*

I dropped my missing person's flyer, looking up into flood lights that exploded in front of me. I tried to cover my face, but my bloodied hands caused me to freeze. His ring finger was caught on my sleeve, the golden band glistening in the headlights. Something called my name, but I could only hear her voice whispering in my ear. *There you go sweet thing, right where you belong.* My potion maker slunk away, leaving me at the edge of a road. The familiar scent of Pink Champagne brushed my nose first…then her face came into view.

"Annabell?" Elywin stared at me.

I was found.

# ABOUT THE AUTHOR

Lizzie Strong is a monster romance author. A Florida swamp gremlin masquerading as a human, she's a dog mom, a previous retail and restaurant manager, and a horror DM for Dumbasses and Dragons, a DnD podcast. She specializes in queer representation, specifically bi&pan representation, with a heavy splash of chaos. Best known for her kink friendly, shenanigans heavy, monster smut, she's also been an avid horror fan since the dawn of time. She has a love of eldritch horror and existential dread, and if it comes with ooze or tentacles? Sign her up. Most of Lizzie's work is on a spectrum from spooky scary to cute and cuddly. However, when she goes horror, it's heavy on the monster gore, eyeballs that don't belong, and that weird tingly feeling that runs up your spine. If you like that, check her out on all socials @Lizziestrongauthor. Or pick up a copy of *How to Marry a Lich*, her gothic monster romance that is for fans of Mary Shelley's *Frankenstein*, the *Addams Family*, and *Crimson Peak*.

When she's not writing she's devouring books, playing RPGs, or doing arts and crafts. Specifically anything that she can paint pink or put glitter on, much to the chagrin of her husband.

# THe RaGe of a Lioness

Fay Jekyll

*.MurdruM.*

*The traveling carnival prowls down,*
*through dying towns in Northern England.*
*In tow, a predator. A lone clown.*
*Trampling heathland asunder in its wake,*
*in the blackness of Hallow's Eve night,*
*canvas apparitions overtake.*
*Perched precariously on the fringe,*
*lies the ghost train, haunted by the clown,*
*with a wide and tormented faux grin.*
*"You're in my universe now, not yours,"*
*growls the clown, an unruly stranger,*
*in the desolate space of the moors.*
*After hours, against a dry-stone wall,*
*the strange, troubled clown vacantly stares,*
*and smoking, at the children he swears,*
*out of character.*
*In anonymity dressed as fun,*
*he could get away with anything,*
*with murder. Soon, the carnival's gone.*
*That monster, with a false painted smile,*
*could have possibly been anyone.*

In every town the American Carnival visited, it was a guarantee there would be at least one woman with a clown fetish; but one was all he needed for an evening.

"If you want to see a real freak show, take a look inside this tent," he growled softly into her ear, pulling her further onto his lap. She moaned and bucked forward to where the seams of his mismatched, garish trousers pitched upward. With one hand, he feverishly reached up her mini dress, grabbing the crease where the top of her thigh met her hipbone and with the other hooked hand, he reached behind her to pull her lace underwear down, and she allowed him to slide them off.

They lay discarded on the filthy ground of the big top, alongside her fishnet tights, which had been ripped apart seconds before in a passionate fever.

She stared eagerly and intently into his black eyes. Underneath layers of cracked white paint, shattered like a broken porcelain doll, were the shadows of a once handsome face, which she pressed to hers, smearing the false red grin over her mouth like a bloodied gash, and when she pulled away for air, she had the remnants of a twisted version imprinted on her own smile.

She moaned quietly again and put up no resistance when the clown took her against the bleachers, driving into her with strong, well-practiced thrusts, giving nothing away save the occasional guttural snarl that contorted his grimy face even more, though he buried his upturned nose feverishly into her slender neck, inhaling her scent of orange blossom and the taste of bitter perfume on her skin.

The fabric of his worn, tired uniform scratched against the cheap nylon imitation of her Halloween costume noisily, the sound of their intense fucking the only thing left to fill the empty void of the big top.

At last, in the bleak early hours of the frigid Halloween night and long since the carnival show closed its curtains, she screamed out in pleasure, loudly and carelessly, to the response of nothing but barking dogs from the depths of the caravan site hidden away behind the colorful carnival facade.

The clown, with his black, empty, and sharklike eyes, straightened out his red-tailed coat calmly, lighting up a squashed, hand-rolled cigarette which had been tucked up behind his right ear all that time from somewhere underneath his wig, and it emerged with a rehearsed flourish like a cheap coin trick.

She watched him awkwardly and redressed, clearing her throat as the sexual tension dissipated, fizzling into the cold harshness of reality that she was now alone, far from the twinkling streetlights of the quiet English town she called home, in the dead of Halloween night with a man whose true face she had never seen; a stormy face that evaded the subtlest of friendly gestures.

"I'm Rebecca, by the way."

The clown took a deep drag from the cigarette and inhaled it all the way down to the last half inch before flicking it with one hand haphazardly onto the straw-littered ground below, showing it the same disinterest that he gave her. It smoked momentarily, eliciting a raised eyebrow from the man, before promptly fizzling out.

"I don't care," he said, finally. With one hand, he reached into a deep pocket and pulled out a pack of stale tobacco and rolling papers. He lay one paper flat on his thigh, pinning it in place with the tip of the hook he had in place of a hand, and rolled himself another crude cigarette, Rebecca watching him intently all the while.

He gave her a cursory impatient glance out of the corner of his eye, and growled low and soft, with the lilt of a lingering American accent.

"What do you want now?"

"You were here last Halloween night, weren't you?"

"You've had your eye on me that long? I'm flattered," he grunted, sparking up the new cigarette, which was hanging downward from his gargantuan faux smile, with a matchstick that lit itself. "I'm Lots-O Laffs," he announced, spreading one hand dramatically across the empty space in the air as if performing. He brought it back down with a loud, harsh slap. "Or if you're feeling formal, Mr. Laughter."

She stared at him blankly, until he finally faced her, with an indifferent predatory gaze as if to punctuate the irony of his own given name. "That was a joke, love. Feel free to smile. I am a clown, after all."

"Were you here when…when that girl died? A year ago, to this very day, wasn't it?"

Lots-O froze, the cigarette losing its orange blaze. With little warning, he stood up and strode down the bleachers, each oversized yellow boot striking against the metal with alarming clangs.

Rebecca came to her senses and tottered after him, pulling at the back of his mismatched frock coat, refraining from grasping too tight onto the loose seams for fear that the ruffles and embellishments might come apart in her fingers.

"I'm sorry, it's just…Halloween means a lot to me these days," she explained and cast him a coy smile, now playing with the mesh of her own underskirt. "I like a good scare."

The clown cast a withering glance at her pale hand clinging to his shoulder with undisguised disdain. In the center of the circus ring, he turned slowly and mechanically toward Rebecca who trembled with a potent mixture of fear and anticipation as the demented figure towered a full two feet above and her stomach roiled from the tumultuous feelings she had toward his presence.

*Curiosity. Fear. Carnal attraction.*

"Halloween means a lot to you, does it?" he asked, cloyingly and unnervingly sweet.

She nodded tentatively, her brown hair tumbling forward despite how pleasantly it might have been styled earlier that day.

"Trick or treat?" he asked, his painted lips barely moving from under the bloody smile, like a ventriloquist.

"What?"

In his hand, Lots-O Laffs fanned out a peculiar deck of battered cards, each edged with a red border and with black, printed writing, barely legible through the unusual cursive font. They were completely unlike any playing card or tarot deck she had ever seen but were fanned out with the ease and the reverence of someone who was well practiced in their dark craft.

He held them up to her vertically, each aligned under the other and overlapping in a neat sequence. Four of the five cards read *treat,* and one card read *trick.* He gave enough time for her eyes to adjust to the flow of the flowery script.

"Do you fancy your odds, Rebecca?"

"Oh!" she smiled nervously. The clown fanned the cards back in with his left hand, and shuffled them deftly against his right wrist, the hook rigid and glinting under stage lights. He fanned them back out, this time face down; the backs decorated with garish demonic lions with forked tongues, their faces bloated and swollen, perpetually screaming.

She pointed at one, which he dutifully and deftly flipped with one spare finger.

"Trick!" she cried, with disappointment, following it up with a short laugh that echoed in the tent. "What are the odds?"

Lots-O Laffs didn't flinch, the outcome entirely as anticipated, but instead he placed two cards back in his cavernous trouser pocket and continued the tired act.

"Let's sway it to your favor then, shall we? Best out of three," he offered tantalizingly, once more displaying two *treat* cards to her and the one *trick*, before presenting them out again.

Somewhere in the distance, the carnival dogs barked once more, setting off the disturbed cries of a few wilder animals, who whooped and hollered accordingly, as if sensing some disquieting happenings.

"It's still a trick card!"

This time, he held just two cards to her, allowing her to watch intently, her focus on the two shuffling cards completely unbroken. He shuffled with a lazy speed, quietly confident. As soon as he halted, she pointed to a card, eagerly tapping at the back onto a grotesque lion.

"It's that one," she insisted. "It's dog-eared in the top corner," she pointed out smugly. The grin wiped off her face and slid eerily onto his as the card flipped over to produce another *trick*.

Beyond the tent, a monkey howled, striking the metal bars of its confinement and a wildcat began a rumbling cry of impatience.

"One more chance," he offered, staring down at her intensely. "One single card to choose from…trick or treat, Rebecca?"

He displayed the dog-eared card toward her, which clearly displayed *treat*, and she felt the rising frustration grow inside, bubbling up from her stomach and all the way through to her fingertips, which reached out as though an electric current were moving them toward the card; the demons on the back taunting her.

*Trick.*

"Fuck me," she gasped.

"That was the treat, love," he quipped, snatching the final card away from her grasp. She was distracted from her protest, jolting as the lion, now awake in the dead of night, roared impatiently. The clown stared intently through the tent flaps toward the sound. "Damned boy Joel is supposed to be keeping things quiet," he grumbled, scratching his ill-fitting wig with the tip of his hook.

"Can I ask…what happened to your hand?" Rebecca said tentatively, and with immediate regret as his eyes slid over to meet hers, brimming with thunder. "It's only that, I also know what it's like to be missing a part of yourself," she elucidated, but the words of empathy fell on deaf ears.

Lots-O Laffs, reeking a potent mixture of stale tobacco, unwashed laundry, and the sickly caramel popcorn, leered forward, his devilish eyes falling flat and predatory, like a shark once more.

"Maybe my family will be wondering where I am…" she began, trailing off as she stumbled backward, forced to walk as the clown stepped forward, each enlarged boot almost treading on her ballet flats, considering that perhaps she didn't need to see this evening all the way to the show's end; yet the tempting call of closure kept her under the clown's thrall.

He raised the hooked hand, glinting in the pale moonlight that pierced through the gap in the open tent.

"Heard the rumors, have you?" he said, so quietly it was almost a whisper, her hands feeling the cold tarpaulin stop her dead in place. He gently held a lock of her brown hair and let it slide over the hook, relishing as she turned her face away from his with disgust. "About my missing hand…" he began, sliding the curved hook down her neck and pressing it hard against her jugular, with a force that stole her breath. The sweet stench of caramel that had once seemed so alluring as it permeated the entire carnival overwhelmed her now. "You can't leave now, Rebecca. I've not shown you your trick, and…" he said, relieving the pressure from her neck at the first signs of feeble protest, "someone has to feed the lioness. Can you hear how she roars?" He cupped the hook to his ear, and the sound of screeching animals replied. He began to sway unnervingly as if dancing to a silent symphony.

"Come, Rebecca. Take my hand," he said, offering her his palm. "I'd rather give it to a pretty little woman than a savage beast, if I had the choice again." He flashed her a wide, performative smile, paint flaking around the mouth, which sent crusted pieces scattering to the floor like a skin disease. "Let me show you around."

She didn't move.

"I thought you liked a good scare on Halloween," he pouted, down-turning the entire bloody gash of the faux smile into a harrowing frown, ever holding a hand out, steady as a statue.

As soon as her wary palm met his, he clamped down with a brute force that crushed her fingers, eliminating any ideas of affection, and dragged her along with a speed that nearly sent her tumbling, had he not intertwined his arm so tightly around hers, supporting her body weight as they strode outside; him setting the pace with enormous footsteps.

Outside, in the frozen fall air, coldness blasted its way under her skin, raising every hair and goose-pimple. The overbearing wooden sign for the American Carnival creaked and groaned behind them, and the big top itself perched on the precipice of the valley, having appeared overnight like a fever dream as it did every year; an eyesore on the otherwise placid landscape, squashing down the moorland scrub and compressing the mud.

In the valley below, streetlights twinkled onwards in the sleepy English village, trick or treaters long since gorged on chocolate, having poisoned their little bodies with sugar in a mad crash.

The world slept while the circus clown whirled on in his aimless frenzy.

He marched her roughly by the arm, stopping her dead at the entrance to the ghost train and let her go by the very start of the track, with its ghoulish Halloween overlay; skeletons swinging by the neck from rusted metal beams and the occasional tinny recorded scream echoing from within the glorified shipping container.

Everything, even in the height of the town's presence, gave off a distinctly undisguisable aura of dereliction, like touching the rides alone would require a tetanus shot. The creeping orange rust smelled of forgotten pennies, soaked in chlorinated water.

"Wait here," the clown commanded, throwing her arm down carelessly and stomping behind the metal unit. After a few seconds, as she stood alone in the howling wind rolling down off the moors, the ride once more became possessed by the spark of electricity, the loud clang of something mechanical switching on. Every metal bolt and joint groaned with all the effort of waking the dead, and an empty cart rumbled forward, a skeletal figure protruding from the front with an outstretched hand beckoned her to climb inside like Charon, the ferryman of the underworld.

She gave a longing glance to the sleepy town in the valley below, thinking how one year ago, that was her; blissful and unaware of the American Carnival that had appeared to plague them all.

The clown had vanished from sight. She could run away, if she wanted to. It was without doubt she knew the clown had given her the chance.

The rumbling roar of the lion, even closer now, served a reminder of why she had come here in the first place.

"I'll play your game for now, Lots-O Laffs," she mumbled, turning her back to the peace of the world under the precipice, and climbing up the steep metal steps to take the bony hand of the grinning skeleton, steadying herself as she clambered inside the tiny cart. The same as she had done hours before to kill some time before the real show started. "It won't be long."

With a fierce shudder, the cart set about its prescribed path on the tracks, into the darkness and cacophony of screaming ghouls, moaning zombies and the swinging of axes followed by a sickening splash of fake blood that accompanied the cheap visual jump-scares; latex demonic masks on poles jumping outwards from behind cinder block gravestones. Each themed room was divided by black plastic curtains that dragged across her face, cold and heavy with a damp sheen of condensation from the plummeting temperature.

The last room she reached had been of particular interest. As the train shuddered through it, she felt sinking disappointment that, of course, the live actors wrenching strings of innards from each other's abdomens had now gone and were asleep somewhere in the caravans tucked away from view, as oblivious to Lots-O's games in the dead of night as the quiet town was to hers.

The room was set out like a butcher's shop, where a man in a white, bloodied uniform swung a butcher's cleaver to the pre-recorded sound of metal hitting wood, the audio of which played on regardless of the absence of murderous cannibals.

Fake cuts of ambiguous meat hung from the walls, dripping crimson dyed sugar water, and assorted chains and handcuffs rattled as the carriage trundled by.

She reached for them on the wall, feeling the cold metal on her fingers with the brief surprise that something in here was real, and pulled a pair of handcuffs from the weak zip-tie that served as a loose preventive measure from would-be thieves on their exit.

They clattered noisily to the bottom of the carriage when the cart ground to an immediate halt, the screeching of metal straining her ears painfully. The room fell into blackness as the power cut out completely, with only a slither of moonlight sneaking in from the exit to the outside world.

Even that dissipated after mere seconds of teasing.

The whistling of her own quickening breath and the smell of dingy plastic kept her company as she waited, waited for anything to happen. It was silent, dark, and bitterly cold.

"Fuck this," she mumbled, reaching blindly forward to hoist herself up and out of the carriage. Two steps, and she could be outside.

"Ladies and gentlemen…well, just lady," a voice boomed, stopping her in her tracks, knees still bent, intending to move upward and creaking in frustration at their lost momentum. "Please keep all hands, arms, feet, and legs inside the vehicle at all times," Lots-O's soft American accent twanged over the grainy speaker.

Tentatively, she sat back down, and as soon as the backs of her thighs touched metal, a fearsome metallic groan cut through the silence, followed by a sickening free fall into darkness below, which churned her stomach violently and shook her spine with a shooting pain on immediate impact with the hidden lower deck. She was spared only a fleeting glance upward to piece together what happened, before the track above closed up, sealing her inside the belly of the crypt-like dungeon.

The carnival freaks had built a hidden level underneath the upper platform of the ghost train, and in the dim, she could just make out the indent of the metal staircase. She'd walked into this trap so willingly, meaning that the chamber's only exit was above her head.

"Lots-O Laffs?" she called into the darkness. The sound of her own pathetic, whining voice crying that *stupid* name stopped short, muffled by something.

With a loud clunk, the power returned, bringing with it cold, burning white light that lingered in her retinas and a manic recorded laughter. Rebecca's own reflection stared back at her a thousand times over and over again in the hidden hall of mirrors.

In her nylon clown mini dress, her own makeup *and* Lots-O's smeared across her skin like a rash. While shielding her eyes from the bright lights, she realized then quite how easy it was to look vulnerable.

She brought the hand shielding her eyes to her mouth in a pitiful attempt to fix some smearing but gasped violently when a shadow appeared behind her with a grim smile she'd begun to know so well.

"Lots-O?"

Rebecca whipped around, faced only by another, jagged mirror.

Clambering out of the cart, she tentatively leaned around the mirror that had been behind her, resting a hand on the corner. The pressure moved the panel; in fact, one touch seemed to send them all spinning, in an endless reflective dance, some showing a thousand copies of her shivering, frightened body, some, the flash of a devilish grin and dark eyes, enlarged and distorted.

In tight circles she spun, daring not to breathe as the mirrors came to a halt. They seemed closer to her somehow, brought inwards in a claustrophobic, endless prison.

A hooked hand raised above her head to the chorus of that dreadful looped laughter and swung down, causing her to flinch and shield her eyes desperately once more, but the attack came from behind, and her opening eyes caught the fleeting retreat of a hook where pressure had scraped across her jugular, leaving a neat, wet trail of scarlet blooming down her neck. The forced adrenaline stole away the pain.

This time, soft, dark laughter broke the loop of the ghost train's record.

"Trick or treat, Rebecca. Do you really think I'd give you a choice?"

Rebecca furiously screwed her eyes shut, blocking out the thousand frightened versions of herself to follow the sound of the American's taunting voice. It was no good; the mirrors incessantly barred a clear path to her escape.

The clown presented her a new image in the mirrors, the dog-eared *treat* card with its unusual, alien font was now enlarged and surrounded her from every angle.

*Treat, treat, treat, treat, treat, treat*, in an endless succession.

"Do you know what an ambigram is?" he asked curiously.

Rebecca shook her head, not knowing if he could actually see her response. "No," she admitted aloud.

"An ambigram is a word written out in such a way that it can read differently depending on your perspective," he explained, the *treat* card still between his fingers, enlarged and illuminated, but from where exactly, she was helpless to know. "This one is a rotational ambigram. What do you think will happen when I flip it upside down?"

With that question, he began to turn the *treat* card; not from face up to face down, but by a hundred and eighty degrees, slowly and deliberately so that the unusual font transformed before her very eyes, changing to read *trick* in the same strange calligraphy.

She cursed herself for engaging and tilting her head sideways to check it read both simultaneously.

"They all read *treat* and they all read *trick*. It's a simple matter of perspective." He held the deck of five up, rotating each deftly, so that the words trick and treat cartwheeled around her, dizzying and inducing sickening vertigo.

"You tricked me," she shouted at the mirrors. Her outburst fell alarmingly short, muffled by the panes that ran the length of the low ceiling to the trailer floor.

"Happy fucking Halloween, Rebecca."

"Bloody hell, I wanted you to show me lions or something, not *this*," she cried, a flailing hand smacking a pane, sending them careening once more and all the mirrors crunched closer inwards, her pathetic whimper lost in the carnival din.

The clown spoke again, thoughtfully and deliberately...almost kindly, if it wasn't for the menacing black eyes that peered out at her from under heavy eyelashes, lost inside the reflections.

"Do you really think you're trapped Rebecca, or is it a forced perspective?"

Rebecca stopped in her tracks, alarmed by the question. It took her a while, and the tips of her fingers had begun to whiten with her stillness and the cold that had seeped into the dungeon of the ghost train, but she got it eventually, tentatively approaching a pane of glass to examine the edges.

She took a deep breath in, crossed her skinny arms over her face, ignoring the twang in her right elbow where Lots-O had grasped it so firmly, and she ran.

The boards of foam hurt when they smacked her, and they bounced indifferently right back up again, their reflective backing glinting menacingly and angrily as movement rippled the surfaces, but even so, the illusion of the hall of mirrors fell down as dominoes would.

She stopped only when a strong hand caught her on the collarbone, pushing her momentarily forward to stop the momentum, then pulled her tight, close enough to smell the caramel popcorn on his skin.

"Not glass," she confirmed with a whisper, staring at the sea of flat black foam in the otherwise empty chamber, each with a reflective surface that faced inwards in a tight circle; reflections she could no longer see from this side.

"Another perspective," the clown said gruffly, directly over her shoulder, the warmth of his body pressed against her back oddly comforting. She despised herself for it and pushed him off.

He coughed sharply once as he inhaled the smoke of yet another cigarette which seemingly appeared of its own accord, and behind her, the chilling draft of an open hatch beckoned her outside. "Now, what was that you said about seeing some animals?"

The crunching of frost on the trampled earth was grounding, and what once had seemed so intense dissolved into reality. Behind her, the back of the ghost train was simply a derelict trailer, transported from town to town with sheer willpower by the rugged band of slumbering carnival freaks, who unlike Lots-O, sought rest on this cursed night.

Lots-O Laffs pressed onwards silently and brooding, darkness encompassing him save for the circle of illuminated orange visible through descending fog on the hillside, transforming his outline to that of a spectre, the mere ghost of a man.

He coughed loudly as the last of the cigarette burned down, and in the following silence there was the wordless expectation that she would follow the disappearing frock coat, its garish colors and mismatched patterns sapped of their fun by England's bleak moorland countryside.

Rebecca's ballet flats grew damp as they moved to the tent, carrying her forward of their own accord as if possessed; roars of big cats, the howling of angry monkeys shaking their fists against bars, and the guttural moan of something inhuman and large emanated outwards. The Amazonian boa constrictor and the venomous vipers, she considered, would not make a sound. Somehow that thought brought no comfort.

Hit immediately by the stench of wet fur and dung once inside the latest trap, the air was noticeably warmer, closed in and stifled, with only a few unseen lights smothered by orange overlays, giving the whole room a low amber haze, to which she lost the trail of Lots-O's cigarette.

The edges of the tent were fringed with enormous square cages, stacked up and covered over with black cloth, but the calls of animals rang on, impervious to the attempts made to silence them.

The groaning of hinges turning forced Rebecca to whip around, gasping as straw fluttered upward to the empty space where a creature had run out behind her.

A loud, singular clunk of a spotlight turning on immediately blinded her efforts to find the thing she was let loose with, and the sudden heat brought fiery pins and needles to her frozen hands.

A lion roared. The padding of heavy feet slammed on the ground, toward its blinded prey. She fumbled backward, cornered by the empty black crate.

"I told you, Rebecca. It's time to feed the lions," Lots-O said slowly, appearing in front of her with the silhouette of his head blocking the light from above, casting his face entirely into one black, cavernous shadow. "Do you know how much they enjoy the taste of human flesh?" he asked, holding up the hooked hand to the spotlight.

For the last time that she would allow, his hand grasped her wrist to draw her in closer. She complied, drawing near enough to the animalistic man that she could feel everything he radiated; the heat of his skin, which was the burn of the most rudimentary and crude form of basic passion. He burned so hot and yet with no warmth, nothing of humanity left.

"I know," she said, the fear in her body language dissipating, her shoulders dropping low, her chin lifting up so she could gaze into the featureless mass of his face.

There was enough stony hardness in her eyes to give the clown a start, his hesitation just long enough to do what she needed to, what she had planned to do for so long; one link of the handcuff she rasped quickly around the empty cage bars and another to the hand that still had purchase on her skin.

The clown slowly and calmly assessed the unfolding situation, poking pointlessly at the locked handcuffs with his hooked hand.

"That's a low blow," he mumbled, gazing curiously at her, unblinking with an unsettling tilt to his head. He patiently waited for an explanation, understanding at once the turning of the tables. "Is the trick on me, now?" Lots-O asked, in that unnatural slow way, ever indifferent and unfeeling, save for the darkness that bubbled just under the surface of his painted illusion.

Rebecca's body shook from the anticipation, but she steadied herself with a breath and the mental rehearsal of a year-long plan.

"Halloween night, one year ago to this day. A traveling carnival came to town," she began, pacing in front of Lots-O Laffs, tauntingly out of reach, and allowing the spotlight to slide across his eyes as she turned her own back to the heat. "A girl died. Eighteen years old. They say," she paused, reining in the bubbling anger, "they say she was found ravaged apart. They say, a man with a penchant for feeding lions human remains, even sacrificing his own flesh to sedate their appetite, roams freely town to town, taking any victim naïve enough to follow—banned from the states for breeding deranged big cats."

She let the statement ring clear in the tent, pausing for the lions to roar with impatience and hunger.

"That girl, she was my sister." This time, Rebecca didn't hold back, her proximity to the hooked hand be damned, and spat right in his face, foam brimming at her mouth as she seethed with anger. "She was my fucking sister and I know what you did to her," she screamed in his face. "I knew I had to get you alone, and I knew I had to make you suffer."

Her voice carried loud enough that even the straw and heavy cages could not swallow the echo, but the cathartic clearing that should have been brought by the confrontation of her sister's murderer was snatched away instantly.

The clown simply ogled at her, slack jawed, with one painted eyebrow raised questioningly. Then, he laughed.

"Are you fucking kidding me?" The clown laughed once more, and then, let out a stream of strangled deranged giggles of disbelief. "That's a story we tell to trick or treaters and naughty children." The clown put on a fake pout and a babyish voice. "Misbehave, and the big bad clown will feed you to the big bad lion," he mocked, and resumed his normal, dead tone, leaning back coolly against the bars to which he was still imprisoned. "Does wonders for PR," he explained with a nonchalant sniff. The sniff turned into another bout of a hacking cough.

It was Rebecca's turn to stare disbelievingly. Her eyes slid warily over the animals hidden away by the black cloth, but through all the questions that flooded her mind, which had been so hellbent on revenge, she could not bring herself to speak.

"The lions are not *real*, they're fucking costumes," he cried, nodding to the cages, cast in shadows by thick black cloth. "Go look!" he insisted, nodding toward them with raised eyebrows of avid encouragement.

Rebecca approached the cages dubiously, the sounds of clamoring circus animals ringing loud; but not from within. The noise just floated around, dead in the air.

*Tinny and grainy. A bad recording.*

She pulled back the heavy black cloth and immediately hurtled three strides back when the enormous sleeping face of a lion had its jaws open wide through the bars.

But the jaws never snapped and the eyes were unblinking. The thick mane of hair was hollowed out, flayed from its weighty skull and leaving nothing behind but the coarse shell of a once-proud beast.

Her hand trembled, refusing her mental command to steady as she tried the padlock, which slid redundantly to the ground. The cage door swung open with a slow, ominous creak, but nothing took the chance to jump outwards.

"It's old taxidermy," Lots-O Laffs shouted, his upturned nose snarling.

"But…but your hand. You said the lions took your hand!" she insisted, rooting through the costumes frantically for signs of living beasts.

"Why should I have to answer your nosy fucking questions? It's none of your damn business how I lost my hand!" he yelled, more ferociously than any lion might, and he strained mightily against the bars, so much that she was suddenly afraid he might be enraged enough to bend them. The clown ceased struggling to hack up something, with a cough so foul that Rebecca feared she'd witness a lung evacuating.

With the strain, the clown's nose began to bleed, a deep viscous crimson that pooled on the straw-littered ground. "Fucking hell, what's happening to me?"

He looked up at her with accusatory and now bloodshot eyes. "What did you do?" he hissed.

"I just wanted to know what happened to my sister. She was my other half—my world," Rebecca began, pacing toward the spot where his legs had buckled out from beneath him and he had begun to wheeze on the ground. She absentmindedly dragged the lion head behind her, its meaty tongue lolling out, picking up bits of grime as it trailed along.

Lots-O laughed again, high pitched like escaping wind, or more realistically, a last gasp for breath. He unbuttoned his tartan shirt as his breath began to shorten and the blue veins in his neck stood out. With his hook, he slid off the bald cap with fuzzy hair at either side, exposing his real, damp black tresses underneath, lined by a crest of fresh pink skin where the bald cap had peeled from his forehead.

"Your sister," he said through catching another stolen breath that bubbled with liquid, "The girl with the blonde pigtails in the clown dress."

"So, you did know her! You did kill her!" Rebecca accused feverishly.

"I didn't fucking kill her."

"Well, you tried to cover it up," she said, clutching at straws.

The clown grinned wide and sarcastically, before sucking his cheeks in with anger.

"That was the local police. How do you think it looks for your failing, miserable little town in the arse-end of nowhere, when the only fun thing that ever happens gets spoiled by a drunk teenager falling off a cliff? Not good for the locals, not good for our business." He hawked and spat out a fresh, phlegmy wad of blood.

All the gusto of rage collapsed from Rebecca's body in a tidal wave, replaced by a sickening, creeping dread that scalded her cheeks and flooded her veins, as suffocating as desire and burning twice as hot.

"The police said that only one local man tried to resuscitate her, even though her body was mangled...shredded beyond recognition for the most part...other parts still missing..." she mumbled, her eyes glassy and vacant.

"Yes, me! Do you think I fucking *live* in this outfit?" he said, angrily scrubbing off the rest of his white and red clown face with his sleeve, the thick sheen of sweat having developed on his feverish skin taking care of most of it. His pink face, though contorted with anger and the chain-smoking of cigarettes, was alarmingly charming and youthful. "I *am* bloody local you idiot, I'm not from the USA," he said, dropping the breezy American lull and donning a natural, flat-vowelled Northern English accent. "I was born in Manchester."

"You…you tried to save her? But you're a horrible person!"

"I guess that's just a matter of perspective," he said with a twisted, sarcastic sneer. "You try watching a kid die, see how nice you feel like being on the anniversary of her death."

The clown wheezed heavily, his pink face taking on a cherry hue as he collapsed to the ground, his one hand held up awkwardly and bent by the restraint.

"What's happening to me?" he begged, a stream of tears forcing black contacts out of his blue, bloodshot eyes.

"I'm sorry," Rebecca began, kneeling by his side on the hard ground. Hot, heavy tears poured down her own face as she took his hooked hand between her own, the obviousness of the costume apparent; the metal tip as blunt as a coat hanger and dipped in crusty red food coloring.

"I'm so sorry," she repeated, cradling the clown's head as he asphyxiated, his veins exploding and his nose pouring out one last torrent of hot blood before his eyes stared up vacantly to the canopy of the circus tent. "I was so *sure* you killed her," she confided to the dead body. "So, I put something in the caramel popcorn."

There was supposed to be relief, empowerment even. That was how she had pictured this moment for a whole year, with the vision of justice so strong in her mind, but now the walls built by the narrative in her head crumbled down into ruins. Instead, guilt sank in her stomach like a stone while grief gripped her by the throat and hot tears burned her cheeks.

She placed the hand that had cradled his head where her tears had fallen on the man's chest, over an unbeating heart.

He was still warm, but as murder swiftly stole his lifeforce, his fingers blanched and blued under the grubby fingernails.

A dog barked again. More accurately, it howled longingly, sensing the truth as only animals could.

Suddenly, there was a chorus of canine mourners, snatching away the seconds of self-pity.

The dogs already knew there was a death in the family, and what was it the clown had said?

There had been a boy, Joel, who was to keep them quiet.

The chorus returned to a solo act, then diminished into a whimper, fading to nothing but the wind whistling through the tent flaps, which provided a pathetic barrier between prying eyes and her crime.

"Shit," she whispered. "Shit, shit, shit."

The hot air of her breath hit the frigid stillness and condensation rose in a white cloud, like a ghost lingering over the obtrusive corpse.

Rebecca cursed herself. Through the whole plan, even if it had been a successful one, she'd failed to consider how to cover the murder up.

Frantically, she patted down the nylon of her Halloween costume, searching for anything of use, but there was only a singular empty vial of a toxic black market concoction in the lining of her bra, which had been emptied mere minutes before her abhorrent weakness led to Lots-O's hand wandering there.

There was nothing left but the unpleasant affair of rooting through the dead man's belongings. In his pocket alongside five cards she knew so well, there was the packet of stale tobacco and a lighter which she fumbled with as the sound of someone else skulking around in the night grew ever more obvious. A caravan door creaked open and slammed shut from behind the frozen Tilt-A-Whirl. The hazy wide beam of a flashlight aimed carelessly flit around like a searchlight, glowing red on the tent fabric.

Rebecca rose to her numbed feet and spun in a tight circle, casting her eyes over the unusual carnival paraphernalia until she found what she was looking for, the box she had seen in one of the carnival freak's acts. The firebreather had left it in a gaudy box lined with orange flames, a tank of liquid paraffin, which she poured over the clown, and as the wet fabric clung to his skin, the outline of his oversized costume became unbearably human in form.

Hastily, she draped the thick lion skin over his body and the man, dressed as a clown, became the beast. Guilt ravaged her as she considered with a heavy conscience that this was the only funeral rite she could offer.

Were there footsteps closer, or was it her mind? Rebecca fought the emotions, which threatened to seize control, and held the dog-eared trick or treat card in one hand and the lighter in the other.

*Treat*, it read. At the last second, she flipped it to light the opposite corner and admired the single flame, which licked upward eagerly; one last *trick*.

"Perspective really is a funny thing, isn't it?" she whispered, holding the smoldering card to the lion skin.

How dry the mane was, baked by an ancient African sun and fried from years of neglect. It sparked up with the offensive stench of burning hair, and not a second too soon. She squeezed herself through the gap where the tent fabric spread taut parallel to the frozen earth.

"Lots-O, are you in there? I can see smoke, man. We've asked you a million times not to light up *inside* the…oh fuck, fire!" Joel screamed. "There's a fire in here! Lots-O, where in hell are you?"

As Rebecca continued her flight down the cliffside away from the fire that had begun to ravage the landscape, the screams followed.

The vengeful lioness fled into the night with the big top to her back, while the sleepy village below awoke to one last Halloween trick. Each tent canopy took its turn to catch the flames Rebecca had ignited, and now the landscape was alight in a blazing funeral pyre for the dead clown, the ghost of whom would haunt her mind she was sure, as eternally as the memory of her dead sister.

# ABOUT THE AUTHOR

*Fay is a psychological thriller author, currently working on her debut novel. Her plots involve magic, murder and probably something else beginning with 'M' to make this sentence flow. She enjoys nothing more than a humorous or sinister twist. Hailing from Yorkshire, England, she has a strong sense of Northern pride which bleeds into the landscape of her stories. Fay enjoys countryside walks, winding up her pet cat and writing in third person.*

*For updates on upcoming projects, follow Fay on Instagram (@fayeliz).*

# COLD Seafoam

Nico Silver

*Carnivals and circuses are liminal spaces. They exist outside of normal life, in a sort of in-between place that isn't really here or elsewhere. They are, therefore, the perfect locations for supernatural creatures to mix with mundane human life and the perfect places for real magic to happen unnoticed. But being liminal spaces where the uncanny goes unrecognized also means carnivals are places where horrors can happen without consequence, where afterward anyone witnessing them will think it was all part of the illusion. Are you sure the mermaid you saw was only a gaff? Are you sure the screaming was only the faint-hearted having a fun scare in a safe space? What better place to set in motion a revolt of the strange against the ordinary? What better place for a supernatural creature to take revenge on the human who wronged them?*

T he first few steps on land were not, as I had been told, like walking on knife blades. That would have been easier. Cuts I could bear.

Instead, it was as if I had pressed the soles of my feet to the edge of a volcanic vent. Burning to the point that I was convinced my skin would be blistered, cracked, and blackened, but I looked, and I was unmarked and whole, my ridiculous pink toes still soft and intact.

A human might have said it was like walking on coals, and my sister and I had listened to many a human over the long years of our existences. Walking on coals, I understood, was possible to do without pain as long as you didn't stop moving, and I didn't plan to loiter on dry land. I had a task to perform, a sister to rescue, and then I would be done with the open air for good.

I looked back to the sea, to where I hoped my other sisters, my aunts and cousins, might be watching, to see me off, but the swells were empty of anything but seafoam. I was on my own, disowned for what I had done as my youngest sister had been disowned before me. Only we had very different purposes, my sister and I, and I hoped I would be redeemed when I brought her safe back to the ocean.

I felt eyes on me, against the naked pink of my skin, the dark of my hair. There. Down the beach, a wolf. A coastal wolf, foraging for fish and crabs and other delicacies among the tide-strewn kelp and the shallow pools. She met my eyes and I saw the more-than-canine intelligence there. Not a mortal wolf, but a wolf woman, what a human might call a werewolf. She didn't approach, only watched to see what I would do. It's not every day a siren sheds her tail to walk out of the sea, and for it to happen twice in a lifetime was a strange thing, indeed.

I straightened my spine and took another step that almost sent me back to the waves, to the cool, safe haven of the green deeps, the kelp forest, the sea. *Keep moving*, I reminded myself, and I took another step and another, and while I can't say the burning lessened, it became more familiar and easier to bear if I kept on taking one step after another after another.

The wolf watched me as I picked my way up the barnacled cobbles, over the tideline of seaweed and stranded water creatures, to the jagged rocks, and finally to where the trees swept their branches down to the edge of the shore. For a long moment, I couldn't see a way in, and I stood with burning feet and the prickle of a wolf's eyes watching me, but then I saw a thin line of dark earth and moss that might be a trail. It was at least a way into the forest and out of the glaring sun.

I walked between branches of fir that smelled sweet and sharp in the summer's heat, stepped and pushed and clambered my way through fallen logs and thick green salal leaves, berries beginning to swell and darken on the ends of the stems. I did not stop to taste them, but kept moving. Bare in the forest shadow, I knew my first task was to find clothes. Humans did not wander the dry world naked.

My sister, when she bargained away her voice and walked on two thin legs for the first time, found a pair of humans camping in a tent and stole clothes from them. She came back to the shore to show me, twirled around on the rocks to display the garments that covered her legs, ankle to hip, and her upper body, torso to neck, but left her elegant arms free. I thought she looked ridiculous and let her know. She stuck her tongue out at me.

She looked human, except for the way she walked, placing each foot with care, as though treading an ancient and particular dance like the selkies did some full moons when they put off their sealskins for human shapes.

Then she smiled at me, kissed my forehead, and left to find the human man we had spent that spring watching, whom she had even dared to speak to, to fall in love with (if a feeling so new could even be called love). He had thought she was human and just didn't feel like coming in from her swim yet. Now she looked human. She looked like the young woman he had thought her to be. That we had thought he thought her to be.

It was the selkies who told me, months later, that her human had known all along what she was, that he had lured her from the sea not to love her, but to keep her, to return her to her oceanic shape and make money from exhibiting her to his fellow land-dwellers. The selkies knew because he had stolen one of their skins and kept one of *their* sisters prisoner, too.

But even the selkies didn't appear to see me off as I stepped burning onto the shore that day. Only one lone wolf-woman who must have had reasons of her own to watch a siren leave home to look for a circus sideshow.

The effort of continuing to move through the forest despite the burning in my feet took all my concentration for a length of time I had no way to measure save by the passing of the morning into afternoon and then evening. It was difficult to judge how far the day had advanced under the trees. It seemed an eternal twilight, and I felt closed in and exposed at the same time. I was used to water cradling me all around, but also the absence of walls. This was like being surrounded by a broken palisade that could not protect.

Eventually, a darkness not so unlike that of the ocean depths took over and I stopped. I had not thought to miss my siren's deep-sea senses on land, but my now-human eyes showed me nothing. I began to stumble. Stumbling hurt more than standing still, so I stopped and felt around for a log to sit on. Taking my weight off my soft pink human appendages eased the burning to something that felt more like the aftermath of a terrible sunburn than the torch-flame of an undersea volcano.

My ears had never been as keen as my other senses, at least not in the open air, unassisted by the carrying qualities of water, but I still heard her coming. And smelled her, damp fur and salt and fish. The wolf sat on a fallen tree only a few feet away. I could feel her there, wondered if she could see any better than I could, or if she had other senses like those I had bargained away, ones that worked better than mine in the deep forest.

I felt a shift in the night, as if something changed, and when she spoke, I realized she had put off her wolf shape and would now have looked as human as I did, if I had been able to see her.

"You should keep moving."

I didn't answer. I could sing, as all sirens can, and I could make the sounds that make up siren speech, but it had been years, decades, since I had spoken in any human language. My little sister was always the one who spoke to humans, when we dared approach them in spite of our family's warnings. I was always a listener. How different things were now.

"There are those in the forest that won't take kindly to you being here," she said.

Finally I drew in a deliberate slow breath and pushed it out through my throat. I had not traded away my voice, as my sister had. I had thought I might need it on dry land. I wondered if I had been wrong. "Like you?" I said, and my voice sounded rusty, unused, ugly.

I heard her make a sound like soft laughter. "I don't belong here any more than you do," she said. "My forest cousins would call me trespasser, too."

"You're a wolf, though," I said. "A wolf belongs in the forest. I belong in the sea." I thought about standing up, continuing on, but the respite from pain kept me seated on the cool mossy log. I wanted to curl up and sleep, but didn't dare. Not with the wolf here, not in this place. Not until I carried my little sister home.

"I'm a *coastal* wolf," she said. "I've lived on the shores of the sea since I was whelped and will do so until I pass into the next world."

"And yet you're here, in the forest, now."

"With you."

"Does that change things?"

"You don't remember," she said, her voice dropping almost to a whisper.

"I forget many things," I said. "Things I don't need to remember. Things that would burden me in the day to day. I've lived a very long time."

She shifted position on her tree. "We were together once," she said. "One summer. You would come into the shallows and I would wade out. We hunted seals and fished for salmon and once we caught a cormorant, but it didn't taste very good. We were together until your sisters came and said it wasn't proper for a siren to consort with a wolf. Until my pack came and said I must choose you or them, only they didn't really give me a choice."

"Then that's why I don't remember," I said. "My sisters decided it would be better to forget." My sisters' rules had driven the youngest of us away, as much as love had called her. My sisters would have had me forget, to pretend all was as it should be.

"I don't have that ability," she said. "And I missed you. And my pack is gone, hunted too close to human houses, poisoned and skinned and driven away to the forest where our cousins took them in or finished them off. I don't know."

"Why wait till now to show yourself again?"

"You were always with your sister," she said. "And watching that human. The one who stole the selkie's skin and took her away to be a sideshow attraction."

She spoke the human words with such familiarity that I wondered if she, too, had spent hours and days and decades watching and listening to the two-legged folk who sought to destroy us.

"They stole my sister, too."

She shifted position on the tree again. "They have done a lot of things," she said. "Poisoned the river, taken all the fish, trapped and skinned and eaten us and tainted every place we live."

"I'm going to get her back," I said.

"I'm going to kill them," she said.

I was silent a long moment, thinking. A siren is a creature that lives in the moment, not one that plans, but I tried to make my thoughts fit into ordered rows, to put them in a shape that might tell me the best way to continue. *Keep moving.*

"Can you find your way through this forest?" I finally said. "Can you find us human clothes and find our way to this sideshow place where my sister and the selkie are captive?"

"I can," she said. "If my cousins will let us pass."

And then I heard the shifting of bodies in the trees all around us, caught the scent of damp fur and spruce needles and blood. Wolves.

"Are they mortal wolves?" I said. I could kill mortal wolves if I had to. Maybe. Maybe my bargain had taken my inhuman reflexes as it had taken my inhuman senses.

"Some of them."

I raised my voice, though I had no doubt they could have heard me even if I whispered. "Will you let us pass?" I said.

"Why should we?" Came the answer, a rough male voice, unused, I think, to speaking human words.

"I'm a cousin," said my coastal wolf woman.

"And a trespasser."

"We're only passing through."

"What for? Go back to your sea."

"To kill the humans," my wolf said, just as I said, "To find my sister."

There was silence. Or not silence, but a pause in speaking filled with sounds of breathing, of furry bodies shifting closer and farther from each other as the forest wolves communicated in some way I could not understand. I wondered if the coastal wolf could.

Finally, "Go," the forest wolf said. "Go and keep moving. If you must return to the sea later, do it by some other route." And then the wolves were gone, melted back into the trees without my ever having seen them.

"I hoped my brothers and sisters found refuge here," the coastal wolf said. "Now I know they did not."

"They might live," I said, because I felt pity for her. Because I know I would be filled with sorrow if I learned my family had been wiped out by another clan of sirens, or by anybody.

"Perhaps," she said. "But I will still kill the humans."

"Then take me to where I can find some clothes, and take me to the human circus and I will help you."

I felt her hand on my arm then and hadn't even heard her move. Just a brief touch, a brush of fingers, but it stirred up a memory from deep down in the sediment where I had buried it. She had brown hair that glowed almost gold in the sun, and dark brown eyes with flecks of green. Her human skin was the red-brown of old arbutus bark and her kisses tasted of salt and periwinkles and desire.

"I remember you," I said, softly. She must have heard but she said nothing in reply.

"Can you follow without holding my hand?" she asked.

"Yes." Though I wasn't sure I could.

"Then come." But instead of walking away, she grasped my fingers in hers and led me into the darker dark.

And I remembered. By her touch, I remembered.

The first time, I had been sunning myself on a rock, combing my hair with my fingers, and dangling my tail into a deep, cool tidepool. My youngest sister had gone to follow a boat, to watch the human men pull more fish than they needed out of the sea.

I felt someone watching and ignored it. There were no humans here, not today, only me and the shorebirds and a trio of wolves hunting in the tidepools. I began to sing softly, a lullaby my mother sang to me when I had nightmares of teeth and blood. Singing was one of the only kindnesses we sirens had. Two of the wolves retreated down the shore, out of sight.

One came closer.

She sat and watched me and then, as I ended my song, she put on human shape. She was lean and muscular, her skin smooth save for a scar on one hip. Her hair was shaggy and caught the light in a way I found strangely appealing, and her eyes were deep and dark and held secrets I found myself wanting to explore.

She came closer, head cocked, like I fascinated and frightened her. I wondered what wolf tasted like.

I didn't move as she got closer and closer, as she reached out a hand to touch my hair, her fingers gentle on the algae-green strands. And then I took her, pulled her into the deep tidepool I had been dangling my tail in, and pinned her under me at the bottom. I smiled, watching her eyes, waiting for her to drown. Her brown eyes were flecked with green and though she was afraid, she just looked back at me and didn't struggle.

Did she not care about drowning?

I let her go and she surfaced, and smiled, and pressed her mouth to mine and I didn't stop her. Not even when she stroked both hands over my chest to my hips. Not even when she took one of my hands and put it on her skin and I felt her nipple crimp and harden against my palm.

Not even when her long, clever fingers found the opening below my waist and slipped inside to caress my soft secret parts.

That first time, half in and half out of a tidepool, we pressed together, lips seeking and tongues tangling, and her fingers stroked me until I wanted to scream. Or sing. I touched her hesitantly, finding soft hair where her legs joined.

She pushed against my hand and the hair parted, soft mounds of flesh parted, and I thought, *She isn't made so differently from me after all.*

Neither of us spoke—I because I only had a siren's language then, and she for reasons of her own—but both of us gasped and breathed ragged breaths into each other's mouths.

I had felt such pleasure before, of course. I was not unfamiliar with sex. But the feel of her fingers, of her lips and tongue, was so much more than the probe of a siren man's erection, so much nicer than my own uncertain touches on myself.

It didn't last long, that first time, because we were both too wanting to go slow, overwhelmed by whatever it was that was starting to grow between us. But each time after, we spent longer exploring each other, touching and trying and testing to see how much we could tease before pushing each other past our limits.

I didn't try to drown her again, and I didn't need to wonder what wolf tasted like.

*My* wolf tasted like the sea.

We heard the circus long before we smelled it, which was also long before we saw it, though the glow lit up the sky from a good distance off.

We earned a few curious glances as we passed. Perhaps we wore the human clothes wrong, or perhaps it was our bare feet. Or maybe humans have special senses of their own that told them there was something different about us, something wrong. But whatever it was that caught their attention, it didn't keep it, and they all looked quickly away. Unless it was that we caused an unease that told their primitive brains, "Don't be noticed, and it won't hurt you."

The wolf's goal *was* to hurt humans, though. Maybe not these humans, maybe not all humans. But she had agreed to do nothing against any of them until I had found my sister. After that, I didn't think much of any human's chances.

Had I followed my own instinct, I would have stayed far away from the bright lights and the noise, the stink of human foods and human waste. But the whole reason I was here was against my instincts as a siren. Live in the now, my brain told me; but for a little while, I needed to live in the what-will-be.

I couldn't read the human letters, but I didn't need to. This circus was exactly what you would expect from a place where other creatures were put on display to be gawked at. Even with only human ears, I could hear the roar of big cats unhappy to be caged, the grumbling of a bear faced with pain at the snap of the whip, the neighing of horses separated from their herd. Even with only a human nose, I could smell a fox's fear, an elephant's sorrow, the pungent desire of a lion to rend his keeper from neck to groin, not to feast on his insides, but to make up for the cruelty.

The wolf had to tug at my hand several times before I realized I had stopped, overwhelmed by the stink and the noise. "Come on," she said.

"We have to keep moving." I finished her sentence, blinked, and made myself really look at the place. A huge tent right in front of us flapped sluggishly as the wind caught its walls. Bright garish red and blue fabric striped the night, so high I had to kink my neck to see the top. The doorway was outlined in lights shaped like tiny skeletons, and each of them seemed to leer at me.

"Not there," I said. The wolf didn't answer. She kept hold of my hand as we moved around the tent, though I could see just fine now in all the burning lights. Her hand trembled, just a little.

"There," she said, and pointed. More tents and wagons clustered on the other side of the big one, all bright colors—there yellow and green, there blue and orange, and there purple. An elaborately decorated wooden wagon had a picture of a glowing sphere on the side, and some symbols I couldn't understand but which I did not think were in any human language. This was also decorated in strings of lights, only they were shaped like vegetables, orange and round, with leering faces just like the skeletons had. Past all that squatted another tent, almost as big as the first one, but not as tall, striped in blue and gray. To each side a small table had a flickering lantern that smelled like roasted vegetables–more leering faces–and I was reminded that humans liked to be frightened, but only as long as they knew it was safe.

This tent had pictures by its entrance, like most of the other tents, but these were things I recognized. A woman covered in fur, a very short man, another man with only two fingers on each hand like the claws of a shore crab, but soft. And a woman with a tail like a fish.

The woman in the picture looked nothing like my sister, save for the kelp-gold hair and fair skin. She looked stiff and posed, where my sister was all elegance and smooth movement. Her tail was that of a salmon, maybe, or a trout, where no fish ever had a tail as flowing or bright as a siren's tail. But it was my sister, nonetheless.

"Let's go," I said, but when I stepped forward my wolf didn't step with me. Her hold on my hand pulled me to a stop once more, and I had to clench my teeth to ignore the burning in my feet.

"You go," she said. "I have to see…" I followed the direction of her look and saw what my own eyes had skipped over in trying to find where my sister was kept. Cages, just visible through a space between a blue and orange tent and the wagon with the crystal ball. The smell of fear and anger came from there.

I nodded and let go of her hand. She hesitated a moment, then touched my cheek, pressed her lips to mine, and then was striding away, towards the caged animals. I made my way towards the other captives.

"Ticket," said the human man standing next to the entrance. His face was painted white and black, yet another leering skull. "Five dollars," he said. "Half-off for Halloween." He held out a hand covered in a black glove with white bones painted on. Halloween, I remembered, was what humans now called Samhain. They tried to turn it from a sacred festival to ward off darkness to a fun event of candy and dress-up. But no amount of sweets or costumes would hold off darkness for them this year.

"No," I said, and looked into his eyes. He went still, stepped back.

"Of course," he said.

I had not bargained away my voice for human legs, as my sister had. I had not even bargained my siren senses. This human shape, these human eyes and ears, and these burning feet, were the price, not the prize. What I had bargained *for* was something even more unforgivable than what my sister had asked for. I had given my siren-self for a measure of the sea witch's powers. And—she said it was only because I was her favorite daughter—she gave me exactly what I asked for.

No human would get in my way. *Nothing* would get in my way.

The summer my sister bargained away her voice for a human shape was the summer my older siblings decided they had been too lax with all of us. It was too late to save the youngest, they let me know, singing a sad litany of broken hearts and human treachery. But it was not too late to save me.

It was improper, they informed me, swirling around and around me until the water was frothy with seafoam, for a siren to love anyone. Humans and other non-sirens—even selkies and wolves—were for luring and drowning, for tearing apart and feasting on, not for sporting on the beach. And sex was for making the next generation of sirens, because we were already so few. Sex was not for pleasure.

I sang my agreement but as soon as I was alone, I swam for the beach, hauled myself up on the sand, and looked for my wolf. She came down the shore in her furry shape, not putting on two legs until she was leaning over me. She grinned and took a small crab, still alive and pinching, from her mouth and held it out for me. I ate it from her fingers and she asked if we would hunt today.

I shook my head and pulled her close, pressing her mammalian warmth to my siren cold, and she seemed to understand what I needed even when I could not have put a name to it—even if I had used words other than siren-song, I could not have described the feeling that made me leave my sisters counsel behind and rush to my wolf. She kissed me, her long human legs straddling my tail to press our lower bodies together. Even behind muscle and scale, my secret parts could feel the pressure of hers, and her slickness against my skin felt like something forbidden and necessary.

I abandoned all subtlety, all the careful exploration we had done together, and devoured her mouth, thrusting my tongue into her softness and drawing her tongue out until our soft moans drowned out even the sharpest calls of gull and sandpiper.

I ground myself against her and she pushed back until we were a frantic, writhing mass on the sand, until we both cried out against each other's mouths, and fell slowly, languidly still.

She curled herself around me; I who had never felt the need for protection suddenly craved it, and she seemed somehow to know.

We were still there when my sisters swam up to the beach and her packmates came around the curve of the shore, and we were driven apart by teeth and claws, by blood and biting, by an ancient hatred that no longer made any sense, if it ever had.

They dragged her away, her packmates, bleeding and limp. She didn't fight them, maybe she *couldn't* fight them, and the last I saw of her was a bloody dragmark in the sand. A clump of fur, skin attached, fluttered from a dead and twisted driftwood log on the beach. I stared at it as I was dragged beneath the waves.

That night, I listened to my sisters, and chose to forget.

And later that summer, when news came to us that our youngest sister had been tricked and captured, it was not my siblings who helped me. It was a lone wolf woman who had *not* forgotten.

Inside the tent it was dark, but not so dark as the forest at night. Bright lights were arranged to lead the viewer from attraction to attraction, so every freak of nature would be seen by following the path from entrance to exit. I walked past the dwarf man. He was entirely human, but must have seen something in me of kinship. He nodded at me and whispered, "Good luck." His voice trembled, but he faced me boldly.

The woman covered with hair was not as furry as she had been on the picture outside, and she was human, too. Unlike the dwarf, she recoiled when she saw me, and stank of fear, but she didn't flee. She must have been more afraid of what would happen to her if she left the too-bright glare of her spotlight. Maybe she didn't know what sirens do to their victims, or maybe the punishment she would endure was even worse. Something had left long, thin, white scars half-hidden beneath her fur everywhere her clothing didn't cover, except her face.

They were all human here, the man with crab-claw hands, the girl with scaly growths on her face, and the beautiful twin sisters who shared one set of legs. All of them watched me pass, and they all seemed to know I was not human, or had been not-human once. All of them were more afraid of what would happen if they ran from me than they were of me. And that, finally, made apprehension build like rancid fish in my belly. What was I about to face if these people would sooner expose themselves to an angry siren?

Near the back of the tent was a small pool and next to it sat a woman on a chair. She, unlike the others, looked human, but was not. I didn't know her, but I knew she must be the selkie who had been stolen. And I knew she was as captive as if she had been chained there, as long as the human man had her skin.

"Will you kill him?" she asked. She scratched her arm and I saw bruises there, dark and painful-looking, forming the shape of a hand, most purple where the fingers would have dug in. "It's Samhain and the spirits are hungry."

I shrugged. "If he tries to stop me." I ignored her mention of the holiday. Holidays are meaningless to sirens and I didn't care what any spirits might want.

"I want to go home."

I stopped and looked at her. "You will go home. Before this night is over every captive here will be free." It had never been my intention to rescue the whole circus; the fates of others didn't concern sirens. But something had shifted in me. Perhaps my wolf had taught me to feel what others felt, or maybe the way these people were treated as possessions to be exploited, just as the land and sea were, made me realize there was something bigger happening. So now it seemed important to *do* something bigger in response, to do something to stop the plundering that humans seemed determined to carry on. But first, my sister. I turned away.

"She isn't well," said the selkie, softly. "I think she's dying." I nodded but didn't look at her. I faced the last glowing light and stepped towards it, towards a final curtained alcove.

A large structure of glass took up most of the area, leaving only space for one person to move around, to see the tank from all sides. It was cylindrical with tarnished brass and copper fittings, and a lid secured with a metal clamp. The water inside was filthy, clouded, and I could smell the waste swirling inside it. I put my hand on the glass, and another hand emerged from the gloom inside the tank to press against the glass opposite mine.

She swam out of the murk. Her porcelain skin was mottled gray and flakes of scales and skin peeled off her tail. She had been all golds and blues and greens, a vision of jewel colors, and now she was a sickly shadow.

"Sister," I said. I don't know how the human had turned her back to her siren shape, but whatever he had done had not restored her voice. She opened her mouth and only bubbles came out.

"Come home with me."

She gestured to the clamped lid, pointed at the padlock that held it shut.

I knew it wouldn't work, but I went back to the selkie's pool, took the chair she handed me without a word, and used it to climb up to the lock. Tugging at it accomplished nothing. Wedging my fingers under the edge of the lid and prying did nothing. I climbed down and stood back. I moved closer and pressed my hand to the glass.

"Move as far back as you can," I told my sister, and she disappeared into the gloom of the filthy water.

I hefted the chair and swung it at the glass.

It bounced off, flinging me away and tumbling me to the ground where I tangled in the curtain. My shoulders burned, wrenched. I hissed. I was a sea witch's daughter, a siren, and even in this human shape I would not be weak.

I got to my burning feet and swung the chair again. I screamed and loosed some of the sea witch's power and swung the chair over and over until the glass cracked and crashed and water sent me to the floor again. My sister lay on the ground, shards of glass surrounding her. She pushed her body up on weak arms and stared at me.

She had no voice, but I still understood when she mouthed, *What have you done?* I knew she didn't mean the glass. I buzzed with unused magic—my own human strength had broken the glass. I crawled to her, ignoring the bite of the shards. How could they compare to the burning in my feet, anyway? I pulled her into my lap. She was so weak.

"I will make you human," I said. "And we will walk back to the sea, and then I will make you a siren again. Our sisters will be so happy to see you, they will forgive you, and our mother will return your voice." I put my hand on her forehead, concentrated as the sea witch had told me to, and began to imagine my sister with legs again.

She pushed my hand away, shook her head violently. *Don't,* she mouthed.

"You're dying," I said. "You won't make it home like this, and I didn't bargain for healing powers. Only changing powers."

*I'm dying,* she mouthed, shaking her head again. *Let me die.*

"No," I said, but I could see she was already slipping away. She wouldn't make it home even if she had a human's legs. She barely had the strength to keep breathing; she could never walk so far.

*Let me go,* she mouthed. *Sister.*

I put my hand on her forehead again. "At least let me help you go as sirens go." I could not be sure that her human had returned her complete siren nature when he returned her tail. She nodded and I let the witch's power flow through me and a moment later I had only a lap full of cold seafoam that slipped away and soaked into the dirt floor.

I sat there for some time. I heard the selkie woman moving somewhere nearby, heard voices as the dwarf spoke to someone near the entrance of the tent. Then footsteps, heavy, angry, and the flutter of the curtain being thrust aside.

"Who are you, and where is my mermaid?"

I recognized his voice. My sister's lover, who had betrayed her after she gave up everything to be with him. I stood, slowly, a long shard of glass clutched in my hand that I didn't remember picking up.

"You," he said. "I know you."

"You don't," I said. "You saw me once, that's all."

"Have you come to take her place? Profess your love for me, and give me everything I want?" I didn't reply. "She did it willingly, you know," he said. "She made herself back into a mermaid for me, to be in the sideshow. Everyone here is a willing actor, fed and housed and paid. I could pay you well."

I stared into his eyes. He wasn't lying, exactly, except about the selkie, though bruises and scars and fear told me the real story was more complicated. My poor sister had not known how thoroughly she had been betrayed. I looked away, studied his clothing, ridiculous even for human garb. Velvet trousers and a ruffled shirt, shiny leather boots, and a cape made of dark-furred leather. I caught my breath, looked him in the eyes again. The cape was sealskin. *Selkie* skin.

"*You* killed her," I said.

"And you, what? You're going to stab me with that shard of glass?"

I glanced at the dagger-like object in my hand, then back at him. "No," I said. I gave him my toothiest smile, and though a human's teeth can't inspire the fear a siren's can, he still took a step back. I followed him, step-by-burning-step until he was backed against the tent wall. I smelled the stink of his fear and saw the tremble of his hands that he tried to hide behind a straight spine and a sneer.

"I'm not going to stab you," I said. I reached out with my empty hand, stroked his cheek, touched the selkie-skin, and let the sea witch's power flow through me again. He flinched and then began to laugh.

"You *are* in love with me," he said. "Just like your sister, just like—" And then he stopped speaking, collapsed to the floor, and looked up at me through his new seal's eyes. I stepped back, was turning away, when I heard another voice. The selkie.

"You gave him my *skin*," she said.

I looked at the seal flopping awkwardly on the floor, trying to speak human words and failing. I looked at the selkie, and held out the hand with the glass shard. "So take it back."

She stared at me, blinked, and then a wide grin tugged at her face. She had long seal canines. She took the glass knife and stepped around me. "The spirits will drink their fill," she said, her voice full of a wild and dangerous glee. "For the first time in generations they will roam free and mortals will know fear again."

We sirens cared nothing for rituals of blood or the business of spirits, but I knew other creatures did. Selkies kept the old festivals, and while they now offered salmon and otter pups instead of spilling human blood, they still remembered. They knew the power of sacrifice, and I wondered if some of that power might spill over to me for the part I played this night.

The fold of curtain separating this section from the rest billowed as something moved beyond it and pushed it aside. The dwarf man looked at me, meeting my eyes with boldness. Behind him, the furry woman and the one with scaly growths waited, fear on their faces until they saw the glass and the man-turned-seal and the look on the selkie's face. Then they grinned and when the man with crab-claw hands pushed his way in and picked up another shard of glass, they followed. Humans do like their bloodshed on Halloween.

I walked away, out of the tent, ignoring the seal barks and wet sounds that came, ignoring the dwarf's laughter and the thud of a foot meeting flesh. But as the selkie woman shrieked in defiance and I heard a wet peeling sound and an almost-human scream from a seal-shaped throat, I couldn't help but smile.

I found my wolf woman surrounded by empty cages, doors open, bars bent, toppled to their sides. All around, I heard screams and running, animal noises. The bear roared, and I turned to watch a burly human man with a long beard snap a whip to keep the huge animal at bay. For a moment, it worked, and the bear crouched down, cowering. But then my wolf stepped forward, grabbed the whip though it cut into her hand, and yanked it away. The bear stood up and the man screamed and ran. He didn't get very far before he was pinned down by claws split from trying to escape. The old bear's teeth were jagged and broken, but they served well enough to rip muscle from bone. He roared again and feasted.

The elephant trumpeted to be free of her chains and walked slowly towards the man who had put them on her. She was in no hurry and the brass knobs on the ends of her tusks proved useful for smashing skulls, though they prevented her from stabbing. The lion growled and stalked the lion tamer and a moment later I smelled spilled entrails and heard wet chewing. The horses neighed, the big cats growled, and all sounded fierce and wild again. I think, if I could have understood their language, they would have sung me songs of revenge. I think they would have told me this was only the beginning of what they would do. My wolf met my eyes and laughed.

I squinted against the bright lights and said, "There are trees over there, and quiet, and I'd like to lie down a while." My feet, forgotten while I smashed glass to free my sister, were burning again, and I needed to get off them, or else keep moving.

I held out my hand and she took it, letting me lead her out of the lights and the noise, the smell of blood and fear. Under the trees it was cold and damp, carpeted with moss and ferns. It was not the sea, but it was not so different, and I have never minded the cold.

"I remembered," I said. "Being with you." She smiled when I moved closer and put my hands on her face. "But I wear a human shape now. I am not as I was."

"I like your human shape," she said, shifting until her body was pressed against mine. "And it cannot hide your siren's heart." We were of a height, and hardly needed to move to touch, lip-to-lip. She still tasted of salt and periwinkles and longing. Of home. She parted her lips and slipped her tongue into my mouth and I pulled away, startled.

"Are you *sure* you remember?" she said, something in her voice I couldn't name, but it made her lips curl up a little.

"I remember." I pressed my mouth to hers again and tugged at her human clothes until I found skin. "I remember you liked this," I said, cupping one of her small breasts in my hand and rubbing my thumb over her nipple.

She made a sound low in her throat and yanked her shirt over her head, discarded her trousers, and arched her back under my touch. I bent lower, put my mouth where my fingers had been, and her fingers threaded my hair, tightened and pulled.

I bit down, gently, and she growled and pulled my head away, guiding me to her other breast. I obliged, teasing her with my tongue and lips and teeth until she seemed to melt in my arms. There was thick moss under the trees, and we tumbled down onto it and when the burning eased in my feet, I realized I hadn't even thought about them, about pain or even sorrow, since my lips met hers.

She pushed me onto my back and tugged my human clothes off and showed me why she liked my mouth on her breasts so much by putting hers on mine. I had not had nipples as a siren, had thought them useful only for mammals to feed their pups, or to bring pleasure to my wolf; now that I had them, I was almost glad to be human, because each flick of her tongue against me sent tingles of pleasure between my legs until I could have screamed. She sucked and I cried out and my voice held something of its old resonance, its siren tones. She lifted her head and met my eyes.

"You sang to me," she said. "We used to lie in the tidepool after, and you sang to me." She stroked her hands over my skin, nudged my human legs apart, and dipped her fingers into my soft, secret places.

How different this body was from my siren's shape. Then, my most sensitive parts were hidden away, tucked under scale and muscle, and she had to push her fingers deep to find the spot that made me sing. Now, she only needed to stroke lightly, to tease with clever fingers until I arched my hips to press against her hand.

Pleasure built under her fingers but I wasn't ready to give in. Not yet. I pushed her away, rolled her onto her back, and licked the salt from her skin. In the middle of her belly was a divot, not quite an opening, and I poked my finger into it. She squirmed and laughed.

"I was attached there," she said. "To my mother, before I was born." I poked my tongue into it. I did not have such a divot in my belly when I was a siren. I had not been born, but hatched. Spawned. I had fought my siblings for a place in the nest until there were only a few of us left out of hundreds. My kind valued strength above all; only my youngest sister had been a companion instead of a rival. Perhaps it was that un-sirenly bond with my sister that had opened me to the possibility of love.

I did not want to remember killing my siblings; I wanted to remember living. I moved my mouth lower, and my wolf opened her legs for me. She tasted like the sea and made wild noises in her throat. She was warm and wet and swollen and I couldn't resist putting my tongue inside her and then my fingers, until she arched her back, buried her hands in my hair—black now and not siren-green—and slowly went still.

I lay with my head on her hip, tasting her still in my mouth, smelling her, feeling the throb of her sex gradually slow. She tugged my arm.

"Come here," she said, and I crawled up the bed of moss to lie next to her. Her hands on my skin were firm and sure. She remembered where and how I liked to be touched and, even though I had legs now and no tail, she figured out how to caress me until I sang out and pushed against her clever fingers again and again until there was nothing but pleasure pulsing between my legs.

We lay together as the night grew deeper and darker and colder. The distant sounds of the carnival faded, the animal bellows and human screams and flesh rending shifting to softer noises as those still alive slipped into the forest. They didn't mean to escape, I didn't think, but to regroup, to carry on the night's work elsewhere until there was no more revenge to be had. Finally the noises stopped entirely and I realized I had been aware of little but my wolf's touch since we walked into this thin copse of trees.

"Will you go back to the sea?" she said.

"Will you?" I had no answer for her. Not yet. Maybe not ever.

She shrugged. "It was good to make them pay."

"Yes."

So we got up and put our human clothes back on and went out into the bright lights and nose-stinging smells, the terrible noise and the waste and rot and filth. She took my hand, and I smiled.

I didn't have my siren-senses anymore, but I did have a share of a sea witch's magic, and I had a wolf woman. There were other carnivals out there, other places where sirens and selkies and even strange humans were captive and tortured and in need of their own revenge. And the burning in my feet wasn't so hard to bear, as long as I kept moving.

# ABOUT THE AUTHOR

Nico is a queer nonbinary writer of urban fantasy, dark fantasy, epic fantasy, and the romantic versions of all three. They like stories with at least a little bit of magic lurking on the edges and tend to write about finding oneself and one's purpose in life, learning to find joy in everyday things, and sweet-but-spicy love stories where two people face down the horrors life throws at them together.

They are also an artist and illustrator (as Nik Sylvan), and the print versions of their Three Realms, Nine Monarchs epic romantic fantasy series (beginning with *A Vision of Air*) are all fully illustrated.

They have also written a dark urban fantasy series called Fictive Kin (starting with *Daughter of Foxes*) and two spin-off series of romance duologies and standalones called Wolves of Autumn (*Chosen of Gods* and *Heart of Outcasts* are out so far) and Autumn & Arcadia (*Waking Pan* should be out by the time you read this).

Connect with Nico on social media, where you'll find them as @nicosilver-books on Instagram, Threads, and TikTok (though they post very rarely on the latter) and @NicSilver on Facebook. Their website is .

After living on both coasts of Canada and places in between (as well as three years in the US as a child), Nico has finally settled down on an island off the west coast with their partner, his two children, an elderly cat, a leopard gecko, and an assortment of fish.

# ABOUT THE SISTERHOOD OF THE BLACK PEN

*The Sisterhood of the Black Pen is an organization started by two female authors determined to lead a group built for indie authors by indie authors. They have made it their mission to be a foundation for women and nonbinary people to utilize in order to gain some exposure in the publishing industry and hopefully begin to gather a readership following. Self-publishing can seem like an overwhelming thing for some, but taking a small first step can lead to a monumental journey.*

### What is the Sisterhood of the Black Pen?

*The Sisterhood of the Black Pen strives to produce quality horror content from the greatest new female and nonbinary voices in indie horror. It is their goal to be a platform for new voices to be heard over the din by providing them with an incredible team of indie authors, editors, and designers who have collective years of experience and want to use what they've learned to help them be heard.*

## Who is the Sisterhood of the Black Pen?

*Faye Knightly and Laurae Knight co-founded this group in 2021 when they became frustrated with the amazing talent in the indie publishing world going largely unpublished and unnoticed. It was time to do something unique. Something empowering. Something twisted. Far too often in the publishing industry, new authors—especially those who identify as women—hesitate to make the leap into the self-publishing world. They decided that they would be a foundation to reduce that leap to a casual skip—one that can easily be made with trusted friends and professionals at your side. Although there is an emphasis on helping new authors, the Sisterhood is proud to say their group also includes seasoned authors who are always happy to share their knowledge and experience.*

*Follow the Sisterhood on Instagram, Facebook, and TikTok (@SisterhoodoftheBlack-Pen) where they make calls for submissions and strive to connect with new talented authors to guide through the publishing world.*

Printed in Great Britain
by Amazon

48270066R00159